Death à la Carte

CW01430738

A Mowgley Murder Mystery

George East

La Puce Publications
www.george-east.net

Death à la Carte

Published by La Puce Publications
website: **www.george-east.net**

© George East 2016

paperback first published 2018
ISBN 9781908747327

Typesetting and design by Fran Brooks

e-pub version ISBN 9781908747334
kindle version ISBN 9781908747341

For Kiosk Jane without whom it would still have been possible but nowhere near as much fun

Bernie Tapin was not a happy man. It was early morning and he had a slight hangover and a nagging tooth. Mainly though, the French fridge lorry was getting on his tits.

He looked again at his watch. Drivers had to take a 45-minute break every four hours, but this was taking the piss.

The parking rules were quite clear and this was one of the busiest service stations in the south. It was free for two hours and then £22 for HGVs. If they paid another £1.50 they got a £9 food voucher, which he thought was very reasonable.

But the driver of the 7.5 tonne fridge lorry was not being reasonable. Or maybe he didn't know the rules, though even a French driver should know better than leaving his motor slewed across two spaces and half-blocking the entry to the lorry park.

It had been there when he'd arrived for the early shift, and no attempt had been made to pay for the overstay in the shop or by phone. Car drivers tried it on all the time when they were journey-sharing, but it just didn't happen with commercials.

The real worry was that it was beginning to look like it was not a driver trying to get away with it or getting his head down or getting a leg over somewhere. The big Renault could have been dumped here after a hijacking, but then who would want to nick a lorry-load of French cheese? He could call the Bill, but he'd look a right pratt if they turned up just as the driver appeared, pulling up his zip and looking pleased with himself.

He looked again at the side of the lorry and the silly picture of a smiling cheese with a website address and telephone number beneath it. He knew enough French to know that 'fromage' meant cheese, but nowhere near enough to call their head office and ask where their fucking driver was.

Stepping up onto the footplate on the driver's side, he pointlessly tried the door handle again. Then he stepped down and walked round the back and looked at the twin-grip doors release. He thought about it for a while, and then reached up. The fridge unit must have been off for hours anyway, so no harm done if it was unlocked.

The levers moved smoothly outwards and together, and the doors swung open with little effort.

Leaning in to the darkness, he gasped with shock and stepped back.

He did not know what sort of cheese Livarot was or what part of France it came from, but it smelled literally like shit. How could people eat such crap?

After a couple of deep breaths, he took his Maglite from its holster and climbed up and into the darkened interior.

The rows of cardboard containers reached to the roof, but a stack had collapsed and a couple of the cases had split and broken open. A number of small square boxes were scattered around, and it was from them that the stink was mainly coming.

Taking care not to step on them, he shuffled over to the gap in the wall and pointed his torch into the void.

Then he saw them.

So many, and all so dead.

1

'Call me Melons.'

'I thought it was "Call me Israel."'

Detective Sergeant Catherine McCarthy shook her head wearily and reached for her drink. 'I shall miss our banter. I think. As you very well know, it was Ishmael. And why are you talking like one of the Wurzels?'

Former Detective Inspector Jack Mowgley gave her his injured schoolboy look: 'Well he was a pirate in *Treasure Island*, wasn't he.'

'Who?'

'Israel Hands. "Thems who dies'll be the lucky ones" and all that.'

She sighed theatrically, playing along with the game: 'You know very well that Ishmael was the narrator of *Moby Dick*.'

'Yes, but what's that got to do with me being allowed to call you Melons again? Is it some sort of farewell treat, or what?'

DS McCarthy put her empty glass on the table and pushed it towards him. 'I just thought it would be nice if you called me Melons and I called you John before you go.'

Mowgley waved a cold chip tantalisingly at a one-legged seagull which was watching them through the large window in the bar area of the car ferry. 'But you only call me John when you've got the hump with me.'

'A woman can change her mind, can't she?'

'True. What about another drink while we debate it?'

The *Mont St Michel* was making ready for sea, and the last of the convoy of cars, campers, caravans and other assorted vehicles were rolling across the link span. It was a sight that Mowgley and his sergeant had seen ten thousand times from the window of their office overlooking the Portsmouth continental ferry port. The realisation that he would never sit in his battered but familiar and comfortable armchair and that this was his first Channel crossing as a civilian gave him pause for thought. He also thought with further regret that, as she no longer worked for him, he would not only have to go to the bar but also pay for the round.

His former bag carrier, drinking companion, fierce defender and best friend caught his mood and looked round for a distraction:

'Blimey, I didn't know you had that many clothes.'

Mowgley looked to where a clearly over-laden rucksack, carrier bag and two mismatching suitcases had been stowed on and around the table next to the one at which they were sitting.

He frowned but nodded to concede that it was certainly an extensive luggage collection for him. Normally the reinforced Supa-Save bag-for-life saw him through a trip across the Channel, and the rucksack was for back-up if he planned to be away for more than a week. Underpants were expensive in France.

'Steady on' he said defensively and as if being accused of dandyism: 'I'm going away forever, remember.'

Melons regarded the cases with overdone distaste. 'I hope they didn't charge you for that one with the missing wheel and the broken handle. And I hope that's not a chuck-up stain on the side of the other one. Which skip did you find them in?'

'It was that charity shop next door to the kebab in North End. Only two quid the pair.'

Melons sniffed. 'You were done. But I suppose they do suit your general demeanour and appearance. Always said you were a charity case.'

'Har-de-har. You'll be sorry when I'm gone and you never see me again.'

'Oh, you poor boy.' She reached out and patted his knee.'

Cherbourg is only six hours away; it takes you longer than that to walk back from Southsea when there's a couple of pubs in the way.'

'Yes, but -.' He paused and glared a warning shot at a middle-aged couple, the female half of which was looking pointedly at his baggage redoubt. The woman had already put a couple of magazines on the table, and the man was looking panicky and resigned at the same time as if he knew a familiar scene was about to be re-enacted. He was holding a tray carrying a couple of croissants and a half-bottle of red wine, and Mowgley's look of irritation deepened into a lip-curling scowl. There was something deeply flawed about even the concept of a half bottle of wine, and even more so about two people sharing one.

The woman had the air of someone who thought she was more important than anyone in range, especially any men. She was thin with a pointy nose and heavy-rimmed spectacles and a hairstyle almost as severe as what was probably her default expression. As Melons shook her head in resigned anticipation, the woman braced her shoulders and took her spectacles off. It seemed hostilities were about to commence.

Before it kicked off, however, a diversion occurred in the shape of a blast of vintage pop music which forbade any exchanges conducted at less than a shout. Luckily, the woman did not look the shouty type.

By now, Mowgley had lost interest in the opportunity for a minor confrontation and was directing a bellicose look at a tall, thin young man who had occupied the stage. He was wearing a very bad shoulder-length wig, a droopy moustache which might be real, a shirt with puffed sleeves under a tight tank-top striped sweater, and his ludicrously flared trousers almost obscured a pair of platform-heeled boots.

The sign beside the stage informed anyone interested that he was 70's Retro DJ Donny; also on the bill were Pirate Pete, Marvo the Mad Magician and a tribute group called *Abbasolutely*.

He winced at the alliteration, tragic pun and the thought of what was to come, then noticed a lonely figure sitting at a table which had been set up outside the News and Book Boutique.

Mowgley had thought he was the oldest person on board by a long shot, but the fat man at the table had at least a decade more of life on his shoulders and face. He had a shock of grey hair, a beetle brow and snout-like nose that looked as if it had been broken at least twice. Along with a silly striped blazer and an instant bow tie, he was wearing a goatee beard as if in an attempt to look intellectual rather than faintly thuggish.

Overall he obviously courted attention, and looked liked the sort of person who wanted you to think that you should know who he was.

From the poster he had seen while picking up the last *Daily Telegraph* he would be reading for a while, Mowgley assumed he was the allegedly famous travel author and star of the ferry company's first-ever cross-Channel book signing.

The PR people who had arranged the stunt had obviously not thought it through. None of the already weary parents in the lounge could have been much over thirty, and all adults were outnumbered by at least two to one by young children. Gangs of little boys swaggered or ran between the tables, getting themselves noticed by knocking things over, mock-fighting and yelling. A dozen small girls had already gathered in front of the stage and were gyrating to the music as they practiced for a night out clubbing in a decade or so's time.

Mowgley sighed as he thought of the next six hours. He never travelled on boats to France in school holiday times for obvious reasons, but this time there had been little choice.

It was a week since he had ceased being a Special Branch - accredited CID Inspector responsible for spotting and suppressing dodgy goings-on at the Portsmouth Continental Ferry Port. The final, final Flying Bandit farewell party at the Ship Leopard had taken place the day before, and he had been sleeping on Melon's sofa since he had paid his dues and said an almost tearful goodbye to Bombay Billy on quitting his rooms above The Midnight Tindaloo restaurant. His official police accommodation in Southsea would also have to be vacated shortly, which would not please the three Romanian taxi drivers he had been sub-letting it to.

Mowgley gave a heartfelt groan, emptied his glass and stood up.

Melons looked from him to the woman with the glasses and back, then took a deep breath to reach the necessary volume velocity. 'What's up? Can't you handle her on your own now you've not got the weight of the law behind you?' 'Don't be silly,' Mowgley bellowed: 'The bloody disc jockey's just picked up a microphone and I think I see a lot of blonde hair and some sequins flashing behind the curtain. It's a bloke so the

Abba tribute band must be coming on. Let's go on deck for a fag before you jump ship.'

~

'Are you sure you're doing the right thing?'

They were leaning on the rail on the lee side, overlooking the quay where the marshals were enjoying sending late-arrival motorists the long way round to the link span.

Mowgley aimed carefully and threw his fag-end at the one-legged seagull, it was easily evaded and the bird flew off with a mocking cry. 'What, you mean jumping before I was pushed?' he said.

He reached for his baccy pouch and thought about the events of the last week, which had sped by before he had had time to draw breath. Like Solomon Grundy, he had been full of life on Monday, but dead and buried by Sunday.

To be fair, his demise had been on the cards since the arrival of his female nemesis. He had got away with his ways of working for a quarter of a century on the job, the last fifteen of them as sheriff of the little frontier town which was the ferry port. He would be fifty six next year and out of work anyway. By taking instant retirement he had at least done Madame Cressida bloody Double-Barrelled Hartley-Whitley out of a scalp. With him gone, the first female Chief Superintendent in the South would see no value in hanging out any dirty washing which might even get in the way of her progress towards Chief Constabledom. The tally and breadth of his technical offences against the Police And Criminal Evidence Act would remain unknown save to those who knew him or had suffered from his highly personal interpretation of the rules.

Mowgley let out a gusty wreath of smoke: 'Am I sure I'm doing the right thing?' Of course I'm bloody-well not. But what choice do I have?'

'Lots. All your friends are here and you've got your pension and you could get a nice little flat and...'

'And what?' said Mowgley sourly. 'Go down the bloody Leopard every day and pretend I was enjoying myself? They all know I didn't want to go, or they will do when word gets out. And every day would be a reminder I was a used-to-be. Not easy for a sensitive man like me, you know.'

DS McCarthy put her hands up in mock surrender. 'Okay, I get all that. But it's a bit drastic moving over to live in a caravan in a country where you hate the food and the people, isn't it?'

'Not at all. I don't hate all the French, just most of 'em. Anyway, I've been meaning to have *La Cour* done up for years and never had the money or time. After a tart-up I can flog it and find somewhere sensible to live. There's been a few enquiries now the market's picked up.'

She looked dubiously at her cigarette end. 'Yeah, but you said the enquiries were mostly about how you had the cheek to ask for money for someone to take a wreck like that off your hands.

'Cheeky cow. It's a fine example of an 18th-century Norman manor house in need of sympathetic restoration. At least that's what my lovely wife said the estate agent said.' He took a reflective drag on his cigarette and held a finger up to mark a point. 'And don't forget my job offer from Yann.'

She nodded and thought it best not to mention the fact that his knowing how to order a large apple brandy and an incinerated burger would not really equip him adequately for his duties as the Cherbourg representative of a distinctly dodgy private investigative agency.

They smoked in silence for a while, then Mowgley said in an attempt at casual interest: 'So what's been happening in my absence?'

'Not a lot of note on the patch. One wife-killer detained on his way out and the usual low-level booze and baccy try-ons. There was an inventive attempt to get a shedload of weed through yesterday, though.'

'What's a 'shedload' amount to?'

'No, literally a shedload. A bloke arrived from St Malo with one of those big DIY wooden chalets in bits in a trailer. He said they were much cheaper across the Channel and he was going to put it in his back garden. When they had a look, the gaps between the walls and the lining were packed with skunk.'

'Actually, I believe they do use some sort of legal cannabis hemp to insulate walls in France.'

'Maybe, but this was definitely for smoking, not keeping the heat in.'

'Ah.' Mowgley thought nostalgically of past cases they'd shared, then said: 'Is that it?'

Melons wagged a finger at a little boy further along the rail who was trying to get the lifeboat release mechanism working. He responded with a single uplifted finger and then wandered off. 'There was a bad case with a fridge lorry which came over from Cherbourg mid-week.'

'What sort of bad case?'

A parking supervisor at Toddington Services had a look in the back of an abandoned French cheese lorry and found ten men in Brittany Ferries overalls.'

'That is interesting. Disgruntled employees trying to escape or a gay sex party or what?'

'Don't know; they were dead.'

'Ah. Any ideas?'

'Not really. The licence plate was puckah and the lorry had started out from Livarot - that's in Normandy - with the usual driver. The passengers were certainly not BF employees, and no ID of any sort on the bodies. They could have got in the lorry on the quayside after any search, or even on the car deck.'

'That'd be a bit risky, would it not?'

'Well, yes and no. Cherbourg's a busy port and lots of swarthy-looking blokes in high-vis company jackets milling around. They could have made their way up the link span separately, tried to look as if they knew what they were doing, then gathered at the back of the lorry after the car deck doors were shut. There's always a time when nobody's about, or they may have had some help from a proper deckhand.'

'Shit.'

'What's up?'

'Nothing.' The truth was that former Detective Inspector Mowgley had realised that none of this was any of his business and he would play no part in trying to crack the case.

He straightened up and eased his back and then leaned on the rail again. 'Just thinking what it must have been like for those poor sods. In the dark and fighting for breath and nobody to hear them. I suppose it was suffocation?'

'It was.'

'How long would they have lasted?'

'With a sealed fridge lorry it depends on how big the inside is and how many people are sharing the air. There were seventy-one people in a chicken truck in Austria last year who didn't make it, and twenty-four very lucky ones in that fridge lorry from Calais this year who did. Someone heard them banging on the walls minutes after it reached the docks. I called your ex-lady friend in Forensics and she said that the average consumption of air is about 300 cubic feet a day. As it happens, that's about the internal volume of a 7.5 tonne fridge lorry. Ten people sharing the air means they would have around six hours each maximum. Just about enough to get from Cherbourg to Portsmouth, but not the onward journey to Toddington.'

Mowgley nodded. Just over a hundred miles due north of the ferry port, Toddington Services was a popular spot for dropping off illegals who had made it across the Channel. 'Poor bastards - and the bloke who found them. And no idea about the driver?'

'No. He either knew they were in there and didn't stop to give them air before Toddington, then panicked and did a runner when he saw the result. Or he was innocent, didn't know they were there - and panicked when he had a look inside after a break.'

'Or it wasn't the proper driver.'

'That's another possibility. It's all up in the air at the moment, but we'll know more in a few days. If you like...?'

She left the obvious question hanging, and he shook his head over-vigorously. 'No thanks. None of my business now.'

He reached for his baccy pouch again to top up his nicotine levels before the tobacco-less six hours ahead. 'So what do you think of the new me?'

'New you?' She decided to try and lighten the mood: 'Didn't notice there was one. Have you decided to turn over a new leaf and start changing your socks every day and buying your round?'

'Very funny. You know I meant your new guv'nor. What's he like?'

She thought quickly but carefully about what she would say. Then: 'Oh, DI Tennent. Too soon to tell, really, but nothing like you for sure.'

'In what way "nothing like me"?'

'To begin with he's taller than you, and younger and much,

much more fussy about his appearance. He's polite, never turns up late and lets me know where he is and always keeps his phone on him and fully charged. Best of all he doesn't fart and blame it on someone else.'

'I sense a big 'but' coming?'

She hesitated: 'He's a bit... predictable - and straight.'

'But you said that's what you liked about him.'

'Yes, but there is a limit.' She spoke more quickly and assuredly now: 'He doesn't smoke, and hardly drinks.'

'What do you mean by hardly drinks? In comparison with normal people, or you and me?'

'Even normal people. When we go to the pub he drinks...'

'Go on, spit it out.'

'Real ale. In halves.'

'Sharp intake of breath. Next you'll be telling me he doesn't like the pies at the Leopard?'

'He brings his own food.'

'What?!' An elderly couple along the rail looked round at them as Mowgley put his hand to his heart as if suffering from a seizure.

'Yes.' Melons gave the couple a reassuring smile and continued. 'His wife makes him low-carb and low-fat and low-taste lunches and sends them to work with him in a Tupperware box.'

'You mean she sends him to work in a Tupperware box? My God.' She did not bother to answer, so he continued: 'So, wifey's a home-maker, eh?'

'Far from it. She sounds like a feminazi.'

'A whatter?'

'An extreme feminist.'

'Like you, then?'

Sergeant McCarthy summoned up a snort: 'Hardly. He said the other day that she won't let him touch her or hold hands in public. She says it'd make it look as if she was under his control.'

'Blimey.' Mowgley stepped back from the rail and gave her a long, calculating stare. Then: 'Has he tried it on yet?'

'What? Don't be daft!'

'He will. If he's already told you his wife doesn't understand him, it's only a matter of time before - what the fuck was that?' A maroon flare had narrowly missed them and the elderly couple as it soared upwards and away from the quay, leaving a trail of bright red thick smoke. As the smoke cleared, Mowgley leaned over the rail and looked down at the quayside. A handful of oddly mismatching characters were standing in a line, waving to him. At one end was Wingco, the diminutive potman at the Ship Leopard. He was as ever wearing his grease-spotted blazer and RAF tie to which he was not entitled. Next to him in donkey jacket, overalls and welly boots was King Dong, winner of countless wagers in the toilets of the pub. Next to him stood the statuesque barmaid, Twiggy. She was wearing a little black dress that would have been big on another woman, and from his vantage point, it seemed to Mowgley he would have been quite safe had he chosen to leap from the boat and into her prodigious embonpoint. Then there were another couple of regulars with whom Mowgley had shared strong drink and duty-free goods over the years. A little way away was Two-Shits, the landlord of the Leopard. All were holding glasses up as if toasting his departure.

Mowgley turned to Melons. 'I wondered what you were doing with your phone just now. I thought you might be checking on messages from your new boss. Are they saying a fond farewell, or just glad to see the back of me?'

'They've come to say it's not too late. You could just walk off the boat and come to the pub.'

Mowgley looked down again at the awesome expanse of Twiggy's cleavage and thought it might be a safe as well as a happy landing. Then, as he watched in bemusement, she turned and started to lift her skirt. This seemed to be a signal, resulting in the others turning their backs and beginning to adjust their clothing.

'Come on,' Mowgley said urgently, you know I get queasy at the start of every crossing - and I don't want to remember them like that...'

~

'So, this is it then.'

The last vehicle and foot passenger had been taken on board, the bow doors of the *Mont St Michel* had been closed, and the boat was securing for sea. They stood at the top of the gangplank, which was being kept in place just for Catherine McCarthy.

'I suppose so.' Mowgley rubbed his chin awkwardly. 'You could come over for the ride, you know. I'll find you a room and you could go back tomorrow.'

She looked at him for a moment. 'Better not. Trev - DI Stretton is waiting to see me about the fridge lorry. But I'll be over next month if you haven't already got fed up and come back.'

'Ah.' Mowgley held out a hand, then withdrew it. 'Okay. See you later, Catherine.'

She opened her arms and stepped forward. 'See you later, John.'

2

At this time of year and with the sun out, the old place did not look at all bad, he thought.

Then he looked again and accepted the truth. It looked really, really crap.

Once upon a time, the vast manor house with spires and twiddly bits and all sorts of embellishments to intimidate the peasants would have been an impressive sight. Now it just looked like another money pit of the type so beloved by Britons with pretentions to grandeur. The sort of people who bought a once-grand ruin not because they loved old buildings or restoring them, nor because they loved France. It was just because of how much you could get for your money across the Channel. What he had paid for the once-grand twelve-bedroom, three staircased and no-toileted folly on twenty acres would not have bought a flat above a fish and chip shop in Hampshire at the time. The trouble was that it was in the hinterland of darkest, deepest Normandy, and would cost the price of a substantial modern home in Hampshire to restore it.

But his wife had fallen in love with the place on sight, and threatened to leave Mowgley if he did not buy it. He had missed the opportunity, and anyway she had left him for the French estate agent who had showed them the place. For all her protestations of undying love for *La Cour*, she had settled for their town house in Portsmouth as her share of the property division, and he had been left with the big old house and the mortgage on it.

Still, being over here full-time rather than arriving once a month to groan at the latest depredations would at least give him the time to get cracking on the basics.

The builders would be coming to audition tomorrow, and in the meantime he had the caravan in the orchard behind the main house.

For the moment, his biggest challenge would be to get the old Citroën to start and to remember that the steering wheel was on the left and that he should drive on the right.

~

The artistically distressed hand-painted Land Rover was in its usual position in the square in front of the church and alongside the Flaming Curtains. The space was officially reserved for the curé, but he and the owner of the bar had long ago come to an agreement involving the source and quality of the Communion wine.

Mowgley liked genuine characters as much as he disliked those who just thought they were. He had read somewhere that the true test of genuine singularity was that the eccentric believed himself to be perfectly normal. It seemed to Mowgley that the proprietor of the *Rideau Cramoisi* measured up to the criteria perfectly. For sure he did not give a monkey's what people thought of him.

A passing driver tooted his horn and he lifted his hand automatically, then remembered he was not on home ground.

St Sauveur-le-Vicomte was the nearest town to *La Cour*, and, if there was such a thing, it was fairly typical of the genre. There was a butcher's shop and bakery, a *tabac* for cigarettes and newspapers, and a curiously outdated DIY store which sold all manner of things people no longer wanted or needed. Newer arrivals were an estate agency which had been set up in the most recent boom in property sales to Britons, and a supermarket outside town which accounted for the many blank-eyed shops along the high street.

Every town has some claim to fame, and St Sauveur's was the regional fire station and the ruins of a castle which had been ruined by one of the first successful cannon sieges.

Another distinction was that a once nationally-favoured author had been born in the town, and the bar was named for one of his books. To the locals it was the *Rideau Cramoisi*, but the closest Mowgley's electronic hand-held translator could come was The Flaming Curtains.

There were other struggling or dying places to find a drink, but the *Rideau* was the only bar in town which was always popular. One reason was the attraction of a probably certifiable landlord, and the other the superb lunchtime specials created by his wife Chantal. There were fifty covers inside the bar and even more in the square, but reservations were necessary all year round.

If asked to describe him, Mowgley would have said that Coco Lecoq looked like an uncomfortable cross between an Old Testament prophet and the mad professor in *Back to the Future.* He had a shock of red hair, a moustache to rival Asterix the Gaul, and possibly the worst set of teeth Mowgley had seen in Normandy, which was saying something.

Coco spent most of his days hunting, collecting mushrooms from jealously-guarded secret locations and combing the marshlands for interesting pieces of petrified trees that he would sculpt into even more interesting works of art. Every week an exhibition was staged in the rooms behind the bar, and everyone was welcome to display the result of their creative urges.

An all-round arts enthusiast, Coco also staged regular open concerts in the square beside the pub. Last year he had arranged an exchange deal which involved the St - Sauveur Ladies Glee Club travelling to perform in a punk venue in East Dulwich, while the club had sent as its representatives a band called We Hate Fucking Foreigners.

Mowgley parked the DS 21 Cabrio next to the near-vintage Land Rover and reached into the glove box for his stash of Curly-Wurlys. As he crossed the square it started to rain, and he would have returned to put the roof up if there was one. If he had the time and money and patience to have it restored, he was told the classic 1970 Citroën would be worth a lot of money. But he figured that, at the moment, he had enough on his hands trying to make *La Cour* habitable.

He had bought the car from Coco, who had taken it as settlement of a year-long bar bill. He had offered it to Mowgley, he said, because the model was created to appeal to eccentrics, and in its state it had reminded him of his English friend. Battered by life, once-handsome, and still somehow in more or less one piece. The car and its condition had indeed appealed to Mowgley, and he felt much happier driving such a pre-battered vehicle. Surprisingly, he also felt more at ease driving in Normandy than across the Channel. This was because the minor roads were virtually empty when compared to Portsmouth, and also because Mowgley was such a bad driver that the locals knew to give him a wide berth.

He reached the door and the giant Airedale accepted Mowgley's admission fee and even allowed the former detective to pat his head.

Coco's dog was, like his owner, a one-off. Morton was elderly but still very active and with the air of authority of a senior military officer with a distinguished service career. When not playing left back for the bar soccer team in informal games in the square, Morton would be keeping order on his patch. Bitches were welcome in the bar, but not male dogs. Owners knew the rules, which included passing the Flaming Curtains on the other side of the road to ensure safe passage.

Inside, the bar matched Mowgley's taste perfectly. As with male dogs, modernity and transient fashion were barred from the premises. But the old oak beams and wood-panelled walls were not an affectation or an attempt to evoke the past. It was just that previous owners for the past century would have seen no reason to bother to update or change the bar, and Coco was not going to start a trend.

At the high, time-shone oak bar, Mowgley gave a thumbs-up when the barmaid signalled with a glass in one hand and a litre bottle of farm cider in the other. It was said that the *Moulin Rouge* in Paris traditionally chose British dancers because the French female shape tended to large hips and small breasts, but Veronique defied that slur. She did not rival the Ship Leopard's Twiggy, but would have given her a good run if centimetres were converted to inches.

It was still early, and the bar was quiet except for a handful of habitués. At the bar were three of them, each with some sign of recent injury or disability.

One of the men was wearing a sling on his right arm, his neighbour had a corrective boot on one foot, and the third was wearing a neck brace. A selection of crutches and other walking aids were propped against the bar.

Mowgley nodded his sympathy and shook left hands with the sling wearer. It was early harvest time and the casualty rate was always high amongst agricultural workers who liked a drink before coming to grips with mostly old and irascible farm machinery. The other two men were not walking wounded from incidents in the cattle maize fields, but were professional invalids. Their crutches and dressings were badges, and proof of an infirmity which allowed them to claim permanent disability benefits.

Their disabilities were apparently sporadic in effect, as the man with the surgical boot actually played for the Flaming Curtains first team under another identity, while the other would often forget his crutches when making his way home after a heavy session.

Mowgley had noted that, as in Britain, those who claimed long-term disability often also claimed they had led an energetic and exotic life before tragedy struck. Amongst disability claimants in the Flaming Curtains there were at least two alleged former French Legionnaires and a past officer in the national CRS riot police.

Mowgley exchanged non-verbal pleasantries with Veronique, picked up the frosted glass and icy bottle and walked to the back rooms. He would settle his tab before leaving, and, unlike in the Ship Leopard, would usually have to persuade Coco that his tab should be bigger than the proprietor's modest guestimate.

Passing a corner booth, Mowgley nodded to a man whose back story was not unusual for expatriates who were actually refugees from life in Britain, or from life itself.

According to himself and available evidence in the form of a learned law book with his name on the cover which he kept as a reminder of his successful self, Oliver had once been a high-flying barrister with a wife and two children and a detached home in one of the leafier parts of Middlesex. For no given reason, he had walked away from his life and wife and children a little over a year ago. The holiday home in the forest outside the town had been sold and the money gone to his wife and her legal team. Now, Oliver had a room above the bar, drinking himself insensible each day in a strictly-observed routine. He would be dry until the *midi*, when he would take a cold beer, sipping it daintily and almost gingerly like a man not knowing what to expect. During the afternoons he would engage regulars in sparkling conversation that they would not understand, then deteriorate rapidly as evening fell. He would sometimes make it to his room before passing out, and could be heard crying when the last customers left. It was very sad, but as Coco said, the page turned and we made our choice of where our lives would go.

Whilst in his cups, it was Oliver's wont to fall quickly and heavily in love. His current fiancée was a sweet-looking Moroccan girl who was holding his hand and looking adoringly at him as he planned the route of the carriage which would take them from the church to their honeymoon hideaway. She could not know it would never happen.

Signalling to Veronique that Oliver's drinks should be put on his tab, Mowgley moved into the back room and found the proprietor of the Flaming Curtains on his knees before a roaring fire. Although high summer, this was not another example of Coco's eccentricity. The blaze of oaken logs was for cooking and not heating purposes. A smoke-blackened cauldron hung from a hook above the flames, and a tray of ham hocks sat on the table nearest the fire, sharing the space with three bottles of cider, a selection of seasonings and a flask of home-made apple brandy. The cider would certainly be destined for the cauldron, but Mowgley was not sure about the Calvados.

Taking a seat a comfortable distance from the fire, he noticed a framed photograph on the mantelpiece. It showed a slimmer and slightly more presentable Coco arm-in-arm with a younger version of the fat and lonely author Mowgley had seen on the ferry crossing.

When asked, Coco explained the man was an *écrivan* who used to live down the road in an old water mill. It was said he had made millions from his memoirs about living in Lower Normandy, and it was thought he was either dead or living in a huge *château* in the south.

~

'Aren't you going to buy a girl a drink?'
Mowgley looked up from his *French for Dummies* and wondered momentarily if his luck had changed.

The woman wore an expensively tousled arrangement of raven-black hair, topped by a small red beret set at a carefully contrived angle. Mowgley did not know if the beret was meant to be ironic or coquettish or both, but then he was not good on female irony or any sort of fashion statements.

Long strands of hair had been teased down and curled round on each cheek, and framed her meticulously made-up face. She appeared to be quite tall, but then Mowgley saw she was wearing vertiginous high-heeled boots which reached almost to the hem of her black trench coat. It was secured with an artfully knotted belt, which emphasised her narrow waist and the flare to hips and breasts.

He tried to think of something clever to say, but she relieved him of the problem:

Her almost painfully white teeth shone in the gloom of the back room as she smiled and said: 'You don't recognise me, do you, Jack?'

This was undeniably true. Mowgley had once learned to his cost how much women could change their appearance. With men it was mainly limited to facial hair; women had a whole armoury of artifices which would not be acceptable in a male unless he was on the run.

Then he realised who the woman was, and how much she had changed since they had last met.

Sylvie Mooney was, according to Coco, the new and sole executive director of Normandy Dream Homes.

French-born, she and her husband had crossed the Channel to start a new life some years before. Like Mowgley, Sean Mooney had been a police inspector. Like Mowgley, it was said that he had jumped before being pushed, or jailed.

DI Mooney had at one time been a leading light in the Met's Drugs Intelligence Unit, and they had met when working independently on a job concerning very large scale importations of Class 'A' materials through the port at Portsmouth and on to the capital.

Also like Mowgley, Mooney had bought his wife a holiday home in her native Normandy. Unlike *La Cour*, the small *château* on a hill overlooking Cherbourg had been totally restored. The work had been paid for, it was whispered in some quarters, by regular injections of cash from DI Mooney's unofficial activities. Other bent coppers used their ill-gotten to buy secret villas in Spain; Mooney had bought a castle in France.

All had seemed to be going well for the couple and their business, but, like Sylvie Mooney, things had changed.

On arrival, they had set up a property exchange business, focusing on the allegedly higher end of the market. The Normandy Dream Homes website showed a cavalcade of photographs and video walk-throughs of grand properties, but most of them were of their own pocket-sized castle. In reality, the couple hoovered up any available properties, promising the owners much and delivering much less. The husband-and-wife team had learned the first rule of French property exchange, which was that the more you had on your books, the more you would sell. There was always a customer for the most distressed cottage or even fairly empty barn at the right price. That was why the company had approached Mowgley some years earlier with assurances they would be able to get top money for *La Cour*, and in a short time. That had not so far happened, though there had been regular inspections by allegedly potential buyers who Mowgley suspected were friends and even colleagues of the Mooneys.

If there had been no change in the situation regarding Mowgley's foreign asset, there had been a speedy and dramatic change to the day-to-day running of Normandy Dream Homes.

For whatever reason (and Coco opined that it proved that mixed marriages rarely worked) Sylvie Mooney had decided to change her sleeping partner as well as her business partner.

This was not hard, as from the start, the company had been entirely in Sylvie Mooney's name. French officialdom only conforming with the requirements of the European Economic Union when it suited them, foreign teachers, violin players and (especially) estate agents often found it impossible to match up to the official criteria for working in France. His wife being a French national, Sean Mooney had to accept that he had, on paper, no official position with the company; he would be a kept man.

The arrangement had worked well until a new agent had been taken on. He was French, and tall and handsome and good at his job. He also proved good at seducing and winning Sylvie Mooney, and persuading her to expel her husband from the family home and the business.

The change of partnership would also account for the transformation of Sylvie Mooney. She had always been a strong and even hard woman. Now, she looked, Mowgley had to admit, at least a million Euros.

By now, he had thought of a pleasantry. Standing up, he held out a hand and said: 'I was just thinking how...French you looked.'

She showed a perfectly aligned row of teeth again, and said: 'perhaps that's because I am. Now what about that drink?'

~

'I was expecting to meet your...friend...Denys?'

Mowgley put the drinks on the table and sat down, noticing the shadow that passed across her face before the smile surfaced again.

'Yes. So was I. Expecting him to be meeting you, I mean.'

In spite of her attempt to maintain her untroubled air, it slipped as she picked up her glass and looked into it as if the answer to her problems may lie there.

Mowgley watched her eyes and asked: 'Is there something wrong?'

Again the teeth. 'No, of course not. It's just that we have been so busy. Denys had a client to see in Honfleur yesterday and was staying overnight so he could do some more work in the morning before meeting you here.'

'So was there a problem?'

The shadow crossed her face again. 'No, I don't think so.'

'You don't think so? Did he not call?'

'No. I came here in case he had arrived to see you.'

Mowgley tried to look reassuring. It was strange how the advent of the mobile phone had been both a blessing and a curse. In the old days, there was usually an excuse for not keeping in regular communication; nowadays people panicked if they did not get a call every two minutes. But she seemed excessively worried.

Perhaps, he thought, it was because of the newness of the relationship. She had booted the old man out, and it could be that her lover had done a runner. The fact she had put so much effort and money into her makeover indicated it was her who was trying to keep him enamoured.

Mowgley had met Denys Simone on a couple of occasions and gauged him as the sort who liked to play the field and who would quickly tire of someone who was keener on him that he on her. Perhaps there was even more to it, and he had taken the car and any available funds as well as himself to other parts. Having said that, it would be strange for even a feckless soul to drive away from such rich pickings. He furrowed his brow as if he were interested and puzzled at the same time, then asked: 'Have you tried his mobile?'

Her eyes flashed with anger and he saw more of who she really was. 'Of course. There was no answer and now it has been turned off.'

He lifted his glass in a hopefully reassuring gesture. 'I'm sure it's nothing. Perhaps it's a flat battery or the car broke down. I'm sure he'll turn up soon.'

She picked up her glass and clinked it against his in a patently empty gesture: 'Yes, I'm sure he will...'

3

'Are you missing me?'

'It was only yesterday. I'm missing the Shit Leopard, for sure, and I haven't had a curry for nearly forty-eight hours. And there's no such thing as pies here.'

'Blimey, you must be having cold turkey.'

'I hate cold turkey nearly as much as I hate turkey curry. Alright in a sandwich with pickled onions, though. They call it dandy over here, you know.'

Catherine McCarthy took the phone from her ear and looked at it as if it would help explain her former boss's drift: 'Sorry pardon?'

'Turkey. It's called dandy. I've seen it in the supermarket.'

'Oh, right.'

'But the funny thing is they don't call Turkey dandy. The place, I mean.'

A pause as Catherine McCarthy wondered how he was going to survive on a day-to-day basis without her, let alone run a private investigation agency.

But it was mostly a game, of course. It was his way to pretend not to be able to pronounce French words or to understand the way things were done in that country when it suited him. Perhaps it was a defence mechanism, or perhaps he just liked to get her at it.

Carefully saying the word as he had so as to play by their rules, she said: 'I thought you just said they call it 'dandy'?'

'No I mean the country. We call the bird and the country the same thing. Turkey. They call the bird 'dandy' and the country-'

'Turquie.'

'There you are, same as us, more or less. How weird is that?'

She gave up the unequal struggle. 'Quite. So apart from that, how's it going?'

'Okay. I saw the agent yesterday, or rather I saw the agent's boss.'

'Is that the woman who's kicked her husband out in favour of a younger model?'

'That's it. And she looks as if she's traded herself in for a younger model.'

Melons decided not to pursue that line of enquiry. 'Ah. And how's the restoration project going?'

'I've got the builders coming this morning.'

'French or British?'

'Both.'

'Well, that's an unusual approach. Dare I ask why?'

Although he knew she couldn't see him, Mowgley nodded. 'They're both regulars at Coco's bar. The Brit speaks the language and can tell me what the French bloke is saying.'

'Well, he can tell you what he *says* the French bloke is saying.'

'Yeah, but I'll know if he's lying. I'm - I *used* to be a detective, remember? And if either of them tries to stitch me up, Coco will not be pleased.'

'And you do love a bit of agg, don't you?'

There was no response, so she continued: 'Okay, I get it. So today is about getting estimates?'

'Yeah. I want to know how much I can get done for what I've got. Then I can move in to the main house and start on the DIY.'

'Hmm. Okay, sounds good. Have you set a budget?'

'Sort of. About half my lump pay-off should do the basics, I hope.'

It was Sergeant McCarthy's turn to nod at her unseen correspondent. She knew that Mowgley had taken advantage of the Police Pension Scheme arrangements to commute some of his pension. 'All good, then.'

'So far. And how have things been going at work? Any news of the fridge lorry driver?'

'Not yet. The factory says he checked in and set off with the lorry as usual. We don't know if he was in on the game or was hijacked by the people smugglers before he got to the ferry port at Cherbourg. But here's the funny thing.'

'Go on.'

'He was originally booked in to go by Caen ferry port. Livarot - where they make the cheese - is only fifty four kilometres away. But Cherbourg is over one hundred and seventy. Someone changed the booking.'

'So an inside job?'

'As far as they can tell, the change was made from the factory. But why change it anyway? They could have loaded the passengers outside Caen just as easily, and it's about the same time for the crossing.'

Mowgley pondered a moment: 'That is strange. Anyway, there's something wrong with all this for sure.'

'What do you mean?'

'Well, switching the ports, organising the Brittany Ferry outfits, and all for ten illegals. What's the going rate now for a lift across the Channel in a lorry? A couple of grand, tops? There must have been others involved even if the driver was in on it. It seems a lot of trouble and risk to go to sneak a few bodies in.'

'You're thinking they were not your run-of-the-mill would-be migrants?'

'Worth thinking about, isn't it? And you've still not got any ID?'

'Too early for that. Because of the circumstances, the heavy mob have got involved, and they'll be checking DNA banks and prints and photos for a match.'

'It's out of your hands, then.'

'Sort of. But you could be seeing me sooner than you think.'

'What, have you chucked it in as well?'

'Don't be silly. Trevor -'

'Who?'

'Oh alright, D.I. Tennant. Anyway, he's said it's okay for me to come over and have a word with our opposite numbers at Cherbourg. Just to box things off so we're in the clear with the Secret Squirrels. In fact, he offered to come too.'

'Told you he'd try it on.'

'Not at all. I think he was just trying to be helpful.'

Mowgley looked at the ceiling. 'Yeah, right.'

'Anyway, I'll probably take a trip to Livarot to talk to the despatch department at the factory when I've done at the ferry port. If you fancy coming along for the ride I'll let you know when it is and I can pick you up on the way through.'

'Actually, I could pick *you* up if you came by foot passenger. Don't forget I've got a motor here.'

There was a silence, then: 'Um, yeah. Very kind. Still think I'll bring mine, though. The budget will stand it.'

'Talking of budgets, I take it Her majesty's Constabulary are paying for this call.'

'They are for my end. But so are you.'

'So am I what?'

'No reason you should know, but in civvy street the person taking the call pays as well as the caller when they're abroad. Time you got a landline in at *La Cour.*'

'Bugger. Speak soon.'

~

An hour later, and Mowgley watched as a V-shape wake spread across the muddy waters of the lower lake. Coco said it was a muskrat, a legacy of the Liberation and a gift from the GI Joes, along with venereal disease and some rather nice abandoned jeeps.

It was his first day as a proper expat and he hoped it would not be long before he wasn't. Around a quarter of a million Britons owned a holiday home in France and whatever they said, most of them would never really want to move over and live full time in it. They liked to drop casual references to their place (it was always a 'place') in the Dordogne or Provence into dinner and wine bar conversations and say how much they would love to live there full-time some day. But they were mostly smart enough to know they'd actually hate it.

But as things were, he would have to go with the flow. The job offer from the private investigator in Brittany had probably been just talk, but he would listen to what the guy had to say.

He heard the sound of a car, and looked round to see a vehicle pulling up at the back of the main building. It could be either, but as it was a badly-beaten white van the odds were very much in favour that it would be the Brit builder.

~

'So, where do you want to start?'

'I reckon it's best to have a walk round, then we can talk about what needs doin' soonest, and how well you want it done.'

The speaker was a small, swarthy and intense-looking man with a shaved head, and a Cockney accent which sounded far too extreme to be genuine. Mowgley had already noticed that Tez the builder occasionally forgot to drop his aitches. Perhaps it was his way of emphasising his Englishness, or perhaps he had a good reason for sounding like someone else.

Tez was wearing a set of ill-treated green overalls, and carrying a clipboard, a mobile phone, and a tape measure that obviously pulled out a long way. His French rival had not turned up yet, but that was par for the course in a country where it was still considered unnecessarily zealous or even impolite to arrive on time.

Mowgley put a hand in the air in the general direction of the main building as if inviting the man to pass judgement. 'What do you think? Is it as bad as it looks?'

The builder looked up at the gaunt and in places crumbling elevation, screwed up his face, puffed out his cheeks and shook his head. 'Have a heart; mate. We've not got through the doors yet. But going by the outside, it's not likely that the inside will just need a bit of a blow-over.'

Mowgley gave the builder a look of encouragement and invitation to frankness. 'So what would you do if you were me?'

The man re-lit his roll-up for the third time, looked at his clipboard and puffed out his cheeks again: 'To be honest, if it's as bad as I reckon it will be, I'd give it away, or blow it up or burn it down for the insurance. Even if there's nothing structural or really bad inside, you're looking at about fifty grand just to get it liveable, and at least five times that if you wanted to do a proper job. With the state of the market at the moment, you'd be lucky to get your money back if you could sell it. There's a saying about big old ruins in France like this, that sometimes free is too expensive. Did you say you'd had an offer for it?'

Mowgley paused to recover from the shock of meeting such a candid and perhaps even fairly honest builder. 'I met the estate agent yesterday and she said someone had shown interest, but what they were offering was much less than I paid for it.'

The man shrugged: 'None of my business, but buyers are rarer than rocking horse shit nowadays. I could lie to you to get the work, but I reckon it would be cheaper to build a new version of this place than do it up properly.' He put his shoulders back as if steeling himself for the ordeal ahead, nodded at the double doors and said: 'Shall we?'

Mowgley nodded glumly, put the giant, ornamental key into the lock, and twisted. Nothing happened, so he tried again.

'Shall I 'ave a go?'

This time the key turned creakily in the lock. Though small, Tez was obviously strong. Or, Mowgley thought, in a past life he might have had a lot of experience at getting through locked doors

As he had not been inside the house for months, Mowgley was surprised at how easily the doors opened for the first few inches. But then they stopped. 'Probably swollen with all the rain.' he suggested helpfully and as if already making excuses for his home.

'Nah. There's something stopping 'em.'

Laying his tape measure, clipboard, torch and phone on the threshold, Tez backed up and made a practiced run at the door. This time they opened a little further, but then swung back.

He rubbed his shoulder and frowned. 'It's like something's behind the doors. I'll shove 'em open slowly, then you get in and see what it is, okay?

Mowgley nodded and waited as Tez put a hand on each door, leaned forward and steadily pushed them a foot or so apart. As he nodded, Mowgley turned sideways, breathed in to minimise his paunch, and pushed his way into the dark interior.

Before taking a further step, he slipped and fell on to the cracked but elaborately patterned tiles in the vestibule. He lay there cursing for a moment, as Tez picked up his torch and pointed it through the gap.

Looking at his sticky hand, Mowgley saw that it was red with what he at first thought was paint.

Then from the metallic smell and a closer look, he realised it was blood.

He cursed again and thought he had probably cut it during the fall before he saw that he was lying in a large red pool.

Then Tez spoke in a curiously dead monotone: 'Fucking, fucking, fucking shit.'

Mowgley looked up and followed the bright finger of the torch beam.

Directly above him, a naked man was swinging gently from a rope attached to an overhead beam. It looked as if he had bled out, and the blood appeared to have come from his groin area. The man also had something red and bloody in his mouth, and it took some seconds for Mowgley to realise what it was.

4

The headquarters of the *Gendarmerie Nationale* in Cherbourg is a post-war cube of concrete; it lies just up the road from the swinging bridge which effectively divides the commercial quarter from the seedier docks area.

Inside seemed like most police stations he'd visited. Especially the interrogation room, which had the familiar bouquet of stale cigarette smoke, cheesy feet and vomit and the strong disinfectant used to mask it.

He was sitting at a burn-scarred table on which was an ashtray advertising a well-known aniseed-based liqueur. Three of the plain brick walls were covered with an irritating shade of gloss green paint. The fourth had a large mirror set in it, which every TV cop drama viewer would recognise as a device allowing those outside to look in without being observed.

There was a door with a peephole in it on another wall, but no policeman standing beside it. As it was a foreign country, Mowgley did not know if this was because he had not been charged with anything, or they did not care if he tried to kill himself.

He waved at the mirror, and started to roll another cigarette. At least you could still smoke in a French nick, he thought. It was not allowed in England nowadays, although the Jocks still saw the sense of allowing a suspect to have a fag.

If it was the right word, he had been invited to come down to the station when the police had arrived mob-handed at *La Cour* after Tez the builder had made a panic call. The senior uniform on the spot had made it clear with a mixture of sign language and bad English that he thought it would be a good idea for Mowgley to accompany him to Cherbourg to make a statement, and Mowgley had seen no sense in putting up a fight.

Although on the whole he would rather be elsewhere, he was fairly at ease with his situation. Even the most ardent Anglophobe would surely not think a Briton of being so stupid as to kill someone and leave him hanging about on the doorstep. As in Britain, a slightly intimidating Q&A in the appropriate nick would be the usual way of trying to get the goods from a witness who might have something to hide. Besides, it was quite interesting to see how things were done this side of the Channel.

So far he had been offered and refused a cup of coffee, then made his statement with the help of the official interpreter.

Racine was a clearly philosophical man of middle years who chose to disguise his Moroccan extraction by dressing as a 1970s Rastafarian, complete with huge striped woollen bonnet and dreadlocks. His army greatcoat and indeed his whole person reeked of cannabis, which obviously did not concern his employers.

As he said after Mowgley had turned down a sprinkle of something interesting for his roll-up, he made a good living from British visitors, but it was not as good as in the hey-day of the booze cruise era.

The cops would usually overlook minor punch-ups or vandalism, but for anything more serious they would arrest the offenders and call him in. At fifty Euros an hour, it was his good fortune that a young male British booze cruiser who could speak French was almost unheard of; indeed, some of his customers seemed to have a problem speaking their native tongue.

Before leaving, he had given Mowgley his contact details. It was not clear if he was offering his general services, or that he thought Mowgley was the sort of person who was going to be in contact with the police on a regular basis.

The statement had been made with no problems, though both the investigating officer and Racine seemed to have difficulty with the idea that even an Englishman would have bought a near-ruin money pit in the middle of the middle of nowhere in the Normandy hinterland.

Now Mowgley was waiting for the inevitable second visit from Monsieur Nasty, who he suspected would be killing time on the other side of the mirror wall. The good cop/bad cop interviewing routine was a stereotype, but had become a stereotype because it was true. Psychologically, it invariably worked to soften a suspect up with a bit of verbal abuse, then to bring on the caring, sharing type to offer sympathy, cigarettes and coffee. From his scant experience with the various branches of the national French police force, Mowgley suspected they did not usually bother with a nice half of any investigating duo.

The plain-clothes officer who had questioned him and overseen the statement-taking either had something against Britons or was an all-round misanthrope. To be fair, he had treated Racine and the woman who typed up the statement equally as contemptuously. It also seemed to Mowgley that Racine had cleaned up some of the man's more offensive comments and remarks.

~

A little after he had made his third roll-up and fifth funny face at the mirror, the door opened and three men came in.

One was Monsieur Nasty, and he was followed in by an older, grey haired man who was obviously more important. The third man had a familiar and welcome face.

Yann Cornec was a Breton who had been a senior officer with the *Gendarmerie* before leaving under similarly muddy circumstances as Mowgley. He had set up as a private investigator in Brittany, and they had met some years earlier when a multiple murder investigation had taken Mowgley to that region of France.

When they met, Yann had said he wanted to expand his agency to take on cases in other parts of the country. He was particularly interested in exploiting the growing British expatriate market, and had come to an arrangement with Mowgley with regards to intelligence-gathering in the UK. The arrangement had worked well, with the CID officer using his contacts and sources to pursue any enquiries on Yann's behalf. It might be a Briton seeking a large loan about whom the finance company was curious, or the tracking of a partner who had returned to England suddenly. The deal had worked well, and had led to an offer of full-time employment when Mowgley took retirement.

This was one of the main reasons Mowgley had decided to move across the Channel, but he had not expected to see his prospective employer until he'd settled in and got the work at *La Cour* under way.

He stood up and held out a hand as the stocky figure walked towards him. 'What is this, Jack,' said Cornec in his near-flawless but sometimes stilted English. 'Just arrived and you are already digging up the dead bodies?'

Before Mowgley could answer, his interrogator stepped between the two men and spoke sharply and almost dismissively to Cornec. The Breton did not reply, but looked at the officer in a way that Mowgley would not have wished to be looked at by someone like Yann Cornec. Almost at the same time, the older man spoke even more sharply to Monsieur Nasty. The officer reddened, looked as if he was about to make something of it, then glared at Mowgley and left the room.

~

'Cheers to all, then.'

Mowgley lifted his beer glass, and the two men sitting opposite him responded to his toast in French and Breton.

They had adjourned to a small and refreshingly seedy bar round the corner from the police building, and going by the photographs and rank badges and newspaper cuttings on the wall it was the station local.

As Mowgley now knew, the grey-haired officer was entitled to his air of authority as he was a full Colonel in a branch of the *Gendarmerie* which investigated serious and unusual crimes when it chose to take over from the local or national police force. There would not be much love lost between the civil and military arms of the service, and this was probably why the original interrogator had been so pissed off.

A former colleague of Yann, René Degas was obviously nearing retirement age, and possibly planning to join Cornec in the private investigation agency.

This, Mowgley had already surmised, could be the real reason Yann was opening the branch in Cherbourg, and perhaps why Degas was being so affable. It might be that Mowgley's real role would be to keep the future boss's seat warm. But perhaps he was reading the situation wrongly.

'So,' Mowgley said when both men had politely declined his offer of the tobacco pouch, 'have you got any ideas about who left the hanging man in my place?'

Degas looked at Yann as if inviting his comment, but the Breton held out a hand in an after-you gesture.

The Colonel nodded, then, as if in afterthought, said: 'By the way, the answer is no, unfortunately not.'

Mowgley frowned. 'The answer?'

The policeman smiled. 'It is the first question educated foreigners ask when we are introduced. The answer is that I am not related to Edgar Degas, the great artist. Degas is not an uncommon name in France, like Smith in yours.'

He smiled again 'As to your actual question, it is as I am sure you would agree, too early to come to any conclusions. But as the victim is - or was - the lover of Madame Mooney, we will of course be speaking to Mr Mooney.'

'A case of "cherchez l'homme" for a change, then?' said Mowgley.

There was no reaction, leaving Mowgley unsure if they had not thought his gag worth a smile, or he had said it wrong. Then Degas said: 'Yes, we are looking for him, but he has, as I think you would say, gone to ground.'

Mowgley nodded. 'Yes. It's an old hunting expression. The hunters say that the fox has gone to ground or earth. It means it has escaped into a hole in the ground, I suppose.'

'Ah yes,' said Degas with a polite smile, 'the pursuit of the uneatable by the unspeakable as your Oscar Wilde had it. He is very popular here, you know.'

Mowgley smiled in agreement, put the roll-up in his mouth and made to stand up, but Yann reached out a hand and laid it on his forearm. At the same time, a woman almost as round as she was high came from behind the bar and headed their way. She smiled at Mowgley, showing an interesting combination of ivory, plastic and gold, then placed a saucer on the table in front of him.

He nodded his thanks and looked across the table. 'It's okay to smoke in here, then?'

Yann Cornec smiled. 'Remember where you are. We are in France and the bar where the off-duty officers like to come.

We believe in liberty, if not always brotherhood and equality. You will see there are no ashtrays available so that precise law is being observed. Also, I do not think that the local officers are going to do a raid on their own bar. Especially as most of them smoke.'

Mowgley nodded and happily lit up. There were some Gallic ways of applying logic of which he approved. For a smoker there was no worse punishment than to stand sullenly outside a pub like a naughty schoolboy.

After he had inhaled hungrily, he tapped his cigarette on the saucer and said: 'Okay, I get that you would be looking for Mooney, but if it was him, why would he go to all that bother?'

Degas looked puzzled. '"Bother"?'

'I mean trouble. Why would he strip the body and hang it up for me to find? And do that thing with cutting his todger off.'

'That's the first time I have heard it called that,' said Degas with mild surprise. 'If it were Mr Mooney, perhaps he thought his wife would find the body. When her lover did not appear, she would probably have taken over responsibility for the sale of your property, and might even have been confronted with the body when she was showing the buyers round. It would add to the pleasure of his revenge. With regard to the people you said were interested in *La Cour*, do you know who they are? Mrs Mooney is of course in shock, so I will not be speaking to her for a day or more.'

Mowgley shrugged. 'Denys did not say. Just that there was a group of people interested in turning the place into a hotel and spa.'

'A hotel and spa?' echoed Cornec. 'There, and in that place? It would be better and cheaper to build a new one.'

'Yes' agreed Mowgley, 'that's what the builder said. But Denys told me that was what the buyers wanted to do. I think he also said they were foreign buyers.'

René Degas smiled. 'In Normandy, that could mean someone from another region. But it could be of interest.'

Before Mowgley could ask why, the phone the Colonel had placed on the table buzzed insistently. He picked it up, looked at the screen, nodded an apology, and placed it to his ear.

There followed the tinny sound of a rapid-fire stream from the earpiece, interjected by the Inspector's grunts of acknowledgement. Then he put the phone down, emptied his wine glass and stood up. 'I am so sorry but, again as you say, duty calls.'

Cornec looked up at his friend. 'Something we should know about?'

'No. Just another thing.' Degas first shook hands with Cornec, then with Mowgley, who felt obliged to stand. It was only as he did so that he realised he had never shaken hands with anyone while sitting down.

'It was good to meet you,' he said, 'even though it was not in the ideal circumstances.'

Degas smiled. 'I understand and me too. Perhaps we can meet later in the week for a drink or something to eat?' He took what looked like an expensive metal credit card holder out of his inside jacket pocket, opened it and removed a small piece of pasteboard with some numbers on it. 'This is my home and work, and my mobile. See you soon, and welcome to France - and Cherbourg.'

Nodding to Yann, he picked up his phone and made a scribbling sign in the air to the woman behind the bar, which Mowgley took to mean she should put their drinks on his tab. Or perhaps there was a special police tab, which was settled in varying ways.

They watched as he walked away, then Yann finished his beer and waved the glass at the barmaid. Then he asked: 'What do you think of my friend?'

Mowgley thought of the best answer: 'He seemed a very nice man. Perhaps too nice.'

Cornec frowned. 'What do you mean?'

Mowgley again considered his answer before speaking. 'Well, here's me, a former middle rank foreign police officer who's just left the force under a bit of a cloud. Then there's him, a senior officer on home ground.'

'And so?'

'In England I don't think a high-ranking officer would be so friendly so soon. Unless he had some reason.'

Cornec looked at Mowgley steadily then gave a slow smile. 'You are in France, remember. We do things differently here. But I am glad to see that you are still being a detective.' He looked around as if checking for eavesdroppers, then said: 'René and I go back a very long way. He is nearing retirement and, though he will have a good pension, he is too young to do nothing. With his contacts and experience he could be very useful to the company in obvious ways.'

'But where does that leave me?'

Cornec's eyebrows met. 'I do not understand.'

'Will he be taking over from me when he retires?'

The Breton gave a short and apparently genuine bark of laughter. 'You need have no worries for your position with us. In his job, René is almost a law to himself. He knows very important politicians and other people. You need not worry that he will want to sit in your seat. And your contacts and experience with the way things are done in England could be most useful to him even before he retires.'

He shook his head and smiled, then waited as the barmaid arrived with two bottles of beer. He poured some into each glass, then held his up in salute. 'Okay, now we should talk business.'

Mowgley nodded. 'I'm all ears.'

'What?'

'I mean yes, let's go.'

'Let's go?'

'Sorry, just being idiomatic, or do I mean idiotic? Boom Boom.' He saw Cornec's brows knit again, and quickly said: 'Sorry, just forget everything I said. So what do you think about the Hanging Man? I didn't want to say too much in front of your friend.'

Cornec sniffed. 'Why not? He is on our side.'

'Of course, just feeling my way. But what do you think it was all about? Mooney getting revenge?'

Cornec shrugged. 'Maybe. Or maybe it was nothing to do with Mooney. Have you been upsetting anyone?'

'Not lately, and I don't think over here. Why?'

Cornec shrugged again. 'As you said, it could not have been to get you into trouble or they would not have done it like that. And why would you want to kill the man who is selling your house? And even if you did, why would you cut off his cock? Maybe it was some sort of warning.'

'Warning?'

'In some countries and criminal organisations, killing someone and leaving them to be found with their cock in their mouth can be a way of showing the dead man had been having sex with someone he should not have been. Or that he had been talking about something he should not have been. Have you been upsetting someone in those ways?'

Mowgley frowned. 'Not guilty on all counts as far as I know.' He saw Cornec's bemused expression: 'I mean I don't think I have done anything like that.'

'Well, I am sure René will soon know something.'

'So he will be taking the case over?'

Cornec nodded. 'Of course, that's why the officer who interviewed you was so unhappy. As I said, René is a law to himself. Soon I will explain to you about the various law enforcement agencies and what work they do, but at the moment you just need to know that René Degas is a very, very useful person to have on your side.'

He let the words hang for a moment, then said: 'But now we must talk about when you can start working for me. Do you need some time to do something with that old ruin of yours?'

Mowgley shook his head glumly. 'I think I'll just try and sell it as it is. Or give it away. When do you want me to start? We still have to work out how it's going to be between us, of course.'

Cornec looked irritated, then shrugged. 'Not really. I have been talking to my feducier-accountant-, and he says the best thing will be for you to work as an associate or a supplier of services. You will not be employed by me, but sell yourself to me by the hour. I will pay for all the costs of running the office, and you will use the micro-enterprise system.'

'The what?'

'It is a new scheme to make the paying of tax for self-employed people simpler, which would be a miracle. It means you do not have to hire a feducier or keep any accounts. You just keep a record of money earned and spent. Then you pay tax on the difference.'

'That sounds simple enough.'

Cornec scratched his bristly scalp and made a wry face. 'Nothing to do with the tax system in France is simple, my friend. Before you can qualify to use the *micro-enterprise* system you must be registered as a self-employed person, and then your turnover can be no more than 32,000 euros each year - if you are providing a service and not running a business like a bar or shop.

'I see.' What Mowgley did see was that, under the arrangement Cornec was proposing and despite what he had said previously, the Breton would be giving none of his company away and could get rid of his 'partner' at any time.

Cornec held up a hand as if he thought Mowgley was concerned only about the turnover ceiling. 'Don't worry about that small amount. Nearly all businesses in France have two sets of accounts. One is for the taxman, and the other is the truth. There will be many chances for us to work things out in cash.'

Mowgley nodded, then asked: 'Okay, sounds good. And when do you think you will have some cases for me?'

Cornec smiled. 'They are waiting in the office already. Do you want to see it?'

~

They did not have to walk too far to the new branch office, as it was next door to the bar.

At first sight, the premises looked like the average estate agency or insurance office found in every commercial area of every French town. So far there was no signage above the shop front or on the plate-glass door; in the window was a line of vertical poles supporting black, felt - covered squares. As yet, the squares bore no information or advertising material.

Inside the emphasis was on minimalism, and the black theme continued with the carpet and a couple of line drawings on one bone-white wall. Against the wall was a glass-topped table with chrome legs on which a single magazine had been artfully arranged. On either side of the table were a couple of black leather bucket seats, and overhead was a row of skeletal chrome spotlights. A door was set into the centre of the wall furthest from the entrance, and on either side of it were identical black leather and chrome desks. One was unoccupied, and using a laptop on the other was a strikingly pretty woman.

'What do you think?' asked Cornec.

'Very...businesslike,' said Mowgley, unsure if his new employer was talking about the decor and furnishings or the lady at the desk.

They walked towards her, and she looked up and smiled, effortlessly managing to make Mowgley think he was the more important of the recipients. He was not good at these things, but he judged her to be somewhere in her thirties, and much more of a natural beauty than Sylvie Mooney. He could not tell if her titian hair was natural, but under the unrelenting spotlight it was easy to see that her complexion was flawless. Against the ivory skin, the crimson bow of her lips was almost startling. She had what people used to say was a pert nose, and a firm but not threatening jaw. If asked to find a comparison, he would have said she looked quite like the Hungarian-born actress Rula Lenska in her early career. Mowgley had always been taken with her combination of beauty, dignity and panache until she had appeared in an episode of Big Brother.

'This,' said Yann Cornec, 'is Cristobel Hardy, or as she prefers to be known, Mimi.'

Mowgley thought about offering a hand and then saying hers was frozen, but settled for a deep nod and a pleased-to-meet-you smile.

'Mimi,' continued Cornec, 'is the office manager and so far the only team member of the Cherbourg branch of SEPC.'

He saw Mowgley's look of enquiry, and said: '"Services d'Enquêtes Privés Cornec"'

'Cornec Private Investigation Services,' explained Mimi, 'It sounds better like that, does it not?' And Mowgley felt a small rush of relief to hear that she could obviously speak English as well as her employer.

She stood and Mowgley saw that she was as tall as he, and that her figure was as impressive and tastefully displayed as the rest of her.

Mimi held out her hand and repeated the just-for-you smile. 'Welcome, Mr Jack,' she said, 'to your new life with CPI.'

~

Mowgley stood and watched as the couple walked away. In her modest heels, Mimi was several inches taller than Cornec, but a man like Yann would not be worried about any threat to his masculinity.

They walked very closely together, and he thought it more

than probably Mimi was sleeping with her boss. He realised he did not know if Cornec was married, not that that would make any difference. It was France, and it seemed to him that married couples without at least one lover between them were the exception. Whatever the relationship, it would be useful for Cornec to have her based in the new office, and she had probably been assigned to assist Mowgley for more reasons than those given. With access to all files and cases and communications, she would be well placed to alert Yann if Mowgley tried to cut out the middle man and deal direct with any British customers. Not that it would be wise to try and fiddle Yann Cornec.

He looked at his watch and wondered what to do next. It was strange to have no ongoing cases to try and avoid, and be free to do exactly what he wanted. He stretched and took a deep breath and became aware of the aroma of the chickens roasting on a rotisserie outside a grocery shop on the other side of the road. An attractive young woman click-clocked past on the cobbles and smiled as if to let him know she knew what he was thinking.

He returned the smile, then decided to buy a chicken and a couple of bottles of cold beer for a picnic by the water.

Remembering to look to his left, he stepped from the pavement and headed for the roasting chickens.

All in all and despite missing so much about his home ground, it might not be so bad to spend some time in this so similar but so different city by the sea.

5

Mowgley had a headache.

The cause was not strong drink - he had not had a hangover for many years - but a close encounter with paperwork of the virtual kind.

In his former life, he had left all that sort of thing to the office admin lady, and unavoidable personal demands had been dealt with by Melons. But his surrogate form-fillers were far away, and this was a country which had made the simplest official process into almost an art form. But then, as an embittered expat had said to him in Coco's bar, what can you expect from a country which insists you keep your electricity bills for the best part of a decade?

It was a week since his first visit to the office and also his first proper day at work. He had spent the morning being gently led through not only the basic office systems and protocols, but also the interminable labyrinth which had to be negotiated before he could become a recognised and approved tax-payer.

For nearly three hours, he had been passing on information to the relevant authority regarding his nationality, age, colour and all other personal details short of his inside leg measurement. Now, he was replete with suffering.

He looked at the minimalist wall clock which had no markings and a single slim hand, and sighed. That was an example of another national trait. The French liked to demonstrate their belief that style often outweighed utility, but a clock which did not show the time seemed a bit strong even for them.

As his shirt front testified, the espresso cups were another triumph of design imperatives over practicality, and had handles with no holes in them. As he had failed to get to grips with the knack of pinching finger and thumb together with sufficient ferocity, the full cup had obeyed the law of gravity and swung downwards as he lifted it to his lips.

As he tired of trying to decipher the clock, Mimi began tidying her desk and preparing to go for lunch. So far, it was all good between her and him. She had increasingly come to his aid during the week, which had always been his game plan. In other ways she was not at all like Melons, but had the same weakness for taking over when he acted like a Category 'A' helpless male.

'Is it that time already?' he asked.

She looked at him and then the clock and nodded: 'It is a quarter of an hour of the *midi*.'

'Ah. Are you going out to eat?'

'Of course.'

'Can I treat you? I owe you for all your help.'

She looked as if she did not understand the question, then again said 'Of course,' but this time in her own language. This was part of the arrangement they had already established that she would repeat common words or phrases in French in the hope that Mowgley would eventually absorb them. He had read somewhere that you needed to hear a foreign word seven times to learn it, but he was living proof that the rule was not universal.

'I wonder, before we go, would you mind calling a friend in England for me?'

She frowned and looked at the phone on his desk.' Do you not know the international code?'

'Yes, but I wanted to surprise her. Look...' he held out a crumpled piece of paper, 'I've written down what I would like you to say. I'll only be a few minutes, then we can go somewhere nice to eat.'

She shook her head in a resigned manner which was remarkably similar to his former sergeant, took the paper and punched out some numbers.

After a moment, she held the piece of paper up at arm's length and said: '*Bonjour*. This is the office of the Normandy branch of *Services d'Enquêtes Privés Cornec.* The director wishes to speak with you.' Without waiting for a response, she pressed a button and indicated with a nod that Mowgley should pick his phone up. As he did so, she pointed at the door to the kitchen and toilet, then tapped her wrist to remind him not to be long.

As she left, Mowgley counted to ten, then said: '*Oui, 'ello. Qui apelle*?'

'Actually it should be "*Qui est la*?"', said Catherine McCarthy, 'but not at all bad as you've only had a week to practice it.'

'Oh, sorry, I thought it was a client. I had asked my PA to call you, but forgot.'

'Bollocks.'

'Quite. Anyway, it's just a quickie before I take Mimi to lunch.'

'Who?'

'Mimi. My PA.'

'You are priceless. Have you done the 'your tiny hand is frozen' schtick yet?'

'Of course not. I'm a changed man, remember? I was just calling to see when you were coming over.'

'I was going to give you a bell later anyway. There's been some developments on the poor buggers in the fridge lorry.'

'Go on, then.'

'They've found the driver.'

'And what did he have to say for himself?'

'Not a lot; he was dead.'

'Oh.'

Melons continued: 'They found him in a ditch alongside a lay-by near the service station. Throat cut, the poor sod.'

'By who or whom, d'you reckon?'

'Whom, reckon,' she said automatically, then: 'Not a clue yet, apparently; there's a few possibilities, though. Maybe someone was with him on the drive to Toddington and did the job so he wouldn't be able to talk. Maybe the organiser was waiting for him and was not best pleased to find all his customers dead. Maybe the driver just panicked when he found them dead and phoned whoever was paying him and Mr Whoever arrived and killed him to keep him quiet. Or, long shot, but maybe there were eleven stowaways and one of them survived, and killed the driver in revenge.'

'Can't see that one. Why would he bother to hide the body

and how would he get it to the ditch? Sounds like it could be any of the rest, though. Any useful numbers in the victim's phone?'

'No. It was gone when they found him. And his wallet or anything else he may have had on him.'

'In that case, how did they know it was the driver?'

'Not too hard. He was wearing a company outfit, and they took photos and wired them through to the factory for confirmation. And then there was his ID photo in the cab of the lorry.'

'Okay, smartarse. So anything else?'

'Not so far.'

'What do you mean 'Not so far'?'

'Remember it's not our - my - case. I'm getting all my info second-hand.'

'Does that mean you're not coming over?'

'Bloody sure. I'm nearly out of baccy and booze.'

'And is your nice new boss accompanying you?'

'No. I talked him out of it. I'll be over on the morning boat on Wednesday, and you can come with me to the Livarot factory if your duties as Normandy director allow. Either way we can have something to eat and drink in Cherbourg in the evening, and I've got a room booked at the Mercure. Does that suit?'

'Well, I don't know about the Livarot trip as one has a couple of cases overdue for action. But we could do the evening. In fact I'm supposed to be having dinner with a very senior *Gendarmerie* officer, but I'm sure he won't mind if you tag along.'

'Most gracious of one.'

'*De rien*. Gotta go now as my PA awaits. I'm taking her to a rather nice little bistro overlooking the water. See you Wednesday.'

'Get you. Can't wait to see your office and meet your 'PA'. What's she like?'

'A bit like you, funny enough. Only younger and a bit better-looking.'

'Thanks a bunch.'

'As I said, *de rien, cherie.*'

~

Mimi locked the outer door at thirteen minutes before the sacred midday. As she said, it was only a brisk walk across the bridge to their destination, and that would give them plenty of time to study and discuss the menu and what they were going to drink.

Mowgley suspected there would be no pies or pasties on even the *à la carte* menu, and while waiting on the pavement he wondered again at the almost religious devotion with which so many French people applied to eating something in the middle of the day. The nation still came almost to a stop for at least an hour from noon, but it did not seem to affect the economy and nobody seemed to mind that so many shops and other places of business were shut when they were taking a break from work. He had even heard of restaurants which closed for lunch, but that was probably an exaggeration.

As Mimi joined him and they headed towards the *Pont Tournant*, Mowgley looked idly across the road. Two men were sitting in a blue Simca parked outside the convenience store, and both looked away a shade too quickly as they saw he was looking.

The turning bridge spanned the narrow channel where the sea flowed from the docks area and marina into a basin lined on one side by rusting and mostly redundant tin-roofed warehouses once kept busy by the local fishing fleet.

The bridge was, to use the French term on the warning notices, 'susceptible' to moving an hour before and an hour after full tide. This was only supposed to happen when there were vessels wishing to pass through, but often it seemed to open just because it could.

It was an interesting feature, unless you wanted to cross it at the wrong time. It was actually a bit of a nightmare at any time, with two lanes taking traffic into the heart of the town in a sort of half-hearted one-way arrangement which many visiting drivers did not understand and some locals ignored.

The remaining single lane which crossed the bridge from the other side merged traffic from two directions, and cyclists and pedestrians and the apparently independently-minded traffic lights complicated matters further. Mowgley had tried driving across the bridge just once, and found himself in the wrong lane and facing a wall of oncoming traffic. He had escaped by doing a five-point turn and going back the way he had come. Since then he had chosen to use the pedestrian walkway.

It being mid-tide and the bridge in a good mood and obviously not feeling susceptible, they crossed it safely and walked along the quayside to the restaurant Mimi had chosen. As she said, she had been spoiled for choice, as there were at least a dozen eating places in a row overlooking the docks and nearby marina.

Some of the buildings had survived for centuries, though like his home city, Cherbourg had been knocked about badly in the War. The dockyard at Portsmouth had attracted the attentions of the Luftwaffe, while it had been friendly fire from the Allied invaders that had reduced most of Cherbourg to rubble. Both cities had been hastily patched up in the post-war years, and it showed.

Like Portsmouth, Cherbourg was acquiring a veneer of sophistication with expensive and expansive waterside development and new and trendy bars, restaurants and stores, but in both cases the veneer was a thin one.

~

After an entertaining if eye-wateringly expensive lunch for the amount of food they had been given, Mowgley had arrived to find his first-ever message on the office answer phone.

Mimi had been an engaging guest, and the food was okay if you liked fish served in very small portions. But he could not see the sense of paying the equivalent of twenty quid for a bottle of red wine which tasted no different from the ones at a fifth of that price in any supermarket. The place she had chosen was next door to one where she said the food was no better and cost twice as much. Strangely, the more expensive establishment was busier, which meant either Mimi was wrong, or all those people were willing to pay the difference just to be seen eating there.

The call was from Sylvie Mooney, and she sounded bad. In fact, she sounded worse than bad. Her voice was shaking and strained as she said she needed to meet with him soon about something that had come up with the sale of *La Cour*.

~

She arrived as Mowgley was getting to know the proprietor of the bar next to the office. This was not easy, as Yvette spoke about as much English as Mowgley spoke French. But, running a dockside bar, she was obviously experienced in sign language and they were already on first name terms when Sylvie Mooney walked in.

She did not look the same woman as when they had last met, and not just because, as even Mowgley could see, she had neglected her appearance.

Asking what she wanted to drink, he signalled for a bottle of the house wine, then led the way to the table in the furthest corner. It would not matter if Yvette tuned in to their conversation, but there were two bored-looking men leaning against the counter. They were in civilian clothing, but Mowgley had been in the game long enough to recognise an off-duty policeman, even from another land.

He could think of nothing to say which could possibly make her feel better about the sudden and grisly death of her lover, so did not try. He filled their glasses and then lifted an apologetic arm to encompass the seedy surroundings: 'I thought it would be best to meet here, because you said it was about a problem with *La Cour.*'

She did not answer immediately, picking up the glass and almost draining it before realising he was watching. As she put it down, he noticed how much her hand was shaking. At their last meeting she had sported blood-red and somehow predatory talons. Now, the varnish was splintered and cracked and on one finger the nail had been bitten to the quick.

When she spoke, her voice was shaking almost as much as her hands.

'Do you think I could have a brandy?'

'Of course.'

He stood up, but before he reached the bar she had called out in machine-gun French to Yvette. Mowgley knew enough to know she was asking for a large one, and was not surprised when the policeman at the bar casually turned round to look at her. Perhaps, he thought, they were wondering if she came by car.

He returned to the table with a glass in each hand and said: 'I thought I'd join you.' As he sat down he looked across at Yvette, held up his baccy pouch and raised his eyebrows at the backs of the two off-duty policemen. She smiled and nodded and came over with an official saucer.

'Silly question,' he said, 'but are you okay? I mean, obviously you are not okay, but...'

'No,' she responded after lowering the level of the brandy by at least an inch, 'it's alright. It's just the shock about Denys, and...'

She left the sentence unfinished and he thought it best not to pursue it at that time.

'So, what's the problem with *La Cour*? Have the people who made the offer pulled out?'

'No', she said again, 'it's not that.' She looked down at his cigarette-rolling activities, then said: 'Could you make me one?'

He held the unsealed tube of paper out for her to moisten with her own spit but she shook her head, so he licked it, finished rolling it, handed it to her and then supplied a light.

She sucked in the nicotine, then exhaled and said: 'It's your wife.'

'My wife?' It was Mowgley's turn to take a slug of brandy. 'What about her?'

He had not heard from The Cow for more than five years. They had parted on bad terms, the divorce had been acrimonious on her side, and they had no children or any other common bond or reason to keep in touch. He had assumed that she was still with her French lover, and perhaps living in France.

'She called the office this morning and said she was your wife and asked about *La Cour* and if it had been sold yet. I suppose she must have seen it on our website. The girl she spoke to did not know that you are divorced, and said she thought there had been an offer, but that your wife would need to speak to me. I have not been in to the office since...Denys, but the girl gave your wife my mobile number.' She shrugged. 'It is something I tell them to do if there is a question or a matter they cannot handle.'

He made an apologetic face as if taking some of the blame for the call, then asked: 'And what did she want?'

She emptied the brandy glass and took another savage draw on her cigarette: 'She asked me to tell you that she would want half the money.'

'Well,' Mowgley held her empty glass up, and Yvette broke off her conversation with the cops to walk over with the bottle. He nodded his thanks, then continued: 'She's got no chance. The divorce deal was that she had the house in England and I took on the mortgage for *La Cour*. It wasn't my choice.'

Sylvie Mooney tried to look interested and said. 'Perhaps, but things may be different under French law.'

'Perhaps.' In her state he did not want to ask her comments on the relevant aspects of post-divorce rights to property in France. He also did not think that, in her state, she would have felt compelled to come and see him just to tell him face-to-face that his ex-wife was after another pay-day. She knew what he had done for a living and probably had not too many people she could talk to about whatever it was that had made her so scared. For sure she would not be confiding in her husband. He looked directly into her eyes and asked: 'Is there anything else?'

'No. She just said she wanted me to call her when the sale was made.'

'Come on, Sylvie. You know what I mean. Do you want to tell me what you are frightened of? Has your husband threatened you?'

She emptied her glass. 'No. I have not heard from him and do not know where he is. That is what the police asked.'

'And have they not offered you protection?'

'Yes, there is a man in the car. I asked him to stay there while we spoke and he said he knows this bar is safe.'

'So it is your husband that you are frightened of? You believe he was responsible for...what happened?'

'I do not know. I am not sure.'

'But who else do you think could have done it?'

She looked across at the bar, then seemed to have an inner struggle. Then: 'I do not know. There is nothing I can tell you.'

Or not yet, he thought. He put a finger up to order another round. 'But you will call me if you want to talk about anything - apart from the sale of the house, I mean?'

She hesitated, looked at the bar again, and said: 'Yes. I will.'

6

'I think you need to speak to the boat lady to solve your problem with your wife.'

'Does she knock people off for a few quid, then?'

'What?'

'Is she an assassin? Will she kill my wife for a fee?'

Mimi shrugged. 'She may do, as I think she is quite mad. But in this case, I think it best for you to speak to her first about the law.'

Mowgley looked meaningfully at the pint china mug he had brought to the office from the caravan along with a jar of his favourite instant coffee. The label on the jar said it was Nescafé *Gold Blend*. The mug had FUCK YOU. I'LL PANIC IF I WANT TO printed on the side. It summed up his attitude towards people who used the imperative. Sometimes he did not want to have a nice day, or enjoy anything.

Mimi looked at the mug with a frown. 'You want more of that *merde*? What is wrong with real coffee?'

'It *is* real coffee,' he protested mildly. 'Somebody in another time and place made it in the approved way. Then they froze it. It just needs thawing out. So what about this boat lady?'

It was the start of the day after he met Sylvie Mooney in the bar next door. He had arrived with the mug and the coffee and a potted plant he had picked up at the 24/7 store opposite. As he had told Mimi, he had been impressed with the range of proper English-style food like ready-made sandwiches and Pot

Noodles on sale. Mimi had been less than impressed with the wilting chrysanthemum, and explained that they were traditionally given to dead family members on All Saints Day.

Mimi picked up the mug with an air of resignation. As she had said earlier, it was part of her job to teach him French, not how to be French in matters of taste. 'Sarah - Madame Campbell - is a specialist in English and French law. We use her when we have a problem with a case involving someone who is English.'

'So she speaks English?'

'Better than you, I think. She is from Scotland and comes from a good family.'

'So why is she living on a boat? And where is it?'

'Mimi gave another low-level shrug: 'It is in the harbour. I guess she lives on it because she wants to. And perhaps because she is a little... mad. I think a lot of your English *aristos* are a little bit mad?'

'I think you mean eccentric; they used to be because of inbreeding. Nowadays you get all sorts of common people in the House of Lords. Do you mean she was -is- a proper Lady?'

'I think so, or so they say in the bar at the *port de plaisance*. She was an *avocat* - a lawyer -, but gave it up and came to live in France with her husband. He is a good musician, and plays in the oldest jazz club in Paris. But she prefers to live here with her dogs and chicken.'

'She keeps chickens on a boat?'

'Just one. It is her pet.'

'I like the sound of her. Is she expensive?'

'It depends if she likes you.'

'Then I will take her some flowers.' He looked at the pot plant. 'You don't want that one, do you?'

'I do not think Madame Sarah would like flowers. She might like a bottle of good wine. I will phone and warn her you are coming...and what you are like.'

Mowgley shrugged off the implication. 'Red or white? They're doing a special offer over the road for two Euros a bottle or twenty for a case. I could take one and keep the rest here for customers we want to impress.'

As he knew she would, Mimi shuddered. 'I think not. Give me some money and I will go and get you a bottle. And a ten euro note will not be nearly enough...'

A couple of hundred years before and because of where it was, Cherbourg had been known as a key to the kingdom. Over time, increasingly extensive and massive sea defences had been added until, by the middle of the 19th century, the small town boasted the biggest man-made harbour in the world.

As well as seeing off a string of would-be invaders, the port has also been a stopping-off point for all sorts of more friendly visitors. In 1912, the SS *Titanic* had called in before heading off for its fateful rendezvous with the giant iceberg.

By the first half of the 20th century, state-of-the-art transatlantic liners would regularly heave-to at the magnificent art-deco terminal, often with what the press liked to call a galaxy of Hollywood stars on board. To Mowgley, it seemed strange that long-dead movie legends like Cary Grant, Clark Gable and Rita Hayworth had walked where he now trod.

Further along the quay was the marina, and the *Bad Penny* was not hard to spot amongst the row of gleaming yachts and gin palaces.

As Mowgley was to learn, the 65ft-long, wide-beamed and solid-looking wooden boat had taken to the water in 1944 to help feed the nation rather than defend its shores. The unromantically-named Motor Fishing Vessel 096 had had a relatively quiet war, then been sold off to the owner of a Humberside fishing fleet as his stylish flagship. She was then bought by a former music-hall comedian who gave her a name which was a double pun on his name and catch-phrase. He had spent more on turning the boat into a luxurious floating home than she had cost to build, with an opulent master bedroom where the catch had once been stowed, and a fully-stocked bar in the wheel house. When he fell overboard and drowned after serving himself at least one too many drinks in the bar, the unusual vessel had passed through a number of hands before reaching those of her present owner.

The *Bad Penny* stood high in the water and it was mid-tide, so Mowgley had to navigate a steeply tilting and narrow gangplank before encountering a large and clearly aggressive cockerel guarding the deck. He knew that the Romans had used geese to warn of potentially unwelcome visitors, and the cock appeared to fulfil a similar function.

The crowing and wing-flapping eventually resulted in a head appearing through a hatchway behind the wheelhouse, followed by a hand brandishing a large spanner.

'Good boy, Chanticleer,' the owner of the head, hand, spanner and boat said, before hauling herself up on to the deck and inspecting her visitor and the bottle he carried.

Lady Sarah Campbell appeared to be around his age, and looked as if she did not care what age people thought she was. Her grey hair was cropped close, and her features, though neat and small, could justifiably be described as strong. Rather than make-up, she chose to wear a smear of engine oil across her cheeks and nose, and her baggy overalls disguised any shape she might have.

'Hello,' she said, apparently addressing the bottle of wine rather than him. He began to reply, then remembered how old-money gentry liked to use the greeting as an exclamation of mild surprise. Next, she said 'Very good' and turned her attention to him, seeming to find him less impressive than the wine. Finally, she asked: 'Did you pick it, or was it Mimi? I shall know if you lie.'

Without waiting for an answer, she took the bottle, handed Mowgley the spanner and led the way into the wheelhouse.

Inside, he was attacked good-naturedly by a manic cocker spaniel with unseemly short legs and a curious tuft of hair on his head which made him look like a canine Tintin. From an obviously top-of-the-range but ill-used Chesterfield sofa, an elderly and obviously very decrepit French bulldog regarded him incuriously.

He looked around and saw that one end of the wheelhouse was occupied with the devices necessary to control the engine and steer the vessel; the other end had become the living area in which he was standing.

Opposite the Chesterfield was a combined wireless and record player which in its heyday in the 60s would have been known as a radiogram. On top of it was a clearly high-end and wafer-thin laptop computer. Alongside the radiogram/desk was a wheeled office chair, and next to it a wood-burning stove, its kinked and rusting flue pipe disappearing through the roof of the wheelhouse.

In one corner of this end of the wheelhouse was a stainless

steel sink alongside a work surface with a chopping board and electric kettle on it. On the wall behind was what he would have thought of as an unnecessarily extensive collection of spice and herb jars. Below it was a small refrigerator and a curtained-off shelf, and the kitchen ensemble was completed by a small and aged gas cooker. A half-open door in another corner revealed the top of a flight of stairs. The walls of the wheelhouse were lined with dark-stained strips of wood, and the large framed windows gave a panoramic view of the quayside and harbour.

While the owner of the *Bad Penny* busied herself with a corkscrew, Mowgley accepted her invitation to take a seat on the Chesterfield next to Bébé. As he did so, the ancient bulldog peered up at him from one rheumy eye, then farted in a somehow disapproving way.

Lady Sarah handed him a glass, sat on the backless office chair, gave him another searching look. 'So you're the disgraced policeman. Or, from what I hear, should that be disgraceful?'

'Probably both,' said Mowgley, lifting his glass and his right buttock. It was good that he would now be able to break wind secure in the knowledge that the French dog would be held responsible.

~

An hour passed swiftly, and the bottle of Pinot Noir had been emptied and added to the collection lining the deck along one wall of the wheelhouse. Another had been collected from lady Sarah's cellar in the bilges.

Nothing had yet been said about the reason for Mowgley's visit, but they had talked easily for two near-strangers from very different worlds. The boat bobbed gently at its moorings, the long dusk was settling in, and Nelson the mad cocker had gone off to explore the quayside. Bebé had moved on to Mowgley's lap, and the cockerel was still on guard duty.

'Does he not get a bit lonely?' asked Mowgley as his hostess opened a follow-up bottle.

'Who, Chanticleer? No, I don't think so. I did move a couple of hens in last year, but he ignored them. I have a feeling he may have homosexual proclivities.'

She leaned over and topped up his glass: 'So how are you liking your new life so far?'

Mowgley reached for his tobacco pouch. He had asked earlier if smoking was permitted on board, and been told it was compulsory. Perhaps, he thought, this was another reason he was getting to like his host: 'It's a bit early to say. I've owned a ruin and been coming here at least once a month for a long while, but the idea that I'm actually living and working here is going to take some getting used to. I thought I'd hate it because I had no job or home to go back to, but that seems to have helped a bit. What about you?'

'Burning bridges can help. It's easier adapting to a new life when you can't go back.' She reached for the cigarette he had just finished rolling, lit it, directed a long plume of smoke at the ceiling, then addressed his question: 'Do I like living here?' She took another extended drag. 'I love France and I quite like some French people. Living on the Penny makes it different, though.'

'In what way?'

'The boat is my home, and this marina could be anywhere in the world.'

'But don't you miss friends and family and...things about where you come from?'

She reached out and gently pulled Bebé's ear: 'I don't have any family, or many friends. I think that's something else that makes moving to another country so much easier. I deal with so many Britons who come over here to live and think it will be like being on holiday all the time. Of course, it isn't. They start to miss people and silly things they have got used to. Loners like you and me do better, because how we feel does not depend on other people.'

She looked at her glass. 'Oh dear, I'm getting philosophical. That's your fault. I usually only have the dogs and Chanticleer to talk to over a glass or two.' She picked the bottle up, held it to the light and frowned.' On that subject, I fear that was the last bottle in the cellar.'

'Mowgley made to stand, earning a sharp reproof from Bebé. 'I can go ashore and get some reinforcements. I need a wee anyway.'

She shook her head, then reached for the mobile phone on top of the radiogram. 'It's okay, as a regular customer I get a special delivery service from the 24/7 opposite your office. But you may want to visit the heads anyway. It appears that Bebé has shat on your lap...'

~

The sea, if not wine-dark was a pleasing shade of velvet. The lights of the clubhouse on the other side of the basin glittered and danced on the water, and mingled with the red and green navigation lights on the yachts and boats still away from their moorings. There was not much of a breeze, but Mowgley was peeing on the lee side to be sure. He had learned that much about seamanship when living on a disused lightship on a quayside scrap yard near Portsmouth ferry port.

It was turning out to be a very pleasant evening, and had seemed rude to turn down Lady Sarah's invitation to sleep on the Chesterfield with Bebé rather than having to drive back to *La Cour*. It would anyway be some time before his trousers dried out and he could put them on again.

During their wide-ranging conversation, they had talked briefly of the claim by his wife for a share of the proceeds of the sale of *La Cour*, when and if it happened. Lady Sarah was of the opinion that natural justice, fairness and their original arrangement and settlement would exclude her from a payoff, but as she also said, French or any law had little relation to justice and fairness. But she would be happy to help, and would bill the company rather than Mowgley.

He threw his cigarette at the reflection of a near-full moon, then saw that blue had been added to the palette of colours dancing on the surface of the water.

Walking along the deck and past the forward end of the wheelhouse, he saw a cluster of vehicles close to the edge of the far quayside. Two marked police cars had their roof lights revolving slowly, and a breakdown truck added to the display with its amber hazard light. The jib of the grab hoist on the back of the truck reached out over the water, and there seemed to be some activity directly beneath it.

He watched for a moment and turned away. Had the incident occurred on his patch less than a month ago, he would have been - and wanted to be - involved in whatever was going on.

Here, it was nothing to do with him and none of his business.

He was not yet sure if that made him happy or sad.

Mowgley yawned, checked the buttons on his boxer shorts, and walked towards the welcoming lights of the wheelhouse.

~

'You need not have dressed to impress me.'

Mowgley scratched his chin, ran a hand through his hair and adjusted the tie that was no longer there. 'Har-de-har. I didn't know the French did irony.'

Mimi grunted with dry amusement. 'And who do you think could be better at irony than the French? We have had lots of practice. First the *bourgeoisie* told us that we must get rid of the *aristos* to have a better life. Then they took all the land and power of the ruling classes and made sure *they* had a better life. We are still ruled by the rich and privileged who live like the Sun King but pretend to be just like us and to hate wealth and privilege.'

The office had been open for an hour when Mowgley arrived from the *Bad Penny* to find a list of calls awaiting his attention. One was from Melons, one from Yann Cornec, and Colonel Degas had phoned three times. He was sounding, Mimi said, increasingly impatient and even a little concerned.

'Are you going to make a habit of turning your portable off when you are not in the office?'

Mowgley tried to look innocent. 'I didn't turn it off. The battery must be flat, or it must have turned itself off.'

Mimi shook her head and held her hand out. 'Give it to me, please. I will see that it is on and regularly charged, and you can take it when you go out and give it back when you return. Okay?'

He complied like a schoolboy handing over a confiscated item. 'I don't suppose you're related to my sergeant, are you?'

'Your sergeant?'

Before Mowgley could explain, a police car screeched to a stop directly outside. They watched as Colonel Degas got out.

'Now you *are* in trouble,' said Mimi. 'The Colonel has come to arrest you for not making yourself available.'

Mowgley waved and smiled disarmingly as the policeman pushed the door open, but there was no response.

Mowgley tried again. 'Allo 'Allo, René. Were you pissing by?'

The Colonel remained unsmiling as he held the door open.

'Can you come with me, please, Jack?'

Mowgley shrugged and looked at the clock. 'I thought we were meeting later this evening. Are you that desperate for a drink?'

'We were meeting. But something has happened.'

'Not a double date? Are you going to let me down?'

'No,' said Degas. 'It is the lady you were with yesterday. Sylvie Mooney.'

Mowgley stopped smiling. 'Is she alright? What's the matter?'

'No. She is not at all alright. She is dead.'

7

In recent years, Mowgley had become a not infrequent traveller in French police cars, but still found himself gripping the back of the driver's seat as the car sped away from the office, its siren and lights at full pelt.

He closed his eyes as they crossed the swing bridge against the lights, then asked: 'What happened to Sylvie?'

Degas turned and looked at where Mowgley sat in the back.

'She was drowned.'

'Drowned?'

'Yes, she was in a car that went into the basin near the yacht club last night. We got her out after midnight.'

'But I thought - did she not have a police guard?'

Degas nodded grimly. 'Yes. One of my men. He was in the car with her.'

'Drowned?'

'No', said the policeman flatly. 'He was shot. In the back of the head.'

'But how could that happen. He would not let anyone get that close, surely-'

The policeman interrupted him: 'Yes, I had thought of that. It appears that the killer shot him from *inside* the car.'

'But that would mean-'

'Yes. Either he had left the back doors unlocked, which is strictly against procedure, or...'

'He knew the man - or the woman - who killed him.'

'Yes.'

'Or he thought he knew the sort of man or woman who approached him.'

Degas frowned. 'What do you mean?'

'He or she could have been in uniform.'

The police officer made no reply, and Mowgley realised that Degas had not considered that possibility, nor that it might have been a woman. From what he knew, murder was increasingly becoming an equal-opportunity career.

As he opened his mouth to ask if he was under suspicion and where they were going, the car braked sharply and slewed through a tall wrought iron gateway above which was a sign indentifying the building as the Louis Pasteur hospital.

~

Mowgley had seen more dead people than most, yet it always struck him as if anew just how empty their bodies were. Even when there was no visible injury, it was immediately clear that whatever it was that had inhabited that waxy shell was gone forever.

He was sure she would have found it another way, but Sylvie Mooney looked at peace now. All fears and concerns had left her with her last breath. She did not look exactly serene, but the pale, sombre face showed no strain, fear or the slightest concern. It would be nice to think she was in a better place, and he envied those who really thought there was somewhere else to go except for the abyss of nothingness.

She lay on her back under the harsh lights, modesty preserved by the sheet pulled up under her chin and her hair neatly arranged. By now, he thought, the forensic people would have done their thing and someone had taken the kindly step to set her face in that neutral expression. It was very unlikely she would have looked so relaxed when she was pulled from the car. The horror of those final flailing moments must have been mirrored on her face, and some unknown mortuary assistant had taken pity on her. Or perhaps did not want to have to look at her face as it had been at the moment of death.

Mowgley looked from her to Degas and the small group of men in the background. Two were wearing green loose tunics and trousers, with caps of the same material, latex gloves and calf-length white rubber boots. Another, probably the porter, had on a knee-length white coat and his hands were resting on the handles of a stainless steel trolley. The face of the body it bore was covered, but Mowgley guessed it was the policeman who had been with Sylvie in the car. On the other side of the trolley was a young, uniformed policeman. He had taken his cap off as if he were in church, and was twisting it between his hands. His face was drawn and his eyes red. Mowgley wondered if it was his first body, or the first colleague he had lost.

Mowgley looked back at the face of Sylvie Mooney, then at the Colonel: 'Yes, of course, that is her.'

'Thank you.' The policeman nodded at the man in the white coat, who stepped forward and drew the sheet gently over the face of the woman Mowgley had been talking and drinking with no more than twenty-four hours before.

~

'I still don't get why you needed me to confirm it was her,' said Mowgley.

They were sitting in the bar next to the office, ironically at the same table he had shared with Sylvie Mooney such a short time ago. The *Bar du Port* was busy, mostly with uniformed and plain-clothes officers, but it was very quiet.

Both men were drinking apple brandy with beer chasers, and René Degas had asked for one of Mowgley's roll-ups.

'I do not know how it is in your country,' he said, 'but here a body must be identified by either a relative or friend or colleague.'

Mowgley smiled wryly. 'I would hardly class myself as a friend - or a colleague.'

Degas looked at the end of his cigarette and leaned forward so Mowgley could re-light it. 'No, but it is only a formality in this case. We know who she was and I did not want to make any of the women at her office have to look at her. Also and strange to say, we could not find Mr Mooney to ask him to say it was his wife.'

'I suppose not. So no sign of him yet?'

'No. But perhaps plenty of signs of his activities.'

'So you think it was him? I can perhaps see the killing of the man who had taken his wife and business away, but it seems a bit extreme that he would be deranged enough to kill a policeman to get at the woman who had betrayed him?'

'That is also what I was thinking. But who can say what happens to some men when they are betrayed?'

Mowgley nodded. 'And what about the man who died with her?'

Degas sighed heavily. 'He was a good man. A local man with a wife and two young children. He had a bright future and had applied to join the close – protection squad. I gave him the job above the head of his superior officer so he would gain experience and stand a better chance of advancing his career and life. Now his wife has no husband and his children have no father.'

Mowgley reached across and awkwardly laid a hand on the officer's sleeve. It was a gesture he could never imagine himself doing on the other side of the Channel when in the company of a senior officer. 'I'm sure you will see they find justice.'

Degas sighed again and then looked up, his face becoming suddenly inanimate. 'Oh yes, they will have justice, if not retribution or satisfaction. I will see to that.'

With nothing to say, Mowgley was about to re-light the policeman's roll-up for the third time when Yvette appeared and laid a packet of *Disque Bleu* cigarettes on the table. Alongside it she placed an expensive-looking slim gold lighter. Degas dropped his shoulders, puffed his cheeks out, looked up at the bar owner then reached out for the packet. She touched him lightly on the shoulder as if giving him a sort of benediction, topped up their brandy glasses and walked away.

Mowgley watched as Degas opened the flap, took out a fat cigarette and lit it, then sucked in a lungful of smoke. He nodded in sympathy. 'Trying to pack it in?'

The colonel took another deep draw and let the smoke trickle from his lips before answering. 'Yes. Yvette keeps a packet for me, just in case. Have you not tried to stop?'

Mowgley shook his head. 'A bit late for that now, I think. It's nearly half a century since I started.' He breathed deeply as if savouring the smoke from the *Disque Bleu*. 'Funny enough, my first cigarette was one of those. The smell brings it all back.

We were on a school exchange trip to Paris. We couldn't believe we could buy cigarettes and beer and flick knives so easily.'

Degas grunted. 'So it is our fault you are addicted to tobacco?'

'I don't think so. A bit like sex, I would have tried it sometime anyway. My sergeant worked out once that I must have got through more than half a million fags since I started. She's like that.'

'Ah yes, your...Melons, you said she was called?'

'Yes; it's a bloody cheek going on at me as she smokes herself.'

'And can I ask why do you call her Melons?'

'Ah.' Mowgley thought about it. 'It's a long story, but that was her canteen name as soon as she arrived.'

'Canteen name?'

'It's a nickname. A whatsname.'

'A whatsname?'

'Yes, a... sobriquet. Do you know what that means?''

Degas smiled. 'I think you will find it is - like so many 'English' words, one of ours.'

'Ah, right. Anyway, in the old days, we used to give all the women - and most of the blokes - nicknames. Sometimes they were quite obscure, like a sort of code. I remember there was one secretary with a huge nose. She was called Cyril.'

'Cyril?'

'Yes, a long time ago there was a football player in our city called Cyril Rutter. He had a really big nose.'

'I see,' said Degas as if he did not. 'And Melons is called 'Melons' because...?'

'As I said, it's a long story. You will know when you see her. But nobody has called her that for years, especially after the last bloke who did to her face had to wear a truss for a long time.'

'She sounds an interesting woman.'

'She is, but please don't ask her about her nickname this evening. If our meeting is still on, that is.'

Degas shrugged. 'Why not? I don't want to sit at home and think about what happened, and there's nothing more I can do today.'

'Well, I don't know if you have a rule about consorting with suspects off-duty?'

'I think we can make an exception in this case, as you are more of a witness than a suspect, and a good *gendarme* is never off-duty. Oh, and by the way...'

'Yes?'

'I think you will find that 'consorting' is another word you have stolen from us.'

~

Sergeant Catherine McCarthy's car rolled over the link span at the head of the queue, she having used her influence to gain the most favourable spot on the lower car deck.

Mowgley was waiting for her at the burger van by the terminal. She parked alongside, got out, stretched, took a deep breath, walked over, took the hamburger from his hand and bit into it. 'Nice,' she said, obviously not meaning it.

'Yes, they're okay, but they're not English, are they?'

She handed it back. 'What do you mean? The owner of this van is from Dudley, isn't he?'

'Yes, but what I mean is that burgers and hot dogs are sort of universal or stateless, aren't they? You can get them anywhere. I read somewhere that France is the second biggest customer for McDonald's after the USA. Pies and pasties are really English, but you can't get them over here.'

'Are you saying that Greggs ought to open a nationwide chain in France? Do you think that the French would really understand the point and purpose of a sausage roll?'

Mowgley shook his head glumly and finished his burger with an air of a man who was doing his duty rather than enjoying himself.

She took pity on him, summoned him to follow with a crooked finger and said: 'Walk this way please, sir.'

Mowgley automatically said 'If I could I would, Ma'am' then followed her to the back of her car, his exaggerated hip swinging drawing the attention of a number of passers-by. At the car, Melons lifted and threw open the boot with a theatrical flourish to reveal her overnight bag and two large cool boxes.

Mowgley tilted his head back and inhaled like a fox taking the scent. 'I do *not* believe it. Lamb Vindaloo.'

Melons stepped back with jaw agape. 'I don't believe it either.

How could you smell a curry that's in a sealed cool box?'

Mowgley sucked at an imaginary pipe. 'A simple matter of deduction, Watson. What else would be in a cool box you were bringing me as a present?'

'The bucket of vindaloo is actually a present from Bombay Billy at *The Midnight Tindaloo*. There's a load of Bombay potatoes, onion bhajis, special rice and mango and onion chutney in there as well. He says all the staff are missing you and you can have your old room in the attic back any time you want it.'

Mowgley sniffed again and ran the back of his hand across his eyes. 'What a man. But what about the other box? More curry?'

'Nope. That's a present from the regulars at the Ship Leopard. They had a whip-round when they heard I was coming over. In no particular order, there's a dozen pork and meat pies and pasties that Two-Shits swears are only a bit out of date, and he said you like them mature, anyway. He wanted to put some cans of lager and cider in as well, but I explained they're not hard to come by in France. There's at least a dozen packets of real pork scratching and some proper Walker's salt 'n' vinegar crisps. Then there's a dozen copies of the Daily Telegraph, the crosswords of which I resisted doing, and a great big block of cheddar cheese from Twiggy the barmaid. I think she's planted a kiss on it. She asked if she should wrap the cheese in a pair of her split-crotch knickers, but I said that might be a bit much for your heart on top of all the other stuff.'

Mowgley stood and regarded the boxes with almost the same level of wonder and excitement as Howard Carter setting eyes on the contents of the burial chamber of Tutankhamun.

'Isn't it funny,' said Catherine McCarthy after allowing him a suitable period of contemplation, 'We've spent the last decade coming over here to take stuff back to England, and now I'm bringing stuff over here for you.'

~

Like a long-term local, Mowgley guided Melons to the bar next door to his office so they could talk business before his old aide met his new one.

Having introduced Melons to Yvette, Mowgley took their

drinks to what had become his table, leaving her to chat with the patron in annoyingly fluent French.

She arrived carrying an ashtray saucer as Mowgley was rolling a cigarette. 'Blimey,' she said, 'you've got your feet under the table here a bit quick, haven't you? Madame says you are the perfect customer and remind her of her first husband.'

'Really? And what happened to him?'

Melons reached into her bag for her cigarettes. 'He died of alcoholic poisoning. But that's not why you remind her of him. So far. '

'I see. And the big young bloke. Does he work here, or is he her son?'

'Neither. He's her toy boy. Or as they say, *jeune étalon*. It means "young stallion".'

'Good for her. So she went from an old boozer to a young stallion. I am well impressed.'

'That's not the half of it. She's had four significant others of various ages and fitness levels in between the old soak and the toy boy.'

'I'm even more impressed. Did she say what happened to them?'

'Some died and some went away is how she put it. But she reckons you could be next when she gets fed up with the youngster. She says he is good in bed but has nothing to say. She said she enjoys talking to you, which impresses me. Your French must have come on leaps and bounds.'

Mowgley nodded non-committedly and decided not to mention the sign language arrangement with Yvette. 'Yeah. But enough of her and me. What's been going on back home? Have you got your new boss under control?'

'Sort of.' She took a drag on her cigarette and a pull on her beer. 'The reefer lorry thing is getting interesting.'

'How so?' Mowgley looked over her shoulder as the old bell on the door clattered, then he lifted an arm in salute to the uniformed police officer who had come in. It was, he saw, the young man who had been at the mortuary. He saw Mowgley, gave a nod and continued to the bar.

Melons looked around and said. 'You are doing well. Here a couple of weeks and you're already well in with the local filth. 'What do you think he's after?'

'Probably a takeaway. The nick's just round the corner. This is their local.'

'And your office is next door. That is handy.'

'Yann Cornec is a clever man. So tell me about the lorry.'

'I think it's a lot bigger than we thought, and going to get bigger. I went up to the Met last week to see the bloke who took over your former lady friend's role at the SPU.'

Mowgley automatically grimaced and rubbed his left shoulder. The Special Projects Unit was a group with virtually unlimited powers when they were investigating a national or international situation concerning guns, drugs or organised murders. He had worked with Detective Superintendent Jane Stanton on a case involving splinter groups of the Russian mafia some years before, and had found himself unarmed and in mortal danger from a man with an AK47 assault rifle. The SPU officer had saved his life by shooting and killing the man, but in the process had also shot Mowgley. He had never been able to decide whether it was an accident, but it had anyway brought their brief affair to a sudden conclusion.

'Before you go any further,' he asked, 'how come you went to see this guy on your own? Have you been promoted in my absence?'

'Not yet,' she replied evenly. Then: 'To tell you the truth, my new boss gives me a much freer hand than you ever did. Anyway, he likes to spend a lot of time in the office, which pleases Jo the admin lady no end.'

'I bet it does. So what did the SPU bloke have to say?'

'For a start, he agreed that as the lorry came through Portsmouth and the poor buggers in the lorry may well have died on the boat, we were entitled to show an interest and be supplied with sitreps.'

'You little charmer,' said Mowgley. 'And what did you get out of him for now?'

'It seems it was in fact well worthwhile for whoever arranged the stunt. My man said that since security had stepped up at Calais, people-smugglers have been looking at other points of departure and entry, and charging punters mega money to get them over and into the UK.'

Mowgley nodded. Seriously high fences now encircled the entire port area at Calais, with police vans at every entrance. The camps of would-be immigrants were still growing in size but it was becoming harder for them to get through. It was inevitable that the gangs would look elsewhere, and had started using high-speed vessels for relatively long-distance crossings, and charging a very high price for a place on board.

'They guestimate that the stowaways would have paid up to ten grand each for the trip and all services to get them to Toddington, which would have meant a nice hundred thousand for the organisers, less a bit for the crossing and the driver, if they ever intended paying him. But there's more.'

Mowgley signalled for a refill. 'Go on, then.'

'The SPU chap said one of the cases was stuffed with class 'A' powder rather than smelly cheese. They'd skimmed off the top half inch of all the rounds beneath the top layer, then filled the boxes with heroin and put the cheese lids on top. Then they'd wrapped the boxes up again. Each box would have looked and felt like the real thing without too much of a close inspection, and the pong of the Livarot would have put any sniffer dogs off the scent.'

'Very clever. So why did whoever it was who slit the driver's throat leave the box in the lorry? It must have been worth a fortune.'

She nodded. 'You can say that again. Each individual box took around two hundred grams of dope. The stuff in the lorry was good quality china white heroin and the going rate on the street - after cutting - is anywhere from £20 a gram upwards. The case had sixty dodgy boxes in it, so at an average street price, was worth coming up for half a million quid.'

'Blimey. So why did he leave it?'

'Dunno. He may have panicked, or it may be that the disguise was so good he missed a case. Unless they were marked he'd have had to go through all of the cases and either open them to find the dodgy ones, or get a clue from the weight.'

'Blimey again. So do SPU have any idea of how many druggy cases there were on board?'

Melons made a face. 'Sort of-ish. They know how many cases the lorries normally set off with, and how many were left behind at Toddington. At a rough guess and if all the missing cases were the same as the one they found, the shipment could have been worth, wait for it, twenty million. But that's street price of course.'

Mowgley took a swig of beer and tried to whistle, but it did not work. 'Still a nice earner for whoever slit the driver's throat, assuming it was him who nicked the dodgy cheeses. Curiouser and curiouser, as the White Rabbit said-'

'It was Alice.'

'What - who brought the drugs in?'

'No, dumbo. It was Alice who said "curiouser and curiouser." In *Alice's Adventures in Wonderland*.'

'Alright, smartbottom.' He paused, sighed, then said: 'I was going to tell you not to speak to a senior officer in that disrespectful way, but now I can't. Never mind. My point is why would a gang with twenty million quid's worth of class 'A' in a lorry risk losing it all for the sake of another hundred grand for stuffing a load of illegals in the back? If they'd shown up on the body-heat scanners or been heard, there was a good chance that the drugs would have been found after the stowaways were arrested.'

Sergeant McCarthy wrinkled her nose and nodded. 'Yeah, that's what I thought was a bit odd.'

'Yes, but this is a bit more than a bit odd. Though of course there's no accounting for the thought processes of the criminal mind. One common factor with drug smugglers is greed - that's why they do what they do and don't give a shit about the people who suffer.' Mowgley looked at the watch he did not wear. 'Anyway, time to meet your replacement.'

'Eh? That's not fair. I've told you all my stuff, but what about yours? What about all these dead bodies turning up around you? And who's this lady Sarah Whatsername? And what about the sale of *La Cour*?

Mowgley drained his glass and stood up. 'All in good time, Sergeant. When you've met Mimi you can bugger off to Livarot to pursue your investigations. We've got a long evening ahead of us when you get back, but now you need to see where Mowgley Private Eye hangs out when he's not on a case...'

8

Most *Cherbourgeois* prefer the centuries-old name of their town, but since absorbing its neighbour at the start of the Millennium, the official appellation has been Cherbourg-Octeville. Because of the joining-up, the town now has a population of a shade over 80,000, making it the second largest commune in the department of La Manche.

When wishing to eat or drink out or be entertained, most residents, visitors and tourist find what they are looking for in the waterside area beyond the swinging bridge. The centre of action is the square with an imposing fountain and overlooked by a truly grand-looking theatre, built in the Italianate style. Set into the bottom left hand corner of the *Théâtre* is an unassuming but impressively appointed and laid-out restaurant, and it was here that Mowgley and his companion were to meet René Degas.

'I wonder if they did this to make it look like a theatre gallery?' asked Catherine McCarthy as she leaned over the chrome railing lining the mezzanine floor.

'Stop pretending you're interested in the design imperatives. You just want to see what he looks like.'

'Not at all,' said Melons defensively. 'Is that him?'

Mowgley looked down to where a man was coming through the double glass doors. He was short and fat, and the light reflected brightly from his tonsure-like bald patch. Mowgley put his age at around sixty, though he looked older. 'Of course not,' he said, 'René is much older, and shorter, and fatter. And he has less hair. Anyway, why should you care what he looks like?'

'I don't,' said Melons. 'Just interested, that's all. Your friend Yvette said he was right fit when I said we were meeting him.'

'Calm down, dear,' said Mowgley,' and tell me about your visit to Livarot. How was the factory?'

'Cheesy. Actually, it was very interesting how they make the stuff nowadays compared with how it was done then. And get this. They actually promoted it then -and still do - as almost a health food. It's a whacking forty percent pure fat.'

Mowgley made a mental note to give Livarot a try and then asked: 'And did you have any joy with the driver?'

'Nobody really knew him at the factory. He'd only been there a couple of months and kept himself to himself.'

'Anything known?'

'No. But guess what?'

'What?'

He got the job on the strength of a testimonial from...Sean Mooney.'

'Eh what?'

'Yes. And there's more. Another bloke had been offered the job, but he backed out at the last minute.'

'So, our man turns up right on cue, clutching his references from the well-known proprietor of Normandy Dream Homes?'

'That's it. The reference said that Guy Ribet had been employed by the company to help move furniture and possessions in and out of their clients' properties. He was found to be diligent and hard-working and helpful etc.'

Mowgley stroked his imaginary beard. 'You look as if you've got even more to tell me.'

'Correct. Monsieur Ribet moved into a nice apartment in Caen soon after starting with the cheese people. Before that he had been renting, but he was suddenly able to come up with a ten thousand Euro down payment for his new bachelor pad.'

Mowgley frowned. 'Poor sod didn't get long to enjoy it though, did he? So what do you reckon happened?'

Melons shrugged. 'Well, for sure we know that Ribet started the journey with a lorry load of box-fresh cheese, but we don't have a clue where the druggy cheese and the illegals were taken on board.'

'What about the risk of checks at Cherbourg when the lorry went through?'

'Because cheese lorries go through virtually every day, they haven't been that scrupulous. And you know they tend not to care what's going from France rather than coming in. And the way it was done with the stacking inside, they'd have had to dismantle a wall of Livarot boxes to see if anyone was behind it. I doubt they bothered '

'You mean they just waved him and all that dope and illegals through?'

'More or less, though the Frogs won't admit it. The driver carefully went through at lunchtime, so most of the people supposed to be checking the commercials were not on duty.

'Surprise, surprise.' Mowgley shook his head. 'But at least we know that the druggy cheese if not the people must have been put on board this side of the Channel.'

'Yes, looks that way. I know Colonel Degas has the local cops looking at all suitable warehouses or units between Livarot and Cherbourg. If it was going to be a regular operation, they'd need somewhere to doctor and keep the cheese and do the changeover.'

Mowgley nodded. 'Very interesting, especially the connection with Mr Mooney. Hello, there he is!'

'Who, Sean Mooney? Where?'

'No; the copper you're so not interested in.'

She looked to where Mowgley was pointing as a tall, slim man in a dark, well-cut suit and a shock of casually arranged grey hair came through the double doors. He looked around and then up at the mezzanine, saw them and smiled and waved. Mowgley wondered if he would have waved so enthusiastically had Melons not been there.

'That's him, isn't it?' said Melons reproachfully. 'Why did you say he was short and fat and bald?'

'Just to see your reaction. Anyway, what is it with you and French policemen?'

She did not reply, and Mowgley thought it best not to pursue the matter. His sergeant had met an officer in the *Gendarmerie* on a case some years before and a torrid affair had commenced. It had ended when Catherine McCarthy found that her *amour* was married with several children.

While they watched, Colonel Degas apprehended a passing waiter and spoke to him briefly before walking up the wide, sweeping staircase. As he approached, Mowgley noted how his former sergeant did all the things that women seem to do when an attractive man is approaching. He stood and introduced them, and noticed that Degas took the seat directly opposite Catherine.

'I think this is where I say that I have heard much about you from our mutual friend,' said Degas, taking a packet of *Disque Bleu* and his gold lighter from his pocket and laying them on the table.

'I wish I could say that he has been telling me all about you,' said Melons. 'But you are not at all as he described you.'

Mowgley nodded at the cigarette packet and lighter. 'Does that mean we can smoke in here as well as your local, then?'

Degas shook his head. 'Regretfully no. There are some things beyond even the power of a senior *Gendarmerie* officer.' He looked down at the table. 'I just do that out of habit.'

Any further conversation was forestalled by the arrival of the waiter Degas had spoken to. He was struggling slightly under the weight of an ornate metal stand holding an ice bucket. In the bucket was a bottle with a napkin wrapped around it. The waiter put the stand next to Degas and looked quizzically at him. The policeman gave an almost imperceptible shake of his head followed by a nod of dismissal, at which the waiter put three tall and narrow glasses on the table and withdrew. He did not actually back out of their ambit, but it was clear from his manner that he knew who or what the Colonel was. Degas reached over, twirled the bottle in the ice, then took it from the bucket. He looked at Catherine McCarthy and said: 'I hope you like Champagne? I thought we should toast the arrival of Mr Jack to work and live in Normandy, and of course, the occasion of your visit.'

He filled their glasses and they drank. Degas and Melons with moderation and appreciation, and Mowgley in one sour-faced draught.

'Did you like my choice?' Degas asked Catherine McCarthy.

'Yes,' she said, reaching over and turning the bottle so she could see the label. I like Oudinot Brut very much, but I won't ask what it cost.'

Degas gave a classic Gallic who-cares shrug, and turned to

Mowgley. 'And you, Jack?'

'Mowgley held his empty glass up to the light and studied it gravely. 'I found it a bit like cider, but without the taste.'

Degas smiled. 'You do a good job of acting as the simple man of the people, my friend.'

'Who says he's acting the simple bit?' said Melons.

Degas smiled again. 'If you are in no hurry, we can look at the menu and order and have another bottle as an *aperitif.*'

The waiter came and went and took their orders after refuelling their glasses.

Again Degas proposed a toast, then asked Melons: 'And may I know why you are here? The official reason, I mean? Is it the Livarot truck with the bodies and the drugs?'

Melons shot a look at Mowgley, who held his hands up in a not-guilty gesture. Then she asked: 'So how did you know about it? You would have been informed about the deaths, but I only heard about the discovery of the drugs yesterday.'

The Colonel smiled. 'I am sorry if I shock you, but I speak with your people in London every week, and we have been working together on a project involving illegal immigrants being taken from Brittany to the UK.'

'Brittany?' said Mowgley, 'that's a bit of a journey isn't it?'

'Yes. But it seems there are so many people wanting to live in your country that they will go to any lengths - and pay any price - to get there. In fact, a lot of French people are rather hurt that all those young men have come right through France and are trying to leave us and find happiness in Great Britain. But the Brittany route is a new one.'

'So how did it work?' asked Melons.

'There are thirteen Breton fishermen - mostly from the port of Paimpol - about to stand trial for taking more than 200 illegal migrants to the United Kingdom. They were able to leave from various small ports without any sort of checks.'

'And did the fishermen act alone?' asked Melons.

'No, they were supplied with their passengers by a gang of Albanians. Interestingly, all the passengers were also Albanian.'

I suppose it was big money for the fishermen?' asked Melons.

'Compared to what they would earn from the sea, I suppose. They had a thousand Euros for each person carried. The people traffickers were charging *ten* thousand for each person, and a 'group rate' of fifteen thousand Euros for a family.

Mowgley winced. 'Ouch. 'And did you get the traffickers?'

'Unfortunately, they will have to be charged and prosecuted in their absence. There will be more Bretons charged in the coming weeks, and two of the accused have already committed suicide.'

'Suicide?' Melons looked shocked. 'Surely that's a bit of an over-reaction? What's the likely sentence?

'There is a maximum of ten years for people smuggling.'

'And do you think that's what they will get?'

Degas smiled. 'I doubt it, even though they are Bretons.'

Melons looked as if she were about to ask what was different about Bretons but thought better of it: 'And how did you get on to them?'

'I am sorry?'

'I meant how did you find out about them.'

'Jack's boss Yann was very instrumental. He acted as an *agent provocateur*. He looked waspishly at Mowgley: 'As I am sure you know, that is another French expression you seem to like to use.'

'So Yann'll be keeping his head down, then?' The policeman looked mystified again, and Mowgley added: 'I mean he'll have to watch his back if the Albanians are on the loose. And are you sure that the two suicides *were* suicides?

'No, we are not sure at all...'

~

Mowgley was content. He was not used to taking his time over eating or drinking, but it had been a very pleasant experience. The long meal had finished with coffee and large shots of Calvados that even he could appreciate was far superior to the moonshine apple brandy he was more used to.

Rene Degas had insisted on picking up the bill and said he could put it through expenses as he had been discussing international cooperation on a case between the *Gendarmerie* and a representative of the British Police Force. Mowgley had seen the bill and was happy to let the Fifth Republic pay for their working dinner.

The trio were standing beside the elegant fountain, waiting

for a police car that Colonel Degas had summoned.

He would be dropping Catherine off en route, and had offered Mowgley a lift to *La Cour*. Mowgley had thanked him, but said he would be spending the night on a friend's boat, and the bonus was that his sleeping companion would be a very flatulent dog. This would mean he would not be held responsible for the pungent odour in the wheelhouse the next morning.

~

The night air was warm and the onshore breeze pleasantly cool. Someone was playing music on a nearby yacht, but it was Sinatra, so the sound aided rather than marred the moment.

Mowgley, Lady Sarah and Bébé were sitting on an old garden bench at the stern of the *Bad Penny*. It was not secured to the deck, and regularly slid an inch or two with the small movements of the boat. But that too was pleasant.

'More wine, your ladyship?'

'Do you need to ask, Mowgley?' She rounded and stretched the vowel in Lady Bracknell style, and he tugged at an imaginary forelock.

'No, mum.'

She held out her glass and made a tutting sound. 'That's what cooks call their mistresses. If you want to play at being my butler, you should call me "Milady"...'

'What, like Parker in *Thunderbirds*?'

'I have absolutely no idea what you are talking about. You are a funny man.'

'I'm funny? What, funny like I'm a clown? I amuse you?'

'Yes, you do. And why are you putting on that dreadful accent? Is your nose blocked? Do you suffer from nocturnal adenoids?'

Mowgley looked hurt: 'That was Joe Pesci. In *Goodfellas*. When he pretends to be angry and frightens Ray Liotta.'

She sighed. 'Again, I have no idea of what you are talking about.'

He shrugged. 'You've no idea how often people say that to me. Especially lately and if they're French.'

They drank in companionable silence while they listened to

Fly me to the Moon, then she said: 'You know, I've never met anyone like you.'

'Is that good or bad?'

'I don't know. You're just different. You are obviously quite intelligent, but you pretend not to be. And you say you are incapable of learning French.

'Old dog and all that.'

'No, I don't think it's that. I've known people who have learned to speak passably when they were much older than you. I could give you lessons, but I think the truth is you just don't want to become familiar with the language.'

'And why would that be, professor?'

'You tell me. I'm not a psychiatrist. Perhaps an ancestor of yours was ravished by a Norman, or you just don't like the new. Are you a creature of habit?'

Mowgley thought about it. 'I suppose I am, or was. A few friends and a local pub and the same Indian restaurant. But now I have to embrace change, don't I.'

'Do you? From what you say, you seem to be attempting to set up a mirror image of your life in Portsmouth on this side of the Channel, if that were possible.' She adjusted her glass, then held up her hand and ticked off the points: 'Local bar, a policeman friend and a strong woman sorting you out at the office.'

Mowgley saw what she meant. 'Mmm. Maybe.'

Another silence and another draught of wine, and then she asked: 'And what about your aspirations for the world? How much do you want to change things and make it a better place? What are your politics?'

'Dunno really. I think a lot of trouble in the world is caused by people who want to change it and make it a better place - in their view. I think more people should be like me.'

'You mean apathetic?'

'If you like. As a matter of fact, I was going to start an Apathy Party, but couldn't be bothered.'

If Lady Sarah got the joke, she did not react to it. 'But what about your work as the man in charge at the ferry port? Did you see yourself as the man in the white hat?'

'I suppose it would be a bit grey. I just think people should not do bad things to each other. I'm paid...I *was* paid to keep a sort of order on my little patch. I was happy to overlook a bit of dodgy dealing and ducking and diving, but I don't like people who hurt people. Especially big people who hurt little people.'

'And did you cut corners to achieve your idea of justice?'

He nodded. 'Of course. What about you?'

'What about me?'

'Did you never bend the rules or tell a few porkies when you were defending someone you thought was innocent?'

'That's another story for another night. But do you think you will be able to adapt and fulfil that role here?'

'What role?'

'Defender of the weak and bringer of retribution and rough justice to the bad guys?'

Mowgley sipped his wine and stroked Bébé's head reflectively. 'Dunno about that. I really don't have much of an idea what private detectives do. But it would be nice to think I could make a difference and help people in trouble - and get paid for it, of course.'

~

The prevailing mood at every cross-channel ferry terminal Mowgley had passed through was ennui, and Cherbourg was no exception. You could smell boredom in the air, and it seemed to have seeped into the walls.

The girls behind the ferry company counters looked permanently bored. It was not their fault, because they had little to do but stand around and look haughty and wait for mostly asinine questions and complaints.

The police and customs officers and the marshals in their high-vis jackets always looked bored rigid. This was probably because they had to stand or sit for long periods on their own with nobody to talk to while trying to look alert. Boredom in between flurries of activity was also probably why they liked taking revenge on travellers. Customs and police officers could spoil someone's journey by intimidation, delay and offensiveness, and the marshals by sending the car drivers in the wrong direction.

The only people working at the Cherbourg terminal who were rarely bored were behind the bar. Passengers ate and drank a lot to pass the time, and the espresso coffee machine was kept as busy as a one-armed bandit in Las Vegas. Constant use did not improve the taste, and Mowgley pulled a face as he peered into and then lifted the tiny cup to his mouth.

'You could always try to persuade Mimi to make a flask of Nescafé instant,' observed Melons, then you could take it with you along with a packet of cold and greasy bacon sandwiches.'

They were at breakfast in the bar area, and it was far too early for a beer. Although the coffee was foul, he had to admit the croissants were good.

'Nothing wrong with bacon sandwiches,' he observed. Then, in retaliation: 'So did you get a leg-over last night?'

She paused with her cup halfway to her mouth: 'Don't start on me because you don't like being here. It's not my fault.'

He realised again that she no longer worked for him and what a good friend she had been across the years. He also realised that she was right that his demise was not her fault, and thought about apologising. He didn't, but rephrased the question.

'What I meant was did he just drop you off at the hotel?'

'No,' she said levelly. 'He came in for a drink in the bar, and then he went home.'

'Ah. Did he tell you much about himself? Like his marital status?'

She put down her cup. 'You just can't help yourself, can you? You've just got to have a dig.'

He tried to look hurt. 'I was only asking.'

She thought about how angry she should be, then said. 'He was married, yes. Then his wife died of cancer three years ago.'

'Oh.' Mowgley tried a contrite look. 'I didn't know that. What about kids?'

'A daughter in the education system with plans to go into the Law, and a son in the *Gendarmerie*. He's serving in Paris.'

'Did he say how old he is?'

'Who, the son?'

'No, Rene.'

'About your age, I think. Although of course he looks a lot younger.'

Mowgley did not rise to the bait. 'Must be coming up for retirement, then?'

She shrugged, 'He said he planned to do a few more years.

Their system is like ours, but he's got a bit of leeway because of his work on people and drug trafficking and how big a problem it's becoming.'

'Did he say where he lives?'

'He used to have a house on the hill overlooking the town. After his wife died and the kids left home he downsized to an apartment in one of the blocks by the quayside.' She looked at her watch. 'Any other questions? They'll be loading in five minutes.'

'Only his birth sign and inside leg measurement. You seem to know everything else about him.'

She shook her head. 'If I didn't know better I'd think you were jealous.'

Mowgley gave up on the espresso, putting the cup back in the saucer and pushing it across the table as if to distance himself from even the idea of drinking it. 'I suppose I am,' he said. 'Not about you and him, but him having got it all right. Must be terrible to lose your wife, but at least they were still together when it happened. And a couple of kids with good futures, and a good job with a good pension and a nice home by the sea.'

She put her hand across the table, then drew it away and said crisply: 'Come on, pull yourself together. Self-pity doesn't suit you.'

Mowgley sat up straighter. 'Yeah, what have I got to feel sorry for myself about? When will I see you again?'

She looked away for a moment and then said: 'Next week, I reckon.'

He raised an eyebrow, 'As soon as that? How will that sit with your boss?'

'Okay I think. René will be having a word with him today.'

'What about, getting you a transfer to the Gendarmerie?'

'Don't be silly. Because of the Livarot lorry and the growth of people and drug smuggling through Portsmouth and from this region, he wants to set up an official liaison deal.'

'Mmm, let me think.' Mowgley put a finger to his lip. 'Who could that liaison officer be?'

She looked almost embarrassed as she gathered her things together. 'I'm the obvious choice, aren't I?'

'Depends on what he wants to liaise about, I suppose.'

She stood up. 'On that note I shall be leaving you. And with all this cross-questioning you haven't told me anything about your lady Thingummybob. Do I sense a romance on the horizon?'

'Don't think so. But it is nice to have a Brit to talk to.'

'Yeah, but what is she like? Is she pretty? Sounds like she's a bit of a hippy if she lives on a boat. Does she smoke whacky baccy or just drink a lot? Or both?'

He stood up. 'Sounds like you've been doing a bit of investigating on this side of the water already. I wouldn't say she's pretty, but she's interesting. And it's someone to talk to and somewhere to sleep when I don't want to drive back to the ruin.'

She moved towards him as if to kiss his cheek and he reared back. 'You could say she's any port in a storm then?'

He attempted a Gallic shrug. 'I suppose so.'

'Be good and see you soon, then.' She walked away, turning to smile and give a little wave. He watched her go and felt that small sense of sadness and loss that comes when a close friend and link with the past goes away.

9

The big house looked as Mowgley imagined *La Cour* could look, given a few hundred thousand pounds of serious attention.

Le Marais stood tall and alone in the vast swathe of marshlands bisecting the Cherbourg peninsula and not far from the D-Day beaches. Many people would think it wonderful to live in such a splendid building and in such splendid isolation, and he reckoned his former wife would have had an orgasm just to see it. That would have been a very unusual event when they were married, he thought, or at least when in congress with him. He had always believed she did not really care for sex. Well, she had certainly not enjoyed doing it with him, that was for sure.

He rang the bell and was disappointed when the big door was opened not by a butler, but a lady who was certainly as well-maintained as and clearly trying to look as grand as the house.

He gave his name and reason for arrival and half-expected her to direct him to the tradesmen's entrance. But after a disapproving look at his shoes, she opened the door a little wider and led him through a high-ceilinged vestibule to a sitting-room looking out across a manicured lawn and lots of bushes cut to look like animals. Beyond lay the sombre visage of the *marais*.

'I bet that takes some keeping nice out here in the wilds,'

observed Mowgley, nodding at the lawn.

The woman did not respond, but looked disapproving at his choice of the word 'wilds'. She pointed at an antique chair which was probably as valuable as it would be uncomfortable, and watched as he obeyed. To get his own back, he waited for her to tell him why she had called the agency and unknowingly become Mowgley P.I.'s first case.

When she spoke, she made hard work of trying to sound as if she came from an environment as grand and exclusive as the one in which she was standing. She was clearly English, but equally as clearly not from old money. 'Did your people tell you what this is about?'

After her frosty welcome, Mowgley was not going to help her: 'My associate said it was about your husband.'

'Yes. Something has happened to him.'

'Okay.' *So far so good.* On the way to see her, he had given some thought to how he would in general approach his new role and this case in particular. He had handled a number of Missing Persons cases in his other life, so there was the standard police procedure and technique to use as a basis. But things were different now. He decided to put the same questions in a slightly different way, and start with a new one: 'I know it's a silly question, but have you been to the police?'

She sniffed. 'Useless. They are not at all interested, and they say they cannot investigate as there are no suspicious circumstances.'

He nodded and tried to look as if he knew all about how French police would act in cases like these. 'I have to say it would be the same in England. Unless the missing person is a child or a vulnerable person and there are indications of-'

'Yes, I know all that,' she snapped. That's what they said and that's why I am paying you so much to find him.'

Now I wonder why he would have done a runner, Mowgley thought, but said: 'I understand how frustrating it can be, but that's the way it works. Can you think of any reason why he might have left voluntarily - or not?'

She shook her head as if refusing to even consider the possibility. 'No, nothing.'

He looked out of the window to where a young man was snipping bits off a bush that was supposed to look like a bird. 'So, no arguments, problems at work or money problems...or anyone else?'

'Anyone else? Of course not. And James is retired. There are certainly no 'money problems.' Mowgley nodded as if he unreservedly believed what she had said. 'Can you tell me exactly what happened? Last week, wasn't it?'

'Last Tuesday. He said he was going to play golf.'

'And is that usual?'

'What do you mean by 'usual'?'

'Does he play golf regularly on a Tuesday?'

'Yes, that is his golfing day. He's a member at the links near Carentan.'

'Do you play? Do you ever go with him?'

She looked at him as if he had made an obscene suggestion. 'No, of course not.'

'Okay. And did he seem his normal self? Did he seem distracted or preoccupied or in any way different?'

'On Tuesday? No.' She gave a wry twist to her lips. 'James is not a great communicator, nor one for a display of mood or emotions. She paused, then said: 'Shouldn't you be writing this down?'

Mowgley smiled reassuringly and made a mental note to pretend to use one for future cases. He had not used a notebook for many years, and then only to make sure he got the story straight with a colleague before a court appearance. Then he said: 'I have a good memory, and I'll start a case file back at the office. Just a couple more questions for the moment, though. I know you said your husband is not a... communicator, but has he said or done anything out of the ordinary lately? Has he been going out a lot more than usual? Has he bought any new clothes or started to take more care with his appearance?

She laughed without humour. 'Do you mean do I think he has run off with someone? Not James. I just know something has happened to him, and that is why I am paying you to find him. Now.'

'I understand how worrying it must be. I'll drop in at the golf club on the way back to the office. And my assistant will be calling to ask for a detailed list of all his and your friends and their contact details. Can I ask how long you've been married? Do you have any children, by the way? And did your husband take any personal items with him?'

'Three years. No, there are no children. And what do you mean by personal items? He took his car and his golf clubs, of course...'

'I meant personal items like keepsakes or photographs or clothing.'

She hesitated and looked away, then back at him. 'He has his own room and en-suite facilities - you can look around it if you think it will help. He takes his own clothes to the cleaners, and we have someone who does the laundry. I don't really know what he had in his room that he may have taken, but –' she paused as if not wanting to continue: 'There is a bag missing from the garage. A suitcase.'

'I see. And did you tell the police it was gone?'

'Of course, they wanted to know...everything.' She looked at him and hesitated and for a moment her face softened and she looked fearful. 'It could have been stolen or he could have moved it or got rid of it without telling me. I just know he would not go off without a word and leave....all this.'

She stepped towards where he was sitting, and her face and voice changed: 'Please. You *must* find him.'

He stood up, feeling almost sorry for her and broke a prime rule of police investigation when dealing with a MisPers case. 'I will. I promise you I will...'

~

'And how was Milady?'

Mowgley frowned. 'My Milady'?'

'No. The fake one in the *marais*.'

'Ah, Mrs deVere with a small 'd'? Why do you say she's a fake? Do you think she knows why her husband left and is pretending he's not run off?

Mimi shook her head. 'No. I mean she is not a proper lady. She just pretends to come from good blood. Your boat lady is a lady *propre*.'

Mowgley smiled.

'What do you find so funny?'

'You French are so snobby.'

'What is 'snobby'?'

'You cut off all your lords and ladies' heads and called each other 'citizen' and accuse the English of being class-ridden, but you're just as bad, or even worse.'

Mimi pouted. 'So what has that got to do with anything?'

'Nothing, really.'

He was back in the office, going through the new routines and procedures of being a private rather than a public detective. By and large, he assumed his activities would be based on the same principles of investigation, deduction and suitable action. There would also be the keeping of records and paperwork, which he had little experience of.

But he had already realised one significant difference. As a police officer he was expected to pare down costs and control spending. Working for an agency like this seemed to be more about building costs *up*; and being creative about it.

He had already got on the wrong side of Mimi by not making a record of his mileage to and from the big house near Carentan. In his previous life, Catherine McCarthy had kept all the receipts for items and costs she thought they would get away with. Now Mowgley was going to have to record every expense resulting from his investigations, and even make some up.

'So run me through it again,' he said. 'I keep a record of all the hours I spend - or pretend to spend - on the deVere case each week, and everything I spend on travel...'

'And on food and drink if you are away from the office.'

'You mean even if I stop for a beer in a bar?'

She nodded, pointing to a paragraph in the sheave of stapled-together papers which was part of his induction kit.

He shook his head. 'Don't forget I can't speak French, let alone read it.'

'Then you had better hurry up and learn if you want to make a living from the company.'

'I'm doing my best,' he said. 'On that note, can we go through how I get paid.'

She sighed. 'It is as I said before. You keep a record of all your costs and time spent on each case, and put them in the correct file in your computer. You send the files to me at the end of each week, with your report on what you have been doing on each case. At the end of each week I send the reports to your boss, and at the end of each month I send the bills to your clients.'

'With a slight addition for administration costs, I guess?'

There was no reply, so Mowgley drained his coffee mug, looked into it and then at Mimi with his little-boy look. She sighed and took it: 'And what do you say?'

'Pretty please?'

'*Non*. You know what you have to do.'

He looked around for escape or the embarrassment of witnesses and finding none, said: '*Encore du café, s'il vous plait, Madame*.' Then he said. Why are you looking as if I just farted? Did I not say the right words?'

She wrinkled her nose with distaste. 'Yes, but it would have been better if you had said '*un autre*' and not '*encore*'. We are not in a theatre. And why did you shout and make the silly voice?'

'Just thought it would help.'

'Well, it did not. When is your first lesson with Lady Sarah?'

'Tomorrow.'

Mimi shuddered. 'Poor woman. You had better take a very good bottle of wine. Now what were your questions?'

'In English?'

'They will have to be.'

'*D'accord*. I get most of what you said about how it all works, but there are a couple of important points.'

She stood up and headed for the door to the kitchen area. 'What are they?'

He raised his voice: 'You said 'your boss' and not 'our boss', and you haven't said anything about how I get paid. And just on a minor point, I find it hard enough to type anyway, and my keyboard has all the letters and numbers in the wrong place.'

She appeared at the doorway to the kitchen: 'That is because you are in France and it is a French keyboard. If you are kind to me I will get you an English one. I will have to translate your words anyway.'

'Good girl. And what about how and when I get paid?'

'I thought Yann went through all this with you when you made your agreement?'

'Yes, but I wasn't really paying attention.'

Even above the sound of the boiling kettle, he could hear her theatrical sigh. 'Again it is simple. He will send the *facture* - the bill - for your time and costs to the customers, and when they pay, he will give you back the money you have spent, then fifty Euros an hour for the hours you have billed. It is up to you to pay your taxes on that money.'

He waited while she made the coffee and reappeared in the doorway. 'Yes, I know. What I meant was how much is it costing Mrs deVere to hire me? What is Yann getting out of it? What's his end?'

'I do not know what you mean when you speak in *patois*. What is 'his end'?'

'How much does he charge the customers for my time?'

'You will have to ask him that.'

'I will. Thank you.'

She put his mug on the coaster next to the computer screen. 'You are welcome. Is that all?'

'No. You did not say why you said 'your boss' and not 'our boss.''

She put her espresso carefully down on her desk, ran a finger over a leaf of the pot plant he had given her, sat and crossed her legs and finally said: 'I say it like that because you and I have a very different working arrangement with Mr Cornec.'

~

Mowgley arrived back from a raid on the cash point in the lobby of the nearby *Credit Agricole* with a problem.

'My phone' he said to Mimi, laying a coffee-flavoured *éclair* on her desk and his mobile beside it.

'What about it? Have you let the battery go flat again?'

'No, but at the bank it started sending out Morse code signals.'

'Morse code?'

'You know, dots and dashes - beeps.'

Mimi shrugged unconcernedly and reached for the *éclair*. 'It is probably a text message. Did you check?'

'I don't know how to.'

Mimi paused in mid-bite. 'Are you telling me you have never learned to read a text message before?'

'Of course I have,' lied Mowgley, 'but not on this phone. It's a new one my friend got for me. I had to give my police one back.'

Mimi laid the cake down with a sigh, and picked up his mobile. She licked her fingers, flipped open the lid, pressed a couple of buttons and handed the phone to him with no comment.

He put his glasses on and looked at the screen. The message read:

Urgent meet me at La Cour 8pm

Mimi wiped her lips then asked: 'So what does it say?'

Mowgley showed her the screen.

She frowned and looked at the skeletal clock 'That's two hours from now. Who is it from?'

'I don't know. It doesn't say. It's just a number '

She spoke as if to a child. 'Then call it and see who answers.'

'Of course.' He looked at the phone. How do I do that?'

'Press the call-back button. The green one.'

He did and put the phone to his ear. After a number of rings an answer phone clicked in, and a familiar voice said: 'Hi, this is Sean Mooney. I'm not around at the moment but please leave a message and I'll get right back.'

~

He became aware of the blue Simca not long after joining the NR13, heading south from Cherbourg.

The driver was keeping his distance, but the constant jockeying to maintain at least two vehicles between them was what drew Mowgley's attention. The average French driver would have overtaken when he had deliberately slowed down, and a more sedate driver would not have sped up to keep them in their relative positions.

To make sure, he pulled off at the sign for Valognes, then rejoined the main route at a later junction. The car reappeared in his rear-view mirror some minutes later.

Mowgley had phoned René Degas as soon as he saw who the text was from, but there had been no answer. He had left a voicemail, and asked Mimi to keep trying Degas. If she did not get him in an hour, she was to phone the *Gendarmerie* and tell whoever was there that Mowgley was meeting a man suspected of murder, and to make sure Colonel Degas knew and that someone would be there by eight.

He looked into the rear-view mirror and scowled at himself. It was a pity he had left his mobile on Mimi's desk.

~

He parked alongside the caravan, walked to the back of the Citroën and opened the boot. From it he took the big rechargeable torch and the short-handled fireman's axe he had persuaded a very drunk man to surrender in the toilets of the Ship Leopard some years before. It had a standard and very blunt chopping edge, but the other end was curved like a raptor's beak and came to a point.

In the caravan, he reached through the curtain covering the front of the makeshift wardrobe and pulled out a shotgun. It was a cheap Russian Baikal, of the type which was known derisively amongst shooting circles as a 'disposable'. Once rumoured to be made from melted-down tanks, the Baikal became popular as a budget gun in the 1980s, which was when this one had probably been made. The stock had at some time been broken, and the hinged joint was very wobbly. If fired it would probably be more dangerous to the shooter than the target, he thought, but that was not a problem as he had no cartridges. Not that his visitors would know that.

Sitting on the bed next to the main window, he rolled and lit a cigarette, and waited.

An hour passed and nobody had arrived. Or nobody he was aware of. In this remote place he would have heard a car approaching from miles away, but it was of course possible they had left the Simca at a distance and would come for him across the fields.

After two more cigarettes, he stood up, stretched and yawned and left the caravan.

As he walked towards the house, carrying the Baikal and the axe and the torch, he saw a light in the first floor window overlooking the courtyard. It was moving back and forward in a short arc, as if signalling something, and perhaps to him.

The front door was ajar, and he set the torch down and hefted the shotgun and the axe, one in each hand. Then he stood the Baikal against the door frame, picked up the torch and slipped through the door.

~

Pressing the switch, he realised the torch was dead, cursed softly and laid it on the stairs. He thought about going back for the shot-less shotgun, but carried on. Taking his lighter from an inside pocket, he thumbed the wheel and went up to the first floor in its tiny pool of light.

Treading carefully to avoid missing or noisy boards on the landing, he reached the door to the room in which he had seen the moving light. Taking his thumb off the button on the lighter, he stood in the dark for more than a minute, closing and opening his eyes to get used to the lack of light.

Then, he slid his hand up the handle of the axe to about half way, raised it to just above his head, stood back and kicked the door open.

~

The light was coming from a lantern. It was the sort powered by batteries but which could be charged by cranking the handle on the side. It was swinging to and fro at about head height, suspended by a length of string from the ceiling. By its light, he could see the room was empty. Or appeared to be. He frowned, automatically reached up to stop the lamp swinging, then walked to the door which he knew led to what had been a changing room for the bedroom.

As he reached for the handle, the door burst open and a black shape came charging at him. Something in its hand flashed in the light of the lantern, and Mowgley stumbled back as he felt a stinging pain in his right cheek. His head struck the lantern and he struggled for a moment to regain his balance, then fell on his back, the fireman's axe knocked from his hand by the force of his fall. The figure swung a foot at his head and raised the knife.

Dazed by the kick and the fall, Mowgley rolled over and away, then felt the handle of the axe. Without aiming or even thinking what he was doing, he swung it in an arc. It landed with a meaty thud and squelch. There was a scream as the beak of the axe pierced his attacker's right foot, and the knife clattered to the floor.

Then, several things happened in rapid succession. The figure gave another scream as Mowgley tore the axe from the floor. There was a shout from downstairs, and the sound of footsteps clattering up the uncovered stairs. The black-clad figure looked wildly around, then staggered to the window and crashed through it. As the door to the landing flew open, there was a shouted challenge from the yard below, a shrieked response, then the sound of a gunshot. Then came silence.

10

Mowgley touched his cheek and winced. 'I suppose it could have been worse.'

'Yes', said Mimi. 'It could have happened in England; then you would have had to spend some time in a hospital there.'

It was his second visit to the Louis Pasteur in less than a week, this time as a patient rather than a witness. At least, he thought, they won't have to ask Melons to identify me.

He reached over, patted the pocket of the jacket hanging over the chair beside the bed, then pulled his baccy pouch out. The pretty trouser-suited nurse who had helped stitch his face looked over from a stainless steel trolley she was tidying and wagged her finger. She said something and Mowgley looked to Mimi for help.

'She is saying it is against French law to kill yourself in hospital, and if she cannot have one, nor can you.'

'So what happens next?'

Mimi stood up and fussed with the sheets and patted the pillow. 'You stay here for the night.'

'Why? It's only a cut cheek.'

'Yes, but they want to see if the kick in your head has done any damage. The doctor said they will let you go in the morning if everything is good. He also said you may wake up in the morning able to speak French because of the blow, which will be a miracle from God.'

Mowgley touched and then shook his head as if testing it.

'Did he really say that?'

'No. I invented the last thing.'

She leaned over as if to kiss his forehead, then straightened up and laid a hand on his shoulder. 'I shall expect to see you in the office by tomorrow afternoon as there is more work for you. But do not forget your meeting with Colonel Degas.'

He nodded and fingered the wound on his cheek as she opened the door and stood back so the nurse could wheel the trolley out of the room. As she did so, Mowgley saw that a uniformed *gendarme* was sitting on a metal chair placed against the corridor wall opposite the door. René Degas was obviously taking no chances that they had removed the threat with the death of the would-be killer.

Degas had been waiting to speak with him after the stitches had been put in. He had said his phone had been switched off while he had been in a meeting with the mayor of Cherbourg and some important government figures from Paris.

They had convened to talk about the possibility and threat of Cherbourg becoming another Calais, under siege from would-be migrants to England. Someone had called him out of the meeting when Mimi had phoned the *Gendarmerie*, but by the time he had reached *La Cour* the incident was over.

The man who had tried to kill Mowgley had been pronounced dead at the scene, killed by a single bullet to the head. Degas said that the undercover officer had had no choice but to shoot him, as it appeared he was reaching for a gun after being warned not to move. There would be an enquiry, but a revolver had been found on the body. Thus it would doubtless be declared a justified shooting, as there was a clear danger to the policeman. Mowgley could not see how a man who would be dazed from falling fifteen feet on to a concrete terrace and probably broken one or maybe both legs would have presented much of a danger, but that was probably not the way the officer had felt, or what the enquiry panel would decide.

The officer who had come up the stairs had got him downstairs and applied a pressure dressing from the first aid kit in the Simca. The ambulance had arrived shortly afterwards, followed by Colonel Degas and an accompanying van stuffed with uniforms. It seemed that the British and French forces were alike in some ways, and clearly liked to turn up mob-handed after if not at the time of an incident.

He had not been too surprised to learn that the two men who had been tailing him in the Simca were undercover policemen. René Degas said they had been given the job to protect him while Mooney was at large, but Mowgley also could not avoid the speculation that the Colonel had been using him as bait.

If so, it had not worked, as the dead man was unknown to Mowgley and so far to the police. Degas had said it was a pity that the man had been killed, as he would now be unable to tell them anything. But it was probable he was known to the police, and they would hopefully have learned who he was by the morning. All they then needed to determine was if he had been working for Sean Mooney, why he had tried to kill a retired British detective, and - if it were also his work - why he had killed an estate agent's wife and her lover.

As Mowgley looked glumly at the bedside table and his tobacco pouch, the door opened to admit the pretty nurse. She was pushing a wheelchair and manoeuvred it alongside the bed. Without speaking, she held up a packet of *Caporal* cigarettes and a lighter.

Mowgley smiled his gratitude, threw his bedclothes off and swung his legs towards the wheelchair. You could say what you liked about the French, he thought, but it was true that they understood and were generally tolerant of the weaknesses of the flesh.

~

After buying a bunch of flowers and a packet of cigarettes for his nice nurse, Mowgley checked into the office and then went next door for his meeting.

René Degas had not yet arrived, and the only customers were a couple of dock workers and an elderly and obviously British couple who looked as if they had wandered in by mistake. The man was pretending to be reading the local giveaway paper, and the woman was looking blankly at a street map of the town. He smiled reassuringly when she looked up, but she quickly looked back down at the map and he realised the stitched gash on his cheek would probably not put her at her ease.

He thought about the restorative powers of apple brandy, but was strong and ordered a coffee without a chaser. Yvette leaned across the counter, stroked his wound and said something which was obviously sympathetic and inevitably suggestive. Then she reached for the jar of Nescafé Mimi had provided, put three heaped spoonfuls of granules in a mug and bustled off to the kitchen and the electric kettle. He sighed and made a mental note to ask Mimi to try and explain the concept of instant coffee to his new landlady.

'*Salut, mon ami* - how are you feeling?'

Mowgley turned and shook hands with René Degas. 'Fine. It was the best night's sleep I've had for a long time.'

They went to the table in the corner, Degas nodding politely and saying '*Monsieur/Dame*' as they passed the British couple. She responded with a tight smile and looked relieved to see that Mowgley was now under the control of a respectable and authoritative-looking man.

Degas exchanged a few words with Yvette as she arrived with Mowgley's coffee, then looked dubiously at the mug as Mowgley reached for his tobacco pouch.

'Is this your regular breakfast?' asked Degas. 'You should eat something, you know.'

'I know' said Mowgley, but I haven't got Yvette to put bacon sarnies with brown sauce on the menu.'

'Sarnies?'

'Patois for sandwiches.'

'Okay.' Degas nodded his thanks as Yvette arrived and put a large, handle-less bowl of milky coffee on the table, together with a plate of croissants.

Mowgley watched as the policeman picked up a croissant, tore the end off and dipped it into his coffee. 'Funny how we live so close together and have such different ways, isn't it?' he said, picking up his mug of instant Nescafé.

They talked of nothing while Degas had his croissant and Mowgley his cigarette, then the policeman pushed the bowl and plate away and dabbed at his lips with a paper napkin. Mowgley saw him looking at the tobacco pouch, and pushed it across the table. Degas regarded it gravely, then shook his head.

'No?' asked Mowgley. 'You're being strong-willed.'

'It is not that,' said Degas, 'I do not know how to make one.'

Mowgley reached for the pouch again, then asked: 'Any

joy - any luck - with finding out about the man who tried to kill me?'

As he spoke, he fingered the wound, looked up and saw that the British woman had heard him. She looked horrified, leaned over and whispered furiously to her husband, who got up and walked quickly to the bar to pay their bill.

'Yes, we know him quite well,' answered Degas. Drawing hungrily on his roll-up, he blew a long stream of smoke towards the ceiling. 'He was not a nice man. An Albanian who was not supposed to be in France.'

'Albanian? Like the gang of people smugglers in Brittany?'

Degas nodded. 'Yes, but it is too early to know if there is a connection.'

'But why Albanians?'

Degas shrugged. 'Why not? The free movement of people and removal of borders means criminals as well as working people can choose where to make a living.'

'Are they part of the European Union, then? I don't know anything about the place.'

'Don't worry; nor did I before the gang arrived in Brittany. Since then I have been doing my homework on the country and how they are exporting criminals. Would you like me to give you a lesson?'

Mowgley shrugged. 'Please do.'

'Okay.' The policeman took a breath as if preparing for a challenging task. 'Albania is one of the poorest countries in Europe. It was a republic until the end of the War, then a Stalinist seized power. Enver Hoxha aligned the country with Russia until they fell out and he changed over to an alliance with China. After Chairman Mao died in 1978, Albania became one of the most isolated and economically underdeveloped countries in the world. Hoxha died in 1982 and since then it has been chaos. There was an attempt at democratic reform and a free market economy toward the end of the 1990's, but it all went bad with get-rich-quick schemes like pyramid selling on a huge scale. There were riots when ordinary people lost billions of their savings. Then the economy collapsed and the country was overrun with gangsters and rebels.'

Mowgley arched his eyebrows. 'Blimey. And we complain about goings-on in Britain.'

Degas nodded. 'Yes, us in France too.' 'I am impressed with

your depth and width of knowledge. So how are things now?'

'Do not be too impressed. My only problem was translating the facts. I am speaking directly from a report by a junior officer who did all the work. As you know, it is one of the privileges of rank to take the credit for other peoples' work.'

'You've been speaking to Catherine. So who did all the work on the report - Mister Nasty? And speak of the Devil...'

'Who? What?' Degas turned to look where Mowgley was giving a blatantly false and effusive smile at the man who had just come through the door. Then he said: 'Mister Nasty? Oh, of course, I understand.'

He turned further in his chair and gave a curt nod to the newcomer, who replied in kind and glared at Mowgley as he walked to the bar.

Degas turned back. 'No, I do not think I would have given Inspector Aittif the job.'

'Aittif?'

'Yes. He is half-Moroccan – and all, as you say, nasty.'

Mowgley raised his cup in tribute. 'Congratulations; you just made a good English joke. Does he just hate all foreigners like me, or is it everyone?'

'Most people, I think. We would say *en vouloir à tout le monde* – he blames or has a grudge against the world. You would say, I think, that he has a chip - a *frite* - upon his shoulder.'

'Sort of. Just a different sort of chip.'

Degas frowned. 'A what?'

'Never mind. But why is he so unhappy with his lot?'

'I don't know. Perhaps because he is of mixed parentage and he thinks it is holding him back in his career.'

'And is it?'

'Not at all. He is just a bad policeman. He is lazy and makes assumptions too quickly and does not think things through. I know he also likes to gamble and is always in money problems. He also likes women and expensive cars. Those are the reasons he has not been promoted.'

Mowgley nodded. 'We say in England that police officers are promoted to the level of their incompetence.'

The colonel smiled. 'I like that. I shall remember to use it when the chance comes. But shall I complete your lesson in Albanian history?'

'Please do.'

'So,' said Degas, 'a new president was elected recently and, to answer your question at last, the Socialist Party are doing all they can to become members of the European Union.'

'But in the meantime the crooks are seeing how well they can do here?'

Degas grimaced. 'That's right.' He looked at the tobacco pouch and Mowgley began to roll him another cigarette. As he did so he asked: 'And is the crime there well organised? Is there an Albanian Mafia like in Russia?'

Degas nodded. 'Very much so and they have had lots of practice. I have had many meetings with a much-respected criminologist called Xavier Raufer. He specialises in organised crime in Albania, and considers the country to have the only true 'Mafia' in the Balkans. This is because of the social structure in the north of the country, and because they have the same attitudes and values as the original Italian Mafia. They are completely ruthless and kill anyone who gets in their way or may threaten any of their projects. They specialise in the trafficking of Afghan heroin, but, like any Mafia group, will turn their hands to anything illegal which shows a quick and big profit.'

'Like people smuggling.'

'Exactly. The reason we are paying so much attention to the people smuggling in Brittany is because of the way the Albanians are moving in and taking over and getting rid of rivals. It is more than a small enterprise.'

Mowgley signalled to Yvette and pushed his chair back as he digested what he had heard. Then he said: 'I get all that, but why would an Albanian Mafia member - if he was one - want to knock off a retired British policeman?'

Degas shrugged. 'Or perhaps a British estate agent's wife and lover.'

'You think that Sylvie Mooney and her boyfriend were killed by the Albanians and not by Sean Mooney?'

Degas shrugged. 'We do not know. We do know about Andrea Berisha, though...'

'Andrea Berisha? Who's she?'

'He was a he. Andrea means 'Warrior' when it is a man. He is the man who tried to kill you.'

'And was he part of the Brittany gang?'

'Again, we do not know, but he had worked for many gangs. He was in prison many times in Albania but had powerful friends. It is thought he has killed dozens of people, and is a professional assassin. He is or was, I think you would say, a freelance killer.'

'So he could have been working for Mooney, or the Brittany gang, or anyone else.'

'Yes.'

'Okay. The only other thing is why he came at me with a knife? Why not just shoot me and make it easy? We were miles from anywhere and nobody would have heard. If he was a professional killer he must have been used to using a gun.'

Degas made a face. 'Looking at his history, it seems he likes to use a knife. Some people do. When you see what was done to Denys Simone...'

'So you think Denys was killed by Berisha?'

'The knife is another link. You know that Denys was tortured before he died. The killer wanted to get information from him - or maybe just enjoyed making his victims scream. Perhaps that is what he had planned for you. '

Mowgley shuddered and tried to think of pleasanter things.

'Okay. So we know who but not why, or on behalf of who...or should that be 'whom'?'

Degas frowned quizically. 'I beg your pardon?'

'Never mind, I'll have to phone Melons for a definitive answer on the proper grammatical choice.'

11

From one of the windows in his new home, Mowgley could see the port. A Brittany Ferries boat was leaving harbour, and he considered how much he would have liked to be on it. If he still had his old job in Portsmouth, there would have been no question.

The big room occupied most of the top floor of the *Bar du Port*, and sat beneath a metal-sheathed mansard roof. It was just the sort of semi-attic room Mowgley imagined staying in when, for a brief period in his extreme youth, he had dreamed of escaping to Paris and becoming an artist. He would live in picturesque poverty in a garret and spend his nights in *zinc* bars on the Left Bank, talking with other artists and other intellectuals while downing great quantities of *absinthe*.

He had been inspired in this ambition by a Tony Hancock film called *The Rebel*, and also a school exchange trip when he was awakening to the attractions and possibilities of adult life.

For a fortnight he had been intrigued and made envious by the differences between his grey world in England and how things were done just a short distance across the Channel. In the early Sixties, he and his schoolmates and even the masters wore grey flannels and coats and shirts which were grey whatever their colour. The French boys of his age had slick Perry Como haircuts and wore brightly coloured tops and narrow, shiny trousers. They smoked in the casual, familiar manner of Alain Delon and Yves Montand, and whizzed around on flashy mopeds which made a lot of noise and smoke. And they obviously got the girls.

It seemed to him then that being French was all about freedom and self-expression and even officially-approved self-indulgence, and he wanted all of it. The clincher was a poster pinned above the bed in his cubicle in the school dormitory. It showed Brigitte Bardot, the Sex Kitten. She was obviously naked, her carefully positioned arms and golden tumble of hair just about covering her pert breasts, and her lips pouting a provocative invitation. He had stolen the poster and put it up in his bedroom at home, but his journey to a new and exciting life in France had never happened. Well, not until now, and somehow it did not hold the promise of those distant days.

He shook his head in regret for an unfulfilled past and looked around at his new billet. Strangely, the mish-mash and age and standard suited him, and he already felt almost at home.

The floor was covered in linoleum, with a roughly central carpet on which stood the metal-framed single bed.

In one corner was a shiny plastic cubicle, its modernity at odds with the rest of the room's fixtures and fittings and decor. It was about the size of an old-fashioned telephone box, and inside they had managed to fit a toilet bowl and a wash basin and a mirror, and above it a shower head.

Nearby, and beneath the window looking across the rooftops towards the *Gendarmerie* building was a barely post-war dressing table with spindly legs, and further along the wall and in complete contrast was a hugely solid and elaborately carved wardrobe. Next to it was an equally imposing if not matching chest of drawers, and on its scarred top stood a dangerous-looking electric kettle and a duplicate of the jar of instant coffee, mug and sugar bowl in the office.

The walls of his lodgings were decorated with the sort and vintage of violently offensive floral patterned wallpaper he had first seen on his school exchange trip to Paris, but rather than a Sixties poster of the Sex Kitten, on one wall was a reproduction of Vincent Van Gogh's local in Arles.

It was not much of a home, he thought, but it was a start. When he sold *La Cour* he should be able to buy a modest apartment in Cherbourg. He smiled. It was actually comforting to think of having a nest in a foreign town where he had only slept in hotels – or on someone else's boat.

He reached for where his coat hung on the back of the door, then paused as he recalled that Plan 'A' had always been to return to England when the ruin was sold. Now here he was, thinking of a home in this foreign port. He shook his head as if to dislodge the thought, then clattered down the stairs to buy a good bottle of wine and a packet of dog treats for the tuition fee for his lesson in swapping his *lingua franca* for the real thing.

~

'I still don't see how a table can have sex.'

Lady Sarah sighed. 'They just *do* in France, Mowgley. Why can't you just accept it? Look, lots of other countries give a gender to inanimate objects. As I keep telling you, the worst possible thing you can do when trying to learn another language is compare it with English and then object to any rules which are not the same. You either want to learn to speak French or you don't. If you do, clear your mind of all the reasons why you believe they have got it wrong and just accept how they choose to do it.'

Mowgley grimaced like a sulky child as he reached for his glass. French lessons did not seem to work for him, mostly because the language did not make sense under any logical scrutiny. He had been visiting France regularly for many years, but had got stuck at his schoolboy level almost from the start. He had made an effort when he got the job at the ferry port, and had attended a couple of sessions set up for officers who had a need to speak French. But he had never mastered more than the basics. He had found himself in like-minded company, and remembered one particularly antipathetic Chief Inspector. When the exasperated teacher had accused him of not wanting to learn, the officer had produced a sheet of paper. He pointed out that the tutor had said at the start of the course that it was only necessary to know five hundred words of any language to get by when speaking it. The DCI had done some homework and written down six hundred words which were the same in English as in French, so what was the problem?

'What are you smiling at?'

Mowgley came back to the present. 'Oh, just another French lesson a long time ago. Are we done?'

'With the lesson, yes. If we go on any longer I shall be driven to jump overboard. But we need to talk about your reading.'

'My reading?'

'Yes, you need to start reading some good French books - in translation to start with, of course.'

He frowned. 'Why?'

'Because it will help you learn the language and even enjoy living here if you understand French culture and why the country and the people are like they are. That's what books can do, you know.'

Mowgley bridled. 'Hang on a minute. I don't intend integrating or becoming French, you know.'

She sighed out a stream of smoke. 'Heaven forbid. Believe me, you just need to read a good French book or two, wherever you are going to live. The French are quite fond of Shakespeare you know, but they still prefer to live here. So what sort of thing do you like reading? Who's your favourite author?'

'Oh, I like to mix it up a bit. I like detective stories-'

'There's a surprise.'

'-but travel and humour mostly. It's best when they come together. Eric Newby is my hero for that.'

'I agree. Anyway, I've been thinking about it. At your age it's too late for Proust. You know what they say - life is short and Proust is long.'

He nodded as if he did know that that was what they said, and she continued: 'I think Zola would not be your cup of tea, and we don't want anything too dense or deep. So, here's a little present to get started with:' She gently persuaded Bébé to move along the sofa, and pulled a plastic bag from beneath a cushion. 'It's *Bel Ami* by Guy de Maupassant.'

Mowgley took the bag and looked inside. 'Thank you. What's it about?'

'It's about a man using his wits to get ahead when he arrives penniless in Paris.'

'Ah. I think I get the plot. 'Beautiful friend' it's called, yes?'

'Well done. But there is a subtitle which might suit you better. It's *The History of a Scoundrel*...'

12

The small square at the heart of the village seemed to be in the process of British colonisation.

Next to the *marie,* a former shop had been transformed into a sort of representation of an English country pub. A hanging sign identified it as *The Red Lion.* Outside was a sandwich board promising Real Ale, Real Food and Real Atmosphere. Tonight, cottage pie and a quiz night were on the menu. Mowgley was slightly surprised to find the idea of a visit unappealing.

On the other side of the mayoral office was an English Tea Rooms and Grocery Emporium. The wording above the subtitle identified the establishment as *La Crème Anglaise.* Even Mowgley knew what that meant, and wondered what the locals thought about a shop calling itself after a sort of custard.

The pub might work, as lonely Brits liked familiar surroundings in which to gather, but he did not think there would be much call for a grocery shop specialising in British favourites like Marmite, Cheddar cheese and white sliced bread.

There had been a need for a vendor of these goods a decade ago when what the French called *l'invasion* was at its peak. But the supermarkets had long ago caught on to the sort of curious things that expats liked to put in their mouths. There were always a few shelves devoted to British and other foreign foods, usually discreetly tucked away from obvious public view like soft porn magazines in a corner shop.

The setting up by Britons of grocery shops or taking orders for food and other items like proper paint and making weekly trips to and from England were projects usually doomed to failure. In fact, most businesses launched by Brits were doomed to failure, and he had read the translation of a rather gloating Gallic report that more than eighty percent failed within a year of opening. The choices for entrepreneurial Brits were actually quite limited.

Many expats too young or poor to retire went for a bed and breakfast operation, which gave them an excuse to buy a big property with more bedrooms and bathrooms than they could otherwise justify. Others went the whole hog and invested in a rural *gîte* complex, and Mowgley reckoned there were now more British-run self-catering accommodation units in France than visitors who wanted to stay in them. Those Britons who thought they could take the French on at their own game and prosper with a restaurant inevitably fared worst of all.

Next door to the grocery shop was another apparently successful British-run business, and it was Mowgley's reason for visiting the village.

There was no name above the modest plate glass window, which showed off some artfully arranged items of apparently antique furniture. A fastidiously blackened foot scraper stood beside the steps up to the brilliantly glossed front door with the dolphin brass knocker, but he could not think that people with muddy boots would want or even be allowed to enter.

He parked the Citroën by a horse trough filled with flowers, and as he got out he noticed two men in official overalls standing by an open manhole. They were looking into it as if unsure what to do next, and beside them was a short man wearing a Tibetan bobble cap and poncho. He had a big guitar held high on his chest and ready for action, and Mowgley wondered if he was there to give helpful suggestions, or entertain them when they had decided on their course of action.

The lady behind the counter in the grocery shop was in her late middle years, wore a trendily colourful apron over a blouse and skirt, and an expression not dissimilar to the men by the manhole. She looked as if she did not know what to do next to escape her situation.

Assuming a brighter expression when Mowgley walked in, she said: 'You look the sort of chap who's in need of a full English breakfast.'

The words did not stick in her throat, but he knew that, before her dream began to collapse, she would have been horrified at the thought of having to cook a fry-up. She would have planned to sell Earl Grey tea and delicate fancies to discerning British expatriates, but quickly come to realise the available custom would rather have a mug of Tetley and a lump of lardy cake.

He promised he would return after calling in to the shop next door on business, but said he would have a quick coffee if she could do an instant.

She almost recoiled in horror, looked at the shiny and obviously hugely expensive machine on the back bar, and said in a faint voice: 'I'm afraid I do not know how to make instant coffee.'

He settled for what she and the French called an Americano, which usually consisted of one or even two espressos topped up with hot water. It was served in the sort of soup bowl with a handle that had become compulsory in fashionable establishments, and which was another triumph of fad over functionality. The near-pint of coffee would be cold before finished, and the weight of the cup would have taxed the strongest man's wrist.

He took a sip and tried not to wince, then asked if she knew the owners of the antique shop. He knew she would, but it was a useful opening gambit to get people to talk about someone.

'Of course,' she said, and he knew from the way she said it that she would take full advantage of any excuse to reveal all.'

Pausing fleetingly to think about and then reject the idea of asking her if it was alright to smoke, he said: 'I've been asked to see Mr Fowldes about something.' He left the sentence to hang, and she effortlessly picked it up: 'Yes, Roger. He sort of attends to all the business side of things in the shop, while Derek - his partner- travels round looking for suitable items to buy.'

She paused, obviously waiting for the opportunity to get to the heart of things and he gave it to her. He did so by asking a question to which he already knew the answer: 'Is he away much?'

'Yes, a lot, lately. He used to go away once a month and come back with a van load of antiques - he's got a very good eye, I have to say. Then he would take them to England and sell them in the trade.' She looked uncomfortable, as if even using the word 'trade' reminded her of what she had been reduced to.

'And do they do much business here?'

'Oh no. Hardly any. It's only the pub which seems to attract people. They use the shop as a storeroom more than anything else. And there's a barn at the back.'

Mowgley steeled himself and emptied the cup. 'So Mr Jardine is spending a lot of time away, from home - and his partner? When did you last see him?'

'Who, Derek or Roger?'

'Derek.'

'Oh, goodness me, it must be a fortnight or more.'

'Ah,' said Mowgley in a hopefully sage manner: 'That sort of thing must put a strain on any sort of relationship.'

'Of course. The atmosphere does seem fraught when Derek is back. And one hears things -' The woman broke off as if realising she had been talking too much to a stranger, and her voice changed as if it were his fault: 'but why are you asking all these questions? Is there a problem?'

'No, not at all,' He put down his cup. 'I'm an insurance broker, and Mr Fowldes has been asking about taking some life cover out on his partner. It's probably because Mr Jardine has been spending so much more time on the road nowadays...'

~

As it was between noon and two, it was predictable that the golf course would be deserted.

In Britain, office workers would be taking advantage of their lunch breaks to work on their slices, hooks or shanks on the driving range, or even trying to squeeze a few holes in before returning to work. Here, a long lunch was par for the course.

At the third ring on the bell push, a plainly unhappy steward appeared from a back room, wiping his mouth with a napkin as he looked pointedly at the long case clock by the changing room door.

'You will have to come back at two o'clock,' he said, causing Mowgley to wonder again how so many French people would know his nationality before he even opened his mouth.

'I don't want to play,' he said. 'I just want some information.'

Looking even more unhappy, the steward reached beneath the counter and produced a booklet. 'It is all in here,' he said brusquely, looking again at the clock.

'Sorry, it's not about the club,' said Mowgley, 'I just wanted to ask you a couple of questions about a member.'

The man's barely concealed irritation turned to near anger.

'That would be impossible. I cannot tell you anything about the members.'

Mowgley had come prepared for the situation, and rested his lightly-clenched right hand on top of the booklet the steward had thrown on to the counter. Protruding from his fist was the end of a twenty euro note.

The steward looked considerably less put out, put down his napkin and said: 'What is it you want to know? If it is not private...'

'I'm enquiring about Mr James deVere, on behalf of his wife. He is an Englishman of around my age who plays here every Tuesday-'

'I know Monsieur deVere,' the man interrupted, 'what about him?'

'I wonder if you have seen him at the club recently, and if you saw him playing here two weeks ago on a Tuesday.'

'I cannot be expected to keep a check on all the members,' the man said testily, then changed his tone as Mowgley's hand tightened around the note. 'But I do remember the day monsieur deVere did not arrive for his appointment. I think that would be a Tuesday? Last Tuesday?'

Mowgley relaxed his grip. 'Appointment?'

'Yes, he plays with the same three Englishmen every Tuesday, and I remember when he did not appear because his friends had to look for someone else to make up the four. They came to me and I managed to find them someone who was free.'

'Ah.' Mowgley gave the man an encouraging look. 'And have you seen Mr deVere since then?'

'No.' The man picked up his napkin and looked meaningfully at Mowgley's hand and then the clock. 'I must go back now.'

'Just another question. Can you let me have the names and telephone numbers of Mr deVere's three friends?'

The steward's eyes widened in a pantomime of shock. 'Of course not. I would lose my place here immediately if any members knew I had given out their private details.'

Mowgley took his hand away, put it in his pocket, then returned it with another two twenty euro notes on discreet show. 'I understand,' he said, 'but I can promise you that nobody will know what you tell me except you and me...'

~

'And how is your new client, the old furniture seller?'

'If you mean the purveyor of fine antiquities, he is, as you said, very worried about what his partner is getting up to.'

'Up to?'

'That perhaps he has found another man.'

'Ah.' Mimi gave a philosophical shrug. 'It happens all the time, whether it is man and woman, woman and woman or man and man. Do you think he is right to be unhappy?'

It was Mowgley's turn to shrug, and he fancied he was getting quite good at it. 'Dunno. But I will find out. It will be the first time I have followed a man,' he said thoughtfully.

'And what did you think about Mr Fowldes?' she said, pronouncing the name as "Fooowld".

'Seemed a nice enough man, and not at all....'

'What?'

'Um, gay-looking, I suppose.'

'You mean he was not wearing an apron and cleaning the statues with a *plumeau*- a piece of wood with feathers on?'

'I didn't see a single feather duster in the shop - or any golden cherubs. No, I don't know what I expected, but he seemed quite...manly.'

'Then he will be the wife.' Mimi said confidently. 'It is always like that. The husband will be much more feminine. And the missing rich man?'

'Proceeding nicely.' He pulled a sheet of crumpled paper from his pocket and dropped it on the desk. 'And I've been keeping a record of my hours and expenses.'

She picked the piece of paper up, smoothed it out, then scanned it. 'Yes, this is fine,' she said. 'I will put it in the computer, add the times and kilometres and costs to the case files. But what is this sixty Euros for?'

'My first attempt at bribery and corruption. I had to give it to the steward at the golf club to persuade him to give me the phone numbers for the people who regularly played golf with Mr deVere.'

She pursed her lips. 'Hmmm. Well, if you have no proof you gave him this amount, I do not think Yann will be happy to pay it.'

'What would he expect me to do - ask for receipts for any bribes I have to hand out?'

She made no comment, putting the rumpled sheet of paper in a drawer, then got up and headed for the kitchen. 'Oh, I forgot,' she said over her shoulder, 'you have had a call from your colleague of the past. She said to tell you to call her in return.'

'I'll do that now, but what's the French for "can you reverse the charges"?'

~

'So have you been out and about solving crimes and gaining new customers, or just skiving in the pub next door?'

'Actually, I've been working on two cases, and I've just been doing all the paperwork.'

'Chin chin. I bet you mean you've given your lady a bit of paper with some stuff scribbled on it, just like you did with me and Jo in Admin.' He heard the click and then the exhalation as Catherine McCarthy paused to light a cigarette, then she said: 'You sound as if you're in danger of enjoying your new life.'

'I wouldn't say that, but it's not as bad as I thought it would be - apart from a mad Albanian hit man trying to kill me.'

'Yes. Quite.' Any news on who Mr Berissa was working for and why he went for you?'

'No. As I said before, he could have been working for the Albanians, or anyone else.'

'But it was Mooney who sent you the text to get you to *La Cour*.'

'Correction. It was Mooney's *phone* that the text came from. But what about you? Any news on the cheesy drugs lorry?

And when are you coming over again? Your mate René has been pining.'

'No he hasn't; I spoke to him earlier and I'm coming over tomorrow. I hope'

'You mean you spoke to him before me? How hurtful is that?'

'I speak to him all the time. It's business. As well as pleasure. You've gone private, remember?'

'Ouch. So you mean you've cracked the case without my help and guidance?'

'No, but there has been an interesting development.'

Mowgley pouted. She would not be able to see it, but it would help with the hurt voice. 'Are you going to share it with me, or are interested civilians not allowed to know?'

'Don't sulk. It's just that I think we know where Mooney could be, and what he's been up to. Maybe.'

'Hang on a minute.' Mowgley nodded thanks as he took the mug of coffee from Mimi, then reached for his tobacco pouch. Wedging the phone under his ear, he opened the pouch and said: 'Alright, then. Tell all. Oh shit!'

'What's the matter?'

Mowgley picked the phone up from the desk and tried to mop up the pool of coffee with his sleeve. Mimi came to the rescue with a box of tissues, pushed his arm away, took the wet tobacco pouch and dropped it in the waste basket, then put the cigarette she had been smoking into his mouth. He took a deep drag, exhaled and then said: 'Blimey, that takes me back.'

'What? Where to? What's going on?'

'I spilled coffee on my baccy and Mimi gave me her fag. It's French.'

'There's a surprise. So do you want to hear my news or not?'

'That's a Roger, sergeant.'

'Okay. Here we go. Yesterday I got a call from my drug squad mate at Manchester.'

'Terry Whatsit?'

'Yep, that's it.'

'And?'

'He'd got the round robin about the cheese lorry and stuff and knew we were looking for Mooney.'

'And?'

'And he said one of his best contacts on the street told him

Mooney had been trying to do business with the big boys up there.'

'Taking a bit of a chance, wasn't he?' Mowgley knew that Mooney had left a few enemies behind on both sides of the sometimes broken fence between dealers and policemen.

'I suppose so, but he apparently had a lot of gear to shift.'

'Go on, then.'

'The word is that he was trying to do a deal for a couple of million for a job lot of Afghan Aunty Hazel.'

'Aunty who?'

'Afghan heroin. It's the latest thing to call it in the trade. Terry told me.'

'Let's have none of your trendy talk here. How good is your mate's street contact?'

'He was very good, apparently.'

'And five mill would be about right for the wholesale on the Toddington shipment?'

'Could be, though of course it would depend on how many boxes there were on board. We know it was good stuff from the case that was left behind.'

'So are you saying that Sean Mooney was in on the shipment or knew about it, met the driver at Toddington, killed him and nicked all the gear? And now he's trying to offload it?

'Could be. But we can't be sure that it's the same stuff or that it was Mooney who killed the driver. It's one line of thought, though.'

'Quite,' said Mowgley. 'So does your mate know if Mooney did his deal or is still in town or even the country?'

'Not yet, and he won't be getting any more information from his contact.'

'Why not.'

He turned up dead of an overdose of guess what?'

'Afghan Aunty Norah or whatever it was you said?'

'Correct.'

'Blimey again.'

As Mowgley took a last pull on his cigarette and crushed it into his ashtray, Mimi waved to catch his attention. She was holding her phone up and pointing at it to signal he had a call waiting.

'I wonder why people do that,' he mused aloud.

'What?' asked Melons.

'Point at the mouthpiece rather than the earpiece when they are letting you know someone is waiting to speak to you. It would be more logical to point at the earpiece, surely? That's where the caller's voice is going to come from, after all.'

There was a moment's silence, then Catherine McCarthy said: I have to say I haven't thought much about that aspect of human activity, lately. Nor the price of cheese, to be honest.'

'What's the price of cheese got to do with it?'

'Exactly. You'd better take your call. See you tomorrow, old boss.'

'Less of the old,' he replied, and hung up.

~

From her desk, Mimi showed what button he should press, and he got it right second time. 'Hello René. I'm sorry, I was talking to Catherine.'

'Yes I know', said the Colonel.

'So how can I help you?' Mowgley held two fingers to his mouth and lifted his eyebrows, and Mimi sighed, shook her head and threw her packet of cigarettes and lighter on to his desk.

'I'm calling to say we have found the place where the Livarot lorry picked up the heroin. I am going there now and am asking if you would like to come.'

Mowgley sat up a little straighter as he fiddled with the packet. 'That's kind of you. Is there a reason?'

'A reason?'

'Why you are offering me a ride? Is there dinner and drinks on the end of it?'

'If you feel like it. I am asking because you have a direct interest in Mr Mooney.'

'That's true. I've just been speaking to Catherine about him. She says he is in Manchester.'

'I think not,' said Colonel Degas. 'I think he is where we are going.'

13

The convoy sped along the RN13, effortlessly spearing its way through the late rush-hour traffic. Each of the vehicles had sirens blaring and blue lights flashing out of harmony, and the motorcycle, two cars and a van barely slowed to turn off the main road and head for the setting sun.

'I see you are becoming a little more French every day,' observed Colonel Degas, nodding at the packet of *Gitanes Blondes* Light Mowgley was opening. 'But they are a little...feminine for someone like you, I think?'

'They're Mimi's. They seem strong enough to me. I spilled coffee on my tobacco. Is it okay for me to smoke? Would you like one?'

'Yes and yes.'

They were sitting in the back of a Renault Laguna saloon, with a shooting-brake version in front and a windowed van behind. The convoy seemed to be maintaining the same speed along the narrow, winding country lanes as it had on the *Route Nationale* trunk road. Mowgley tried to keep his hand from shaking and to look unconcerned as the high hedgerows flashed by.

Degas handed Mowgley's lighter back and apparently mistook his fixed stare of apprehension for casual curiosity: 'This type of countryside is called the *bocage*. It is typically Norman, with small fields and high hedges with trees in them. It is good to stop the wind, but it was not good for the Allied troops when they were trying to break out from the peninsula after the D-Day Landings. The Germans had their tanks and machine guns in the fields and could shoot down at the road.'

Mowgley winced as they rounded another blind corner. 'I should think the *bocage* stuff is not helpful nowadays for seeing a tractor coming out of a field and on to the road.'

Degas smiled. 'That is why we have the motorcyclist in front to clear the way. Everyone gets out of the way when a police *moto* approaches at speed with its lights shining. Even tractors. Anyway, we are nearly there.'

They reached a crossroads, and Mowgley moaned softly as the driver executed a wheel-wrenching turn and followed the lead car on to an even narrower road.

After racing past a sprinkling of old farm buildings and cottages, they arrived at the centre of a village, with a huddle of houses, a large church and opposite it a small bar and grocery store. A short, dumpy middle-aged woman was fiddling with the chain around a row of gas canisters in front of the window, and she stood upright and watched as they sped by.

Suddenly, they were out of the village and into the marshlands, a flat and desolate area and, in contrast to the *bocage*, there was not a hedgerow or tree to be seen as far as the distant horizon.

After crossing a bridge over a river, the lead car braked sharply and the convoy clattered over a wide, flat sheet of metal across a fast-flowing channel of water and then into a yard in front of what looked like a group of deserted factory buildings.

Their outrider had already dismounted and was standing next to his motor cycle, its blue light lazily turning as he talked to a uniformed officer. Nearby were a patrol car and two unmarked vehicles. One was a pristine white van, and the other a muddy and obviously badly-treated Peugeot pick-up. In the back was a single bale of hay, which Mowgley guessed was destined for the small herd of cows watching incuriously from the other side of the road cutting through the *marais*.

An elderly, worried-looking man in brown overalls and gumboots was standing by the driver's door, listening to an irritable-looking Inspector Aittif. As he saw Mowgley sitting in the back of the lead car with Degas, Aittif looked even more irritable.

Their car stopped sharply a few inches from the back of the pick-up, and Degas and Mowgley got out. As the Colonel walked over to speak to Aittif, Mowgley looked up at the gaunt, flat-fronted building. There was some barely-discernible lettering along the top of the front elevation, and many of the small panes in the metal-framed windows were broken. Whatever it had made, the factory had clearly not been making it for some years.

Drawn to a subdued roar coming from the back of the main building, he walked around the gable end to where a frothing waterfall tumbled from a concrete chute to a lower level. It was obviously an offshoot of the river they had crossed, its power magnified by the narrow channels and then the plunge over the weir.

'It was a mill.'

Mowgley turned. He had not heard Degas approaching. 'Of course. What did it make - flour?'

'No, electricity. It has been unused and empty for many years. All the small and pretty water mills in the area have been bought by English people or Parisians. I cannot imagine why anyone would want to own such damp and awkward places, but they do.'

'But not an ugly one like this.'

'No, it is not quaint enough and not much good for anything else than what it used to do. It was empty and for sale or rent for twenty years, and then someone bought it.'

'A mad Englishman?'

'You could say that. It was your friend Sean Mooney.'

'You're kidding?'

'It is not his name on the documents, but we already know he was involved. Our friend the farmer -' Degas nodded towards the man by the truck '- keeps a close eye on this part of the *marais* because of his cows. He was naturally interested when a car made several visits here some months ago, so he took the registration details. Norman farmers are like that. Then he saw the Livarot lorry stopping here. This morning, he came to look after his cows, and thought he would have a look around. He saw something through a window at the back of the building and made a call to his local police station.'

'So this was where the switch of cheeses was made?'

'It looks that way. This place is on a direct line two hours from Livarot and just thirty kilometres south of the port. It is in plain view but few cars use the road, and the lorry could be hidden behind the factory while the change was made. But they did not think about a curious farmer.'

Mowgley nodded. 'The best laid plans and all that. And Mooney is inside?'

'Perhaps. Shall we look?'

~

Degas led the way to a single storey extension running the length of the back of the main building. Aittif was following, and paused to reach through the open widow of a gleaming, low-slung black sports car parked behind the mill.

'Blimey,' said Mowgley, 'I see what you mean about him liking fast cars.'

A policeman was standing to one side of a pair of studded metal doors, which had apparently been forced open. Next to the doors was a small, broken window at head height through which the farmer had probably seen what he had seen. Below the window was a shiny new mobile generator, with leads running from it through the doorway.

Inside, Mowgley narrowed his eyes against the bright light from a trio of lamps on tripods, their satellite dish-style reflectors aimed at a long wooden workbench in the middle of the room. On the bench were several cardboard cases bearing the Livarot logo. One was open. Two figures in white coveralls and hoods were examining the area around the boxes and another was taking photographs.

'The cheese in those boxes is all normal,' Degas said. Our friend is through there.' He pointed at a wide doorway in a wall beyond the bench. From the lintel hung a series of overlapping vertical strips of heavy plastic. Degas pushed his way through them and Mowgley followed.

They had entered another room of a similar size, which also had a wooden work bench occupying its centre; it too was surrounded by portable arc lights. On its surface were not cases of cheese, but there was a body.

Mowgley had not known what to expect, but it was certainly not this.

The corpse was wearing a dark blue suit and a white shirt with a blue tie. The black shoes were highly polished and the soles showed hardly any signs of wear. The body had been neatly arranged, with arms at its sides and feet close together and pointing upwards. Rather than a murder scene it looked as if the body had been laid out as in a chapel of rest, arranged and put on show in new clothes for visits by loved ones.

Then it occurred to him that the body on the bench was more like a shop window mannequin or a waxworks dummy being prepared for display. The comparison came to mind because there were no hands protruding from the cuffs of the sleeves, or head from the collar of the snow white shirt. The sterility of the scene and the figure were enforced by the lack of blood on or around the body.

Mowgley shook his head as if it would help him better understand what he was seeing, then reached for a cigarette. He hesitated as if it might seem disrespectful to smoke in the presence of the corpse, then offered the open packet to Degas. The policeman took a cigarette and a light, and the pair smoked in silence as they took in the bizarre scene.

Eventually, Mowgley spoke. 'Was this how they found him? And are we clear to move around?'

'He was found exactly like that. I am told that the forensics people have done their work on the surroundings, but not on the body...except the preliminary search and going through the pockets. But they took a DNA swab this morning and sent it off.'

'So why do you think it is Mooney?'

Degas pointed to a see-through plastic evidence bag at the end of the bench, near to where the head should have been.

'In there is a passport, a driving licence and even some credit cards. They are all in his name.'

'That's a bit obvious, isn't it? And no keys or car outside?'

'No.'

'So he didn't get here under his own steam - by himself, I mean.'

'No.'

Any distinguishing marks?'

Degas waved his cigarette in the direction of the fully clothed, headless, handless corpse as if indicating the obvious. 'Not that we know of yet. Mooney was never arrested in this country so we have no information on him, but it will be with us from Manchester and Europol soon.'

Mowgley nodded. As a police officer, Mooney's blood type, fingerprints, distinguishing marks, dental records and DNA would have been added to the Europol data base. Europol was the law enforcement agency of the European Union, and held data on all officers as well as millions of known criminals.

Keeping his distance, Mowgley walked slowly round the bench, looking at the body and the surface of the bench and the concrete floor beneath it. Degas followed him, each man using a cupped hand as an ashtray.

'Not a trace of blood, so he was not killed here. Or at least, not in this room.' Mowgley smiled grimly. 'How's that for a priceless piece of deduction?'

Degas echoed his smile. 'Exact. They are looking elsewhere in the building, of course for any signs of blood - or the missing parts. And he must have been dressed after the removal of the hands and head. The shirt collar and sleeves are completely clean, or they are to the normal eye.'

Mowgley took a last draw on his Gitanes, walked over to the nearest wall, stubbed the end out and slipped it in his jacket pocket 'So someone went to a lot of trouble to set up this little tableau. The question is why?'

Degas followed Mowgley's action with his cigarette, then took out a handkerchief and wiped his hands. 'You are right.' He looked at his watch 'There is nothing I can do here until the forensics have done their work and Europol and Manchester have responded. I saw a bar in the village we passed through. Shall we see if it is open?'

'Good idea.'

~

Once upon a time, Mowgley knew, even the smallest village in France would have its own shop and usually it would be a combination of provisions store and bar. On entry, customers would usually turn one way to do their shopping, and the other for a drink. As in Britain, the ineluctable rise and rise of out-of-town supermarket shopping had killed most village stores, but some determined owners battled on. The determination of the owner of this one could be seen in her face, Mowgley thought.

When the two men entered, she had been serving an elderly lady, dropping a handful of dirty potatoes into the old wicker basket the woman was clutching to her breast. While Mowgley looked round at the range of perishable and household goods, bottles of wine, toys, china ornaments and even picture postcards of the church opposite, Degas asked a question and the woman nodded. He turned and led the way into the bar, and Mowgley felt immediately at home.

It was certainly not the sort of artificially quaint and rustic sort of place which middle-class British lovers of *France profonde* would have rhapsodised over. In fact, it was the opposite, and the lack of pretence and pretention was what appealed to him.

The floor was covered in time-worn linoleum, and the handful of chairs and tables were of 1970s vintage, made from peeling tubular steel with plastic covered seats and back rests. There was an empty fish tank on an old sideboard, and another wall was taken up with a huge fireplace. Last winter's log was still in the grate, and would doubtless see service in a few month's time. Normans, and especially Normans with small businesses were renowned for wasting nothing.

Above the mantelpiece was a flyblown mirror, and the other walls were almost covered with mostly hand-made posters for events which had taken place long ago. Mowgley had noticed how attached Norman bar owners became to posters, and the oldest here referred to a village fete in the August of 1997.

As he debated the wisdom of encouraging the cat sleeping on the nearest table to move, his eye was caught by a frameless photograph pinned to the wall next to the mirror. Like the photograph in Coco's Bar, it showed a younger version of the grey haired author Mowgley had seen sitting glumly on the ferry-boat waiting for a book to sign. Clearly in a bohemian phase. The man was wearing a bushy beard and shoulder-length mousy hair, and was toasting the camera. On each side of him were a collection of mostly elderly men, probably locals by their overalls and air. They were also holding their glasses aloft. On the bottom border of the photograph, someone had printed in large letters:

JOLLY BOYS CLUB - AUGUST 1994.

'What is it?' Mowgley turned away to see Degas watching him looking at the photograph. 'Nothing,' he said, 'just a coincidence.'

They left the cat in peace and took seats at the bar as the shop bell signified the exit of the customer. Shortly afterwards, the owner pushed her way through a more delicate and colourful version of the vertical strips which had hung from the doorway in the factory. Mowgley had noticed how short the woman was when she was serving in the shop, but in the French way there was a raised platform behind the bar so the patron could look down on her customers.

After consulting with Mowgley, Degas ordered a couple of beers, then nodded at the cigarette packet and lighter Mowgley had laid on the bar. The owner reacted as if he had suggested group sex, shook her head so hard it dislodged a curl of hair above one ear, and swept off through the plastic drapes. Degas shrugged. 'Sorry, but it is up to her.'

'Perhaps she knew you were a policeman, and did not want to be seen allowing the law to be broken.'

'I think that lady makes her own rules for her bar and will not change them for anyone,' observed Degas dryly.

The rule maker returned through the plastic strips, put two bottles on the bar, then reached beneath it and produced two glasses. She left as silently as she had arrived, leaving her customers to pour their own drinks. Mowgley took a long pull of cold lager and let out a sigh of contentment.

Automatically, he reached for his cigarette packet, then withdrew his hand as he remembered the house rules. 'So,' he said, 'what's your guess about the body? Who is it - and why the head and hands were cut off... and why there was no blood at the scene?'

Degas placed the cold glass against his cheek. 'I do not have an idea at this moment. What about you?'

'*Moi aussi.*' He felt and looked pleased with himself at his pronunciation. 'How was that?'

'Very good, but you might have said '*moi non plus.*' To make it better understood.'

'Okay,' said Mowgley. 'I am nonplussed too. But something tells me it is not Sean Mooney laid out on that bench. In fact I would give you odds - I would bet you - that it is not him.'

Degas raised his glass again. 'I accept the challenge. The loser will pay for a tour of Cherbourg's most infamous bars so you will feel at home. But why are you so sure it is not him?'

'Dunno. It's just a gut feeling. The passport and the other stuff in his pockets. If they were trying to disguise who it was by going to the trouble of cutting off his head and hands, why leave the identification in the pocket? It's all too obvious.'

'Ah.' said Colonel Degas: 'Perhaps that's why they did it. What if they wanted to confuse us - as they have? Or perhaps they had need of the head and hands.'

'*Needed* them? What, like trophies, you mean?'

'Perhaps they wanted to show someone that Mooney was indeed dead. Or get fingerprints from the hands to prove it Or perhaps it is something the Albanian Mafia likes to do to remind others how barbarous they can be.'

'Hmmm.' Mowgley looked discontented with those options. 'I think it could have been done a lot easier with a mobile phone camera, then sending the picture to whoever the interested party was. Or-'

He was interrupted by an insistent buzzing coming from Degas' jacket pocket.

The policeman took out his phone, flipped the top open spoke rapidly into it, then responded to the information he was obviously getting. '*Oui...Oui...Oui... d'accord...okay...merci bien.*'

'Problems?' asked Mowgley when Degas had returned the phone to his pocket.

'Not enough to stop us having another drink. We will need a rehearsal for, as I think you say, our pub crawl when we find out who the body belonged to...'

14

The house sat somewhat haughtily above its distant neighbours, looking down on the rocky beach of what looked like a fairly private cove. A stream passed beside the house's high walls on its way to making a small but regular contribution to the English Channel, or what the French preferred to call The Sleeve.

Cherbourg could be found along the coast a dozen miles to the west, and Mowgley's home town of Portsmouth was something like seventy nautical miles in a roughly northerly direction. A sailor friend had once tried to explain the difference between sea and land miles to him, but he had either had too much to drink, or his friend had. For sure, there was nothing between where he was standing and his old office but water; because of it, what would have been little more than a commuter's drive had become an unbridgeable gulf between cultures and attitudes.

He left the car where the lane came to a dead end, and paused to look at a shrine set in an alcove in the wall a little way from the gate. The colours on the figure of the Virgin had faded, and there was a posy of dead flowers in a vase at her feet. There was no glass or security screen, and across the Channel the old and probably valuable effigy would have been long gone, and the vase with it.

But things were different here. As Colonel Degas had said, there were more than enough criminals to go round in rural

France, but they did not seem to bother as much as the English with stealing small things just because they could.

Mowgley pressed the button on the box next to the gate, which was a solid sheet of metal made decorative with a framework of wrought-iron scrolls. Obviously, the owner thought there was a significant risk of burglars, or perhaps the overt nod to security levels was just because he was British.

Mowgley waited and watched a flurry of gulls fighting over something on the beach, then there was a crackle and a squawk, and a tinny, irritable voice said '*Oui*?' Mowgley felt a flush of pleasure that he could tell that the speaker was not using his native tongue, but perhaps that was because he knew the owner of the house was from Northampton and not Normandy.

'Mr Ferris? John Mowgley.'

Another squawk and then: 'Okay. I'm in the greenhouse.'

There followed a buzz and a click, but the gate did not move.

After a moment, he pressed the button again, and the voice returned, this time sounding even more irritable. 'What is it?'

'The gate's not opening.'

A heavy sigh issued from the box, then the voice said in a talking-to-a-child tone: 'For fuck's sake; I thought you were supposed to be a detective. You have to push the gate open after I unlock it,'

The buzz and click followed, and Mowgley petulantly kicked the gate open, feeling that he had somehow lost an opening skirmish.

~

A more pretentious owner might have called the long and ornate tunnel of glass behind the house a conservatory. An even more pretentious person would have said it was an orangery.

It was at the end of a footpath cutting through an immaculate lawn, beyond which a line of magnolia trees guarded a triple garage and a gravelled driveway leading to a larger version of the gate through which Mowgley had passed. He would have had a bet that, unlike the pedestrian entrance, the double gate opened itself when the big and shiny Range Rover Discovery outside the garage drew near.

Seeing the house close to, Mowgley reckoned it would cost at least a million in the same sort of setting in even the northernmost parts of England, and double that on the south coast. He wondered if that was the reason Ralph Ferris had chosen to live on this side of the Channel.

After observing the species for a number of years, he had concluded that Britons who chose to retire to France - or any other foreign country where property was not an obsession - fell into two broad categories. By far the biggest was influenced predominantly by price. If they traded in their house in the United Kingdom for a similar-sized home, they could usually bank a nice nest egg to augment their pensions. Or they could swap their homes for somewhere far grander. Either way, the lure of cheaper property usually turned out not to be a sound reason to spend the declining years of one's life away from friends, family and familiar way of life.

By far the happiest expats were those who moved to live in another country because they liked it there better than in their homeland. Blurring the boundaries were those Brits who would rather be in Britain, but had come to terms with being a forever foreigner.

Mowgley had no idea into which category his interviewee fell, but he seemed to have made the best of his voluntary – or perhaps involuntary – exile.

Ralph Ferris was a small, stocky man with a foxy face and slicked-back hair, and like many short people he gave off a whiff of aggression. Mowgley had no information on what he had done for a living in his past life, but he would have had money that it was not the law, accountancy or any other middle-class profession.

He was standing by a raised bed containing a row of exotic-looking plants bearing clusters of small round fruit which may or may not have been oranges. From his right hand dangled a pair of secateurs, and the expensive short-sleeved shirt showed off a frequent golfer's tanned and powerful forearms. With the white slacks and tasselled loafers, he was dressed for a post-round drink in the bar rather than a gardening session, and looked as if he might feel more at home in Southern Spain than in northern France.

Mowgley nodded as he wondered if Ferris had chosen to receive his visitor in the greenhouse by design. At the back of the house, a wide flight of marble steps led up to a terrace, on which there was a metal table with a very wide umbrella attachment over two recliners. One of them was occupied by a middle-aged woman in shorts and a sleeveless top. She was wearing sunglasses and looking at a magazine, and had given him no more than a cursory glance when he had passed by.

'Alright, then,' Ferris laid the secateurs on the brick ledge formed by the raised bed, and turned to face Mowgley like a man with better things to do, 'what's it all about?' He walked over to where a glass topped table held a packet of cigarettes and a tray with a bucket of ice, a bottle and several tall glasses on it, then sat down in a recliner that matched the two on the terrace. He made no gesture or invitation for Mowgley to take the other one.

'As I said on the phone, I'm being retained by Mrs deVere to look into the disappearance of her husband...'

'"Retained"? "Mrs deVere?"' Ferris's voice flew high with derision, and Mowgley noted he had a vaguely south London accent. 'Do you mean Annie Cross?'

'I don't know her maiden name-'

'Cross is not her maiden name, it's her real name. She married plain old Jimmy Cross.'

'So where does the deVere come from?'

Ferris paused to light a cigarette with a sleek and very slender silver or platinum lighter, blew out a cloud of smoke and sat back in the recliner. 'She made it up after they came over to live here.'

Mowgley frowned. 'Do you think she - or he - needed to change their name?'

Ferris said nothing for a moment, regarding Mowgley steadily through the haze of smoke. It was as if he was considering telling the truth, making something up, or merely telling the investigator to fuck off.

In the end, it seemed to Mowgley that he had settled for the truth. 'Jimmy bent? I think not. Straight as an arrow, our Jimmy. But he might have a reason for not wanting people to find him. Dunno about her, but I bet she's got plenty in her past she wouldn't want getting out.'

'So do you know how long they had been married and why they came over - and where the money came from?'

Again, it looked as if Ferris was considering how to respond to the question. Then he said: 'Best part of ten years, I suppose. Jimmy was in property in London. Made a fortune and everything was going great till his wife died suddenly. It took The Cow five minutes to sniff him out, and get him up the aisle. As to why they came over, I haven't got a clue. Jimmy loved London and was a true Brit. It was either her idea or he had a good reason. I did hear things were not going too well for him.'

'Did you know him before he moved over?'

'Yeah.' Ferris nodded, then his face seemed to soften and he looked at his glass: 'Do you want a drink?'

Mowgley shook his head and half-raised a hand to say thanks but no thanks, and Ferris continued. 'I knew him a bit, because of business. I was in building supplies and I'd take him out for a beer and a meal pretty regular. Then she turned up and pretty soon she'd got rid of all his mates. Then after we moved over I got a call saying he was thinking of relocating and would I look out for a place for him. He didn't say why, and never has. I got in touch with the people who found us this place, and they came up with that lairy pile on the marshes.' He took another draw on his cigarette. 'Shouldn't you be writing all this down?'

Mowgley smiled. 'No, that's only on TV cop shows. And old ones. I'm recording our conversation.'

A sudden change came over Ferris's features and Mowgley held his arms out in front of him in a placatory gesture. 'Only joking. I've got a good memory.'

Ferris looked as if he was considering losing his temper, then sat back again and said: 'Is that it, then? What else do you want to know?'

'Only if you've got any idea why Mr deVere - Mr Cross - would want to disappear. Did he ever talk to you about anything to do with his marriage, or his finances?'

'Yeah, I been thinking a bit about that,' conceded Ferris. 'He never said much about anything, really. We played golf once a week and then had a couple of beers in the clubhouse. The other two were always there so he wouldn't have said anything anyway. He was a private sort of bloke. We never got invited over for drinks or dinner, but that would be her doing.'

'So did he seem preoccupied or concerned about anything when you last played?'

Ferris thought about it and then said: 'No, don't think so. I remember he played a blinder and we won the pot. He didn't seem to have anything on his mind.'

'And what about money worries?'

Ferris screwed up his pointed, foxy nose. 'Who can say? He must have had plenty when he came over after selling the company and cashing in on his place over there. But she's done a good job of spending it on the house and herself.'

'So you've got no idea of why he might want to disappear?'

'Only to get away from her. I suppose she might have done him in, but then why would she bring you in if she had?'

'Only as an alibi and because she thought I'd never find him.'

As Mowgley had intended, this gave Ferris something to think about. After a pause to let it sink in, he asked: 'Do you know if he was seeing anyone else?'

'Jimmy? I wouldn't have thought so. I don't reckon he was ever that sort of bloke, and he never said anything about a bit of spare. Not that he would.'

'Okay. Well, thanks for your help. I'll give you a call if I think of anything else. I can see myself out.'

'Alright,' said Ferris, who obviously had had no intention of leaving the recliner. 'You press the button by the gate to unlock it.' He waited a moment, then added: 'But you've got to pull it open...'

He had reached the greenhouse door before Ferris called after him: 'By the way, how did you get my number?'

Mowgley rested his hand on the door handle and smiled. 'That was no problem, Mr Ferris. Remember, I used to be a policeman.'

He made as if to push the handle down, then, as if in afterthought, said: 'Oh, just a final, final quickie. What was the name of the estate agency you used to find the Crosses a place to buy?'

Ferris looked puzzled, then said: 'Normandy Dream Homes. Why do you want to know?'

Mowgley smiled again as he pushed the handle down. 'Nothing important, just thinking about selling my house...'

15

The rain came as they left the *Bad Penny* and walked towards the town centre. It was a heavy downpour; with the dancing drops glittering as they bounced from the cobbled quayside.

Mowgley liked weather, as did Sarah Campbell. She too was bareheaded, occasionally turning her face up to the pewter sky to greet the rain. Nelson was enjoying the elements, biting at the big drops and snuffling at the odours intensified by the heavy fall.

'Now remind me,' said Mowgley, 'where are we going and why?'

She reached out and wiped his brow almost fondly. 'You look like a drowned rat. We are going to the Musée Thomas-Henry, and the purpose is to take another step on your road to assimilation and integration into Gallic culture.'

Mowgley grunted, wiped a finger down the side of his nose and flicked a spray of raindrops into the gutter. 'I'm thankful you didn't say my "journey". So who was Thomas Henry? Another French artist I've never heard of?'

'Actually he was a town councillor in the 1830s and fancied himself as an art critic. He wanted young people in the area to learn to appreciate art. Now there are more than three hundred paintings in what they like to call the 'little Louvre'. Whoops, I sound like a tour guide, don't I?'

She broke off as Mowgley pulled her sharply away from the kerb. The bus thundered past, sending up a sheet of dirty water and causing Nelson to bark joyously.

The couple stood close to each other, the rain streaming down their faces, Mowgley found himself reluctant to leave go of her arm, and she did not seem eager to free herself.

'So is Bébé going to be okay on her own?' asked Mowgley, searching for something to say which would hold the moment.

'She'll be fine. The nice man next door promised to keep an eye on her.'

'"Next door?" I take it you mean on the next mooring.'

She pulled away. 'I mean next door. He is my neighbour. Don't go all nautical on me just because you've spent a lot of time on a car ferry. I brought the *Bad Penny* across the Channel virtually on my own, which was fun and quite instructive.'

'Sorry, skipper. I must remember I'm only the cabin boy. Is romance blooming with your next-door neighbour, then?'

Don't be silly. Guido is gay. And what would I need a man for?'

'Quite.'

She smiled. 'You men are funny, aren't you? You find it impossible to believe that a woman can be content or even prefer to be on her own. I think that's because being alone is a natural state for woman and the opposite for men. I've often wondered why that is. Perhaps they don't want to lose their mothers.'

Mowgley did not respond, and they walked on towards the statue of Napoleon, astride his horse and pointing out to sea and across the Channel at the old enemy.

~

'Well? Did you enjoy it?'

Mowgley gave the question serious consideration, then said: 'I don't know if that's the right word, but it was interesting. I liked the one by Millet.' He lifted his glass, then looked into the past and his face darkened.

She leaned forward. 'What's the matter? A bad memory?'

'Yes. I found someone dead in a bath once, and it was like his painting of the woman lying in the river.'

She touched his arm. 'I know what you mean, but I think you are thinking of Millais, not Millet. They sound the same but were very different in style.'

'Oh, right. Fancy another one?'

They were sitting in a bar time seemed to have forgotten, or at least overlooked. It was ironic, Mowgley often thought, how so much was spent on creating trendy 'retro' bars. Some even featured the classic stand-and-deliver lavatory cubicles which consisted of not much more than a square of porcelain with two footprints showing the user where to stand, and a hole between them. When he had first encountered a *turque*, he thought someone had stolen the toilet pan.

This bar was fitted with one, but that was because the owner had never updated it. The toilets were entirely in keeping with the rest of the establishment, as the fixtures, fittings and decor had not been affected by passing fashions and fancies

Like any town, Cherbourg had changed over the decade or so that Mowgley had been a regular visitor. But the pace of change seemed slower than in Britain, and perhaps in the rest of France. Boutiques selling outrageously expensive clothes and shops with silly names came and went, but the traditional restaurants and department stores remained stubbornly the same. Nobody had as yet tried to launch a vegetarian restaurant in Cherbourg, and if it happened, he would place a bet it would be a short-lived venture.

Le Derby was tucked away down an alleyway leading from the Theatre Square, and was patronised almost entirely by people who had been of drinking age when its decor had first been fashionable. After exposure to a million or more cigarettes, the ceiling was a pleasant shade of gold. The varnish from the wood-panelled walls had long eroded, and the mirrors and posters advertised drink brands which had quit the shelves several decades ago. The chest-high counter maintained its original zinc surface, and at the end of it sat the proprietor.

Sarah had told him that she had heard that the lady owner had been sitting in the same place, dressed in the same two-piece suit for nearly forty years. While her barmaid looked after the customers, Madame sat with knees modestly pressed together, a shiny and commodious handbag on her lap, and on her head a pill-box hat of the same style and colour as the one worn by Jackie Kennedy on that fateful day in Dallas in 1963.

Local legend had it that Madame and her husband had come

to the bar full of enthusiasm and very much in love in the early Seventies. Business had not lived up to their expectations, enthusiasm and love had waned, and he had run off with the barmaid. Since then, Madame had sat, Miss Haversham-like, in her unchanging surroundings with the unchanging hope her man would return.

It was obviously too good a story to be true, but Mowgley preferred the romantic fiction to the probable verity that the old lady felt the cold, liked familiar garments from her youth, and could not afford or be bothered to update her bar.

He paid, nodded to the proprietor and left a couple of Euros on the counter in appreciation of the service, decor and prices. Though not set at the levels when the decor was in vogue, the drinks were cheaper than in the more trendy parts of town.

Sarah smiled as he returned. 'I think you are going to like it here - or could do.'

Mowgley put their glasses on the table and looked round the bar. 'What's not to like? Cheap beer and pleasant surroundings - and no no-smoking rule.'

'I meant France - or Cherbourg - not the bar. It's only been a month and you look almost content. Or should that be resigned?'

He sucked at his beer, licked his lips free of froth and thought about it. 'Somewhere in between, I think. The funny thing is that all the time I had a job and some sort of life in England, I couldn't see myself ever being at home here. Now I've got no choice, I can see the good bits. What about you?'

'Can I see the good bits?' She looked out of the plate glass window at a young couple walking hand-in-hand along the narrow alleyway. They seemed oblivious of their surroundings or anything else in the universe except each other. 'I like France.'

'Yes, I can see that. But why?'

She shrugged in an almost French way. 'Why does anyone like France? More people come here on holiday than to any other country on earth. The French can't be bothered to travel abroad, and who can blame them? They know what they have, and think we should be grateful to share it. Apart from the literature and art and wine and food, I think I like it here because of people's indifference. You can be yourself.' She picked her glass up and raised it as if in a toast. 'That should certainly suit you.'

He smiled and ran a hand across his nascent beard. 'Maybe it's a honeymoon period, but I am enjoying being able to be myself.'

She toyed with her glass and observed dryly: 'I can't see that being a problem for you anywhere.'

He sniffed. 'Pot and kettle. So how long have you been living here - in this bit of France?'

'About three years.'

'And before that?'

'Paris.'

'So your husband would be able to play in the jazz clubs?'

'More or less.'

'And you brought the boat over?'

'Yep.'

'So why is it here and not in Paris?'

'It was in Paris.' Her look warned him not to take this line of questioning any further. 'Now I know what it's like to be grilled in a police station.'

'I think you should know what that's like well enough anyway.'

She smiled. 'Yes, but not on the receiving end.'

'That's true. Last few questions, then.'

'That's what you people always say.'

'True. So when did you retire?'

She reached for his cigarette packet. 'I didn't. I got the sack.'

'I thought barristers were self-employed?'

'They are. But you can be disbarred.'

'I knew that, but it's pretty rare, isn't it?'

She reached down to stroke Nelson's head. 'Not any more. It's the most common sanction nowadays. It was more unusual in my days, especially for a woman to get the chop.'

'Can I ask why?'

She repeated the Gallic-style shrug. 'I trusted someone.'

'I didn't think you could get disbarred for that.'

She looked at him, then seemed to make up her mind. 'It was a big drugs trial. I got involved with the accused, and he told me he was guilty.'

'But that's okay, isn't it?'

'Not really. You can defend someone you know is guilty, as long as you enter that plea for them. He went for not guilty and

I did nothing about it. I got him off by leading him the right way and letting him tell what I knew to be lies. After it was all over he dumped me and sold his story to a tabloid from his safe haven in Spain. That was it for me.'

'Ah. So that left a bit of a bitter taste, then?'

'You could say that. But it was my fault for being such a bloody fool.'

They sat silently for a while, then she said. 'Can we have another drink? All this interrogation is making my throat very dry. It's cheaper and easier to buy a bottle here, by the way.'

'Of course.' He stood up. As he turned to go to the bar, she put her arm on his and asked: 'Where are you sleeping tonight?'

He frowned. 'In my room I guess. Why?'

She reached for a cigarette and waited while he lit it. 'The boat's closer, that's all.'

'Yes,' he said, 'I suppose it is...'

16

'Don't you dare even *think* about it.'

'What?'

'Growing a beard.'

Mowgley ran a hand over the dark stubble. 'I'm not growing one,' he lied. 'I just haven't shaved for a couple of days.'

Catherine McCarthy frowned: 'Well, kindly do so. Only men with fat faces or something to hide like a weak chin should be allowed to grow beards. All others look like rats peering through a hole in a horsehair mattress, and it should be against the law. Now I think of it, I like the idea of a Beard Police with powers of immediate arrest and execution.'

'You mean you'd execute someone for growing a beard?'

'No, I meant the arresting officer could issue a compulsory shaving order and have it executed on the spot.'

They were sitting at a newly-acquired addition to Mowgley's room. The table had been bought with the assistance of Racine the police interpreter from a nearby second-hand store. Though having the required number of legs, it was an unremarkable example of 1970s design, and made an interesting if uncomfortable match with the two mock Henry II chairs Racine had scavenged from a squat.

The coffee they were drinking came from a gleaming and sleek new machine, which looked decidedly out of place on the cumbersome sideboard.

'This is nice.'

'What, the coffee or the room?'

She looked around. 'Well both, really. I mean the room is nice and large and there's a lovely view. And the coffee's really good. Was the machine a flat-warming present?'

'No. I got it at the hypermarket on the hill - it was on special offer.'

'And you were able to understand the instructions?'

'No problem,' he said, not adding that an English version had been included.

Catherine McCarthy took another appreciative sip, looked at the packet of cigarettes on the table top, then puffed reflectively at an imaginary Holmesean pipe and said: 'So, let us look at the evidence, shall we, Watson? Proper coffee, proper French fags and the beginnings of a bohemian beard. I trust the Breton beret is on order?'

She reached out and took a cigarette from the packet of Gitanes, lit it, then nodded at the wall above the sideboard: 'That's a nice print.'

Mowgley bridled. 'It's not a print. It's real. You should recognise the scene. It's market day in the Theatre Square. By a local artist.'

Melons blew out smoke and raised her eyebrows: 'An original? You've been splashing out, what with the furniture, the new fridge, the coffee machine *and* an original painting. Have you had your commission from solving your first case?'

'The painting was a present.'

'Oh really? Someone must think a lot of you. Was it from your landlady?'

'No.'

There was a pause, then Melons said. 'It was from your Boat Lady, wasn't it? Is it all happening with her?'

'Not at all,' Mowgley said stiffly. 'She's just –'

'– a good friend? Yeah, I know. From what you tell me, she likes lame dogs.'

'What's that supposed to mean?'

'Nothing. So how's your new career going? Have you been paid yet?'

'Not yet, and it's all a bit different from what we're used to.'

'In what way? Not getting paid? Not having the authority and resources of the Force? Having to go down those mean streets alone and do what a man has to do? Or what? I would have thought doing things your way would have been right up your mean street.'

He reached for the Gitanes. 'Yeah, it's a bit of that, but mostly it's the way the rules of engagement are so different.'

'What do you mean?'

He lit his cigarette and blew smoke at the ceiling. 'For a start, in the Job you have to keep on top of the budget and clear up cases as soon as you can or you're in trouble from above. With this sort of work you have to build up the exes and string the case out as long as you can or as long as the punter has the funds.'

'And you don't like that?'

'Not that bit. But the more I ponce around and build up the bills, the better Yann likes it. Next week I'm going to England to tail…'

She sat up straight and pantomimed a shocked expression. 'Excuse me. Did you just say 'tail', Mr Spade?'

'Ha ha. Anyway, I shall be flitting around Surrey and hiding behind lampposts and thinking of inventive ways to build up the costs.'

'Sounds fun to me. And you can take me out for dinner while you're over. That'll help build up the overheads.'

Mowgley took their mugs and walked across to the sideboard. 'As a matter of fact, I was going to ask you for a bit of help on this one, using the data base and stuff.'

'Done. I shall find the most expensive restaurant in Surrey. One that sells pasties, though. Unless your conversion includes developing a craving for frogs' legs, that is.'

'Har de har.' He returned with two small cups and put them on the table with a flourish. 'I've done espresso this time. Hope that's not too sophisticated for you?'

'Cheeky sod. So where is René taking us to dine this evening?'

'I don't know. And you'll be on your own.'

'What? You're turning down a free meal?'

'I have other plans and have no wish to play the raspberry.'

'You know very well it's gooseberry.'

'Yeah, but I wonder why?'

'Why what?'

'Why it's gooseberry and not any other fruit.'

'Quite. But anyway, if you're going out with Lady

Whatsername, why not bring her along? I bet René would like to meet her.'

'No, I'm on my own tonight, and I've got to do a bit of local research in the seamier side of town.'

'You mean going on a pub crawl and getting paid for it?'

'Yeah, I suppose so. A bit like the old days, really...'

~

It was a little after one in the morning and Mowgley was in a mellow mood. He felt almost at home as he made his way back to his lodgings after his first proper Cherbourg pub crawl.

Or, as it would appear on his expenses sheet, familiarising himself with the area and local contacts. He would have had a hefty bet that Yann would not agree, but it was worth a try.

He and Racine had done their best to visit all the bars in the docks area as yet unknown to him, but it had soon become clear, even after only a *demi* in each, that it would have to be an ongoing project.

During his voyage of discovery he had also discovered the ultimate in American-French fusion takeaways. Run by an enterprising Moroccan, the outlet specialised in big, slightly underdone hamburgers, sliced into strips to suit being served in a crispy baguette. Also sandwiched in with the burger (or burgers) was a nod to healthy eating in the shape of an oiled lettuce leaf. For those feeling more than peckish, a mass of chunky Belgian-style chips, liberally coated in salad cream could be squeezed in. There was also an option to find room for sliced gherkins, sautéed mushrooms and even a fried egg or two. It was the sort of gargantuan indulgence that Elvis Presley would have returned from the grave for, but seemed somehow more sophisticated because it was enclosed in French bread.

Having passed the same fountain twice, Mowgley had finally taken what he believed to be the right direction for home when he saw a man on the other side of the road.

He was kicking a dog, and Mowgley was about to protest when he saw that the dog-kicker was not alone. In the shadows at the entrance to an alleyway, another man was bending over a figure which lay slumped against a wall. Mowgley looked regretfully at the remains of the baguette, then laid it carefully on the pavement.

It is a natural reaction for passers-by to shout at someone engaged in a criminal activity in the hope that it will cause the offender to desist. Sometimes the offender will take note and make off, but the shout also alerts and prepares the evil-doer for any approaching menace. Mowgley knew this from many past engagements, and crossed the street silently, keeping out of the nearest assailant's eye-line.

Another laudable action by passers-by when trying to stop an attack is to lay hands on the attacker. This invariably ends in a struggle which the have-a-go hero may lose. Much more effective is to damage the assailant as quickly as possible and thus render him less capable of retaliation.

Mowgley did so by opening his arms wide, cupping his hands and then bringing them together very hard on the dog-kicker's ears. At the same time, he used his body to push the man against the window of the shop outside of which the action was taking place. Several things then happened in quick succession. The window gave way, an alarm blared out and, frightened by the noise, the dog bit into his saviour's calf.

The dog-kicker occupied with bleeding copiously and trying to extract himself from the shop front, Mowgley was free to turn his attention to his colleague.

He was the smaller of the two, and had been bending over the man on the floor and going through his pockets. When his friend had gone through the window, he had stood, turned and reached for a pocket on his own jacket. This potentially dangerous development did not give Mowgley the time to disengage himself from the dog, but he was able to launch himself across the space between himself and the target.

In his youth, Mowgley had been an undistinguished pub team soccer player, but admired for his talent and willingness to use his head to take on an often wet and heavy ball. He had continued to practice and hone his natural ability after his football-playing days were over.

When attempting a head-butt, most people aim in the region of the target's forehead. This is not the most effective action, as a collision of heads can cause as much damage to the nutter as the nuttee. Mowgley had learned this basic rule early on, and had a jagged scar between his eyebrows as evidence.

So, as recommended by the Glasgow Kiss instruction

manual (had there been one), he aimed for the middle of the man's face with the top of his head.

It was too short a distance in which to build up much momentum, but there was coming up for seventeen stone of bone, muscle, sinew and fat behind the blow.

Although he could not see what was happening, Mowgley was aware of the splintering and crunching of bone giving way. The man screamed with a mixture of anger and pain and fell back, tripping over his victim.

He did not take long to roll over and start to rise, but his scream was even louder when Mowgley's knee caught him in the vicinity of the already damaged area.

There was another nasty crunching sound, then the man slumped alongside his victim.

This left Mowgley panting heavily, leaning against the nearest wall, with pains of differing intensity in the top of his head, right kneecap and left calf. At least, he thought, the dog had let go of his leg.

Kneeling to tend to the victim, he gave a grunt at the sudden pain in his kneecap, stood up and turned towards a streetlamp. Protruding from a bloody torn patch on the right knee of his trouser leg were two small, yellowish teeth. As he debated on the wisdom of trying to extract them with his fingers, the wail of an approaching siren cut through the shrill demands of the shop alarm.

To this noise was added an enthusiastic bark, and Mowgley looked across the road and swore. The remains of his fusion burger were disappearing down the throat of the dog which had bitten him, thus adding insult to injury.

17

It was Mowgley's third visit to the Louis Pasteur, and he felt the staff were beginning to look upon him as a regular.

After being handcuffed at the scene of the altercation he had been thrown into the back of a police van which followed the ambulance taking the men he had injured to the hospital. A telephone call to Colonel Degas had resulted in the cuffs and any possible charges being removed, and he had spent the night in the Pasteur to ensure the self-inflicted wound to his head had caused no lasting harm.

Before calling in to see René Degas the next morning, he had checked in at the office and then the *Bar du Port*, where the story of his encounter had already grown with the telling.

Now, he was sitting with a black coffee and cigarette in the office of Colonel Degas, being updated on events subsequent to his arrest.

'It seemed a bit pointless mugging a beggar,' he observed.

Degas shrugged. 'It was not so much a mugging as a falling out amongst friends.'

'Beg pardon?'

'The three men are all very small criminals, not much up from *les mendicants* - beggars. They use the dog to excuse their behaviour or presence down *allees* at the back of shops or houses they think might be a good idea to break into. Last night they stole money from an English sailor who was drunk, then spent most of it on wine. They had also taken a telephone and passport and a boat ticket from the man with the yacht and had an argument about what best to do with them. The man on the floor was stabbed and beaten. He was the owner of the dog, who was trying to protect him when you arrived.'

'Oh.' Mowgley fingered the wound on his head. 'A bit silly of me to get involved then. I should have let them get on with it.'

Degas shook his head. 'I do not think so. You could not know the circumstances, and acted like the Good Samaritain.'

'Samaritan.'

'I beg your pardon?'

'It's 'Samaritan' in English, not 'Samaritain.''

'I see,' said Degas somewhat stiffly. 'Thank you. Anyway, the men will be charged with the robbery of the sailor, and you will not be charged with the damage to the shop or the cost of replacing the man's teeth and mending his nose.'

Mowgley looked to see if Degas was serious, then decided he was not, and said 'Phew. That's a relief. Fancy a drink, or is it too early?'

'It is rarely too early in France, as we like to take our time over drinking- as with other leisure activities.'

They rose to leave, then Mowgley asked 'So what will happen to the dog? Will it go back to its owner?'

Degas took his jacket from the back of his chair, putting it on and shrugging at the same time. 'I do not think so. They say the man who owns it will be in hospital for a week, and then in custody and probably in prison afterwards. The dog followed the ambulance to the hospital and is in the yard now. It will be put in the place for strays, then put down if nobody wants it. Why do you ask?'

Mowgley rubbed his chin. 'Well, I sort of feel a bit responsible. If I hadn't come along, he would still be with his master.'

Degas smiled grimly. 'Yes, but his master could have been dead if you had not intervened. Then his friends would be in prison for a very long time, and the dog would still be killed. Are you saying you want to keep it?'

Mowgley puffed out his cheeks. He knew the dog was in the yard as he had seen it when he arrived. It had looked at him, and they both knew then that some things in life just had to happen. 'Well', he said casually, 'if Madame Yvette has no objections, I suppose I could look after it for a while. Just until he's found a good home.'

Degas shook his head. 'I had heard about you English and your indulgence with dogs. And this is to be his reward for biting you? I am sure Yvette will have no objections - although she might want some extra payment.'

'I don't mind paying a bit more...'

'I meant what you call payment in kind, my friend.'

~

'What is that dreadful scruffy object you have at the end of a lead?'

'It's a dog,' said Mowgley defensively. 'I'm looking after it for a friend.'

Sarah Campbell wagged a reproving finger. 'I was talking to the dog, not you.'

He grunted. 'They say the old ones are the best.'

'It depends on what old things you're talking about.' She waved an invitation for Mowgley and his companion to come aboard. 'Take his lead off - if it is a he - so we can see how he gets on with Nelson.'

'Are you sure?'

'Of course. It's the best way to find out if they are going to be friends or foes. Dogs are much more honest than humans. What's his name?'

'We're not that well acquainted yet.'

Sarah nodded her thanks for the bottle Mowgley produced with a flourish from his jacket pocket, then asked: 'How did you meet?'

As Nelson and the newcomer sniffed at each other's rears and Bébé looked on unconcernedly from a cushion on her mistress's lap, Mowgley replied: 'It's a long story, but basically I tried to save him from a kicking, he bit me, then followed me home.'

She started to unwrap the foil from the neck of the bottle. 'That's settled then. If he liked the taste of you so much that he wanted second helpings, he'll obviously eat anything.'

'So?'

'So that's what we shall call him. Nelson, Bébé – say hello to Mangetout...'

18

Mowgley leaned on the portside rail and watched a man in orange overalls struggling with the giant hawser which was the last obstacle to the *Mont St Michel* leaving port. He was working alone, and the choppy sea was making it difficult for him to pry the hawser from its bollard. Eventually, a couple of men also wearing orange overalls strolled across the quayside towards him. They were obviously enjoying watching his struggle as much as Mowgley and the other spectators.

On the mooring alongside, an Irish Ferries boat was unloading, and a steady stream of vehicles was crossing the link span before bumping on to French territory.

As Mowgley lit a final cigarette before going below, a sports car edged out from behind the former terminal which now housed the *Cité de la Mer* museum. The car was an Aston Martin, and he had seen it recently in another place.

He screwed up his eyes, but could not see more than the outline of the figure at the wheel. The DB5 remained static, its engine running as the last vehicles emerged from the innards of the ferry boat. One was a white Range Rover with tinted windows, and it did a looping turn as it left the link span and headed off towards the port exit. After a moment, the Aston Martin drove off in the same direction.

Mowgley was writing on the back of his hand when the main refrain from *Ring of Fire* emerged tinnily from his inside breast pocket. He put the Biro between his teeth, took his phone out, flipped the lid open and spoke with a very bad American accent.

'*Enterprise* bridge: Captain Kirk speaking.'

'Are you trying to escape your obligation?'

'Oh, sorry Réne, I thought it was Scotty in the engine room. How did you know I was on the boat? Am I being tailed?'

There was a pause, then Degas said 'Tailed?'

Mowgley sighed theatrically. 'Sorry, I thought you understood Private Investigator talk. I meant are you having me followed?'

'Not at the moment.'

'Then how do you know I'm just leaving port?'

'Simple. Your assistant just told me.'

'Ah. So why do you think I'm trying to escape?'

'I thought you might have heard from Catherine that you owe me a pub crawl and one of those hamburger baguettes you were talking about.'

Mowgley threw his cigarette butt at a polystyrene cup floating past the ferry. As usual he got the speed of the tide and boat wrong and forgot to allow for the wind. 'I take it you've had the DNA report and the body in the mill was Mooney's?'

'That's right.'

'Are you sure?'

'It was a DNA test, not an opinion. They used his blood. There can be no doubt.'

'So if the killer or killers left the passport and other stuff in his pocket because they were not worried about anyone knowing who it was, it still doesn't explain why they would have cut the head and hands off.'

'No, but as I said before, it may have been as evidence they had killed him or as a trophy, or a warning to others. Anyway, we can now concentrate on catching the Albanian people smugglers - who are perhaps the same gang who tried to kill you and did kill Mr and Mrs Mooney and her lover... and her protection officer.'

Mowgley frowned: 'Sorry, but am I missing something? Why does the discovery of Mooney's body a few days ago put him in the clear for the killings of a couple of weeks ago?'

'Because he had been dead for more than a month when we found him.'

'What? I don't remember any decomposition or maggots or even a smell.'

'That is because he had been kept 'on ice' as we say. The forensic examiners could tell that he had been frozen after death and then thawed before putting in the mill.'

'Charming. And could they tell if the hands and head came off before or after they froze him?'

'I am impressed by your thinking. That is what puzzled me. They say that the head and hands were removed *after* the body was thawed.'

'Hmmm. Curiouser and curiouser.'

'I am sorry?'

'Never mind. I'll give you a call when I get back from Blighty.'

'Okay. Speak to you then, and happy tailing.'

Mowgley held up a hand. 'Hang on, mate. Have you got a pen?'

'Of course, why?'

'Can you run a couple of numbers for me? I mean check out the licence plates of two cars.'

'Yes but why? Are you trying to use *Gendarmerie* resources to help with your private detective work?'

'Not this time, but I hope to in the future.'

'Okay. I have my pen ready. But why do you want to know about these cars?'

'Tell you when I get back. It might be something or it might be nothing - but worth a look, I think...'

19

It was good to be back.

Not back home, yet. But back to where he had a job and a place to live and had already got to know some interesting people. And some interesting bars.

He also liked to live somewhere where they did things so differently. Best of all, he felt he could live and act how he liked without censure or comment. As Sarah had said, the French left you alone. He might not admit it, but so far he quite liked being a foreigner.

Another curiosity was how he was feeling much more at home on the wrong side of the car and road. Over the Channel he was a nervous passenger and an even more nervous driver, but it was different here. Perhaps that was because he was a foreigner and could be expected to drive badly. Or perhaps it was because all French drivers seemed to be worse than him at using the road, only in different ways.

So buoyant did his thoughts make him feel and so deserted the highway that he put his foot down and watched the needle reach the 80kph mark with almost a sense of wonder at his own temerity. That would still not satisfy the occasional motorists - and even once a tractor driver - who daily tried to bully him to speed up with impatient blasts on their horns, but there were relatively few vehicles in this part of the department. In fact there were relatively few people in this part of France.

In the city where he had lived and worked until recently, there were 140,000 people and nearly as many vehicles swarming around on an island no bigger than some of the fields he was passing. In Greater London where he had spent the past three days, more than 5000 people fought for space to live and breathe in every square kilometre. Here in Normandy, it was just over a hundred.

With the sun shining and the road ahead clear, he took the old Citroën up to very near the speed limit. He was feeling very Toad-like, and had the hooter on his car worked, he might have sounded it.

~

He found the village and roadside restaurant after three attempts. This was an improvement on his usual performance, and he saw it as more evidence that he was settling in.

The person he was meeting had already arrived, as signalled by the twee 1950s-style delivery van parked opposite the bar. It must have cost several times the asking price of a modern version, and would have cost even more had it been an original.

It stood out amongst the array of lorries, tankers, rigs, tractors and cars spilling out from the car park and lining and often obstructing the through-road. It still lacked a quarter of an hour to noon, so the place was obviously as popular as Mimi had said.

When he had asked her to recommend a place on neutral territory, she had given the matter careful consideration before coming up with the *Plat d'Or*. She had obviously not chosen the venue for its mutual proximity – it was at least thirty kilometres from Cherbourg, and even further from his client's antique business. Clearly she had not chosen the place for its ease of locating or parking facilities. She had, she said, chosen the *Plat d'Or* because it served the best *ouvrier* in the area. Twelve Euros would buy a four-course meal, complete with cheese board and coffee and a bottle of robust red wine or local cider. She also knew who he was meeting, and said the low price meant Yann would be able to charge the client at least three times what the meal actually cost.

She had also explained that *ouvrier* meant 'worker' and was used to describe any bar or restaurant that put on a low-cost lunchtime meal. Unlike the *Relais Routiers* system, there was no official association or guide, and standards varied vastly. If you chose badly, you could end up with a supermarket burger and some formerly frozen chips. An informed choice could unlock the key to a gastronomic journey of discovery and delight. The trick was to look at the type and number of vehicles outside any establishment offering an *ouvrier* lunch. She had eaten at the Plat d'Or and would rather dine there than in many of the overpriced and pretentious restaurants in Paris.

Given the potentially unpleasant meeting that lay ahead, it was quite likely there would be no luncheon, but it would be interesting to see how the drivers of all those lorries and cars could find room inside, and what they would be eating.

What must have been the original bar was small and cosy and almost club-like. The walls were lined with wood panelling punctuated by imitation candle wall lights, and under them sat a handful of mismatching easy chairs and low tables. The chest-high bar along one wall doubled as a reception and drinks servery. To one side of the bar was a port-holed swing door, permanently in action as at least half a dozen women bustled to and from the kitchen, bearing over-burdened trays. Some would disappear and reappear through an archway leading to a room containing around twenty tables and twice that number of diners. Others would take the flight of stairs up to another dining area, and a further flight indicated there were full dining facilities on at least one other floor.

Amongst the swirl and comings and goings of servers and served, the person Mowgley had come to meet sat stony-faced in an armchair facing the entrance. The chair was backed up defensively against a wall and gave an all-round view.

When he saw Mowgley, Derek Jardine's face became even stonier. Mowgley walked over, greeted him cheerily and held out a hand. It was not accepted, and neither was the offer of a drink. Mowgley shrugged, lowered his hand and went to the bar to order a coffee, returning to draw up a chair.

He deliberately did not speak, and they sat in silence until Jardine said: 'I suppose you want money?'

Mowgley kept silent and studied the man opposite. It was the first time he had seen him close to. He knew Jardine was in his mid-fifties, but his attempts at looking younger had the opposite effect. The severe, razor-cut college-boy haircut did not suit his probably plumped-up and definitely fake-tanned face, and the formally casual outfit of designer bomber jacket and jeans, ankle boots and floral shirt would have looked better on a younger man.

Eventually, Mowgley smiled disarmingly. 'At least you haven't asked me how I manage to sleep at night, doing what I do.'

Jardine did not speak, and Mowgley waited until the barmaid had brought his coffee before saying: 'As a matter of fact, I'm already getting paid - by your partner.'

Jardine's expression did not alter, so it was obviously no surprise. He might be a vain man, but he was obviously not a stupid one. He would have known his older partner would be suspicious about the increasing frequency and length of his absences in England. It would not have taken much of an analytical mind to make the connection between Mowgley's appearances in Lewisham over the past three days.

The former police officer had spent many hours and days on observation duty in his early career, and was well aware that a red, left-hand-drive 1970s convertible Citroën with French licence plates was not the best vehicle in which to blend in with its surroundings in England. This was fine as, once he had established the address which Derek Jardine was spending so much time at and why, Mowgley wanted him to know he was being watched. It had made yesterday's call to Jardine's mobile much easier. During it, he had explained that he was a private investigator and needed to talk about a personal matter. When the other man had begun to bluster, Mowgley had silenced him by giving the Lewisham address he had been visiting the day before, and the name of the resident.

This would also be why Jardine had not been surprised to learn that Mowgley was working for his partner. He would probably have been surprised to learn how much Mowgley knew about him, thanks to the resources available to Catherine McCarthy's friend in one of the darker and undeclared sectors of the Met.

What Mowgley knew was that Derek Jardine had never been arrested or charged with any criminal offence, but had totted up an impressive array of penalty points on his driving licence, mostly for speeding. Deeper investigation revealed that, in his twenties, Jardine had been briefly married before realising his true sexual orientation. A child had resulted from the brief union, and Jardine had moved out and on to a new phase of his life.

What Mowgley could not know was that, after spending the ensuing years working variously as an airline steward, a tour guide and manager of a gay club in Ibiza, Jardine had found his first long-time partner in Roger Fowldes. Up until recently, they both had thought they had found their eternal soul mates.

The pair had been together for fifteen years, using Fowldes' experience in the trade and Jardine's natural flair for spotting sellable items to build up an envious reputation. On holiday in northern France in the early days of their relationship, they had discovered what treasure trove could be found in the places where people brought their unwanted household effects to be sold on commission. In any *salle-des-ventes,* there would be a wealth of uninteresting tat, but the odd very special piece. Next to the modern divan with the broken springs and the leopard skin effect headboard you might find a solid oak 19th-century Napoleon day bed in mint condition. Often it would be the same price as the divan.

This was because, at that time, children were eagerly divesting themselves of their parents' and grandparents' furniture and possessions when the family house was passed on to them, and ditching all those beautifully crafted tables, chairs, sideboards and wardrobes in favour of self-assembly furniture made from veneered chipboard. So, the partners in love and business spent a happy decade hoovering up unconsidered items and selling them on to trendy London antique shops at sometimes ten times the price they had paid for them.

All good things come to an end, and as more and more British dealers flocked to cash in on the trend for French period furniture and fittings, the bargains became increasingly scarce. This accounted for Derek Jardine spending more of his time on the road, but not for his frequent and lengthy visits to apartment 14, Telmar House in Catford Road, Lewisham.

Jardine put his brandy glass on the table and Mowgley noted that his long, thin fingers were shaking, as was his voice. 'So why are you here? What do you want? Why haven't you told my partner what you think you've found out about me?'

Mowgley turned and caught the barmaid's eye and pointed at Jardine's glass. Then he said: 'I wanted to speak to you before I spoke to him.'

Jardine let out a gust of a sigh. 'So it *is* about money. You want me to pay you not to tell him about who you think I'm having an affair with.'

'No,' said Mowgley, I wanted to give you a chance to tell your partner about your son before I do.'

This time, Jardine's face registered real shock and his face paled beneath the fake tan. There was a loud silence as the barmaid arrived. Then Jardine said: 'But I don't understand why you want me to tell Roger?'

'I just think it would come better from you. But, I would like to know why you kept it a secret and had him worrying and suspecting for months. Why not just tell him when you first made contact with your boy?'

Jardine took another swig from his glass, then looked at Mowgley for a moment.

'I'm sure you know a lot about people and their ways, but perhaps you haven't come across circumstances or a situation like this before. When I walked out on my wife and son, she made sure I couldn't see him. I'm not blaming her, because, quite honestly, I was not interested in any contact. I probably did not want to be reminded of the other me.

'Then, about six months ago, I got a phone call...and it was James.' Jardine paused and gave a wry smile. 'He told me later he had used someone like you to find me. He said he had called to let me know his mother had died and he thought I should know, even if I was not really interested.

'I went to the funeral in England without telling Roger. I could see no point and thought that would be the end of it. But, when I met Jamie I realised what a bastard I had been and what could have been. He was obviously in a bad place with losing his mother so suddenly, and other things which were going on in his life. I realised I could help, and the more I was with him, the more I realised what I had missed and how I had wasted all those years. But I don't expect you to understand that.'

He paused, picked up his glass again and sat there, looking into the past.

Mowgley did not contradict him, but leaned forward and said. 'Okay, but I *still* don't get why you didn't tell your partner?'

Jardine gave a humourless smile. 'Nobody can really know about a relationship and all the things which make it work - or threaten it. Even sometimes those involved in it. Gay couples are no different from straights in many ways. I know Roger knew something was going on, and Jamie got a strange call about a month ago. He told me he had answered the phone and there was silence and then the caller hung up. He saw that the call came from a landline in France and this region. Obviously, Roger must have got hold of my mobile and been checking out the frequently called numbers.'

'Yes, I understand' said Mowgley, 'But what I still don't get –'

'- why I didn't tell him it was my son I was seeing? The truth is I was frightened of what it would do to us and our relationship. I thought he might be jealous. I meant to tell him at the right time, but the longer it went on the harder it became.'

'You thought your partner might be jealous of your *son*?

Jardine gave another sad smile and nodded. 'It happens. You must understand. Roger is well into his seventies. When we met, he was the age I am now. He was strong and self-confident and secure. Now, he's full of fear and doubt. It would perhaps seem to you that knowing the young man I had been seeing so much of is my son would relieve his anxieties. Perhaps you're right, but over recent years Roger has become more and more dependent on me. He simply doesn't want me to have any friends, or any relationships that he thinks would threaten ours.'

Jardine broke off to signal the barmaid for more drinks, and this time Mowgley chose a glass of Calvados.

After she had left, Jardine asked: 'Are you married or in a relationship, Mr Mowgley?'

'No. I was - married I mean. But that was a long time ago, and there's nobody now.'

'I thought not. Anyway, what are we going to do about this?'

Mowgley frowned and ran a hand through his hair: 'Well, like I said, I can hang on for a few days or even a week before I have to send your partner a report of where I went and what I did with his money while in England. But, as I said, I think it will come much better from you. He's going to find out anyway.' He took a drink, then said: 'Look. If you don't say you know about me, and that you just felt it was time to tell him, he may get in touch with me to call me off the job. Then he'll think you'll never know he was checking up on you.'

'And what if he doesn't call you off?'

'I'll tell him the truth.'

Jardine shook his head, then raised a finger to the corner of his eye. 'You know,' he said, 'when I first saw you I thought what a nasty piece of work you looked.'

Mowgley raised his eyebrows. 'Surely not? And what do you think of me now?'

'I think you could be a really nasty bit of work if someone upset you. But underneath, I think you may be a good man. Shall we have a drink to seal our deal?'

'Only on the condition that you pay for a long lunch, and I can send the bill in to your other half...'

20

Colonel Degas could resist no longer, and reached for Mowgley's packet of Gitanes.

He lit up, drew the smoke in hungrily, sighed, then asked: 'So, how was your meeting at the *Plat d'Or*?'

'Excellent. We started with a terrine, then it was some sort of roasted pork with fried apples. The rice pudding was a bit sweet for me, but the Camembert was perfect. The waitress said it was all to do with the rain and the grass, and last year was a very good year.'

Degas smiled. 'I think you are becoming French. What I meant to ask was how did it finish with the antique man. Is the case concluded?'

'Oh. Yes, it's all settled now. I just need to write up the report and work out the costings. The meal was a bit of a celebration.'

The office had been closed when Mowgley got back from the longest lunch he had ever had. He was not used to taking his time while eating and drinking, or even doing both at the same time. Standard practice in his home town would be to fill up on beer and then arrive with taste buds anesthetised at an Indian restaurant when the pubs chucked out. He hesitated to use the word even to himself, but It was somehow very civilised to eat and drink slowly and make the pleasure last.

It had also been good to rub shoulders with ordinary working people - some still in their overalls - who took their food seriously without an ounce of pretension or preciousness. It had been a very convivial atmosphere, and he had felt he fitted in. Jardine had acted as interpreter when necessary, and Mowgley had even managed *Happy Birthday to You* in French for an eighty-year-old at the next table.

Now, five hours on, Degas and he had met in Yvette's bar for the start of the proposed pub crawl, but Degas had suggested a postponement. There had been, he explained, some developments.

As Mowgley had thought, the Aston Martin on the quayside was the same one he had seen at the mill where the headless and handless body had been found. It was the latest indulgence of Inspector Aittif.

'And what was he doing at the docks? Following a suspect or meeting somebody?'

Although they were the only customers and Yvette was not behind the counter, Degas looked around the bar before he said: 'It seems he was meeting somebody.'

'Officially?'

'No, and that is the problem.'

'Why?'

'The Range Rover he followed was a hire car from a company in Belfast.'

Mowgley frowned. 'So what?'

'It was rented by a Stuart Thompson.'

'And do Europol know him? I bet you checked.'

'You are right. We did.' Degas took a pull on his cigarette and tapped it against the edge of the saucer on the table between them. 'He is not known, but the company is.'

'In what way?'

'It is a fake company.'

'A fake. Do you mean a front?'

'Thank you. Yes. For processing illegal money.'

Mowgley looked thoughtfully to where the door had opened to admit an off-duty *gendarme*. 'I wonder if there are any laundry companies set up to launder bent money.'

'What?'

'Nothing. And whose money is this company processing? A car hire company can't turn over that much.'

Degas tapped his cigarette on the saucer again. 'It can if it is one of many. The company has offices in the Republic of

Ireland and in a dozen European countries. And they are growing.'

'So who's behind it? Rentabent? Eurocrook? Gangsters R Us?'

Degas did not even bother to ask what he was talking about, and said almost matter-of-factly: 'It is the Irish Republican Army.'

Mowgley stopped with his glass short of his mouth. He knew that the organisation might no longer officially exist, but the years of extorting and stealing lots of money had given some of its members a taste for it. After the Good Friday Agreement, the IRA had officially disbanded and its weapons surrendered. Banners were still unfurled on the anniversary of the Easter Rising, and veterans would gather in bars to talk of the good old days and exaggerate the part they had played in them, but it was in reality all over. Sort of.

Gangsters will be gangsters, and the organisation which had been set up to win freedom had become something else. The members had no slogans or rankings or uniforms, and were now an army of mere criminals. Other countries had their mafias; Ireland had a ruthless and experienced organisation forged in bombs and blood and bullets.

'Blimey,' he said. 'And what is your interest? What was Inspector Aittif up to?'

Degas stubbed his cigarette out. 'That's the problem. We knew of them and that they had become more organised and were growing in strength, but they were not considered a particular problem in France. But now they are becoming so. They deal mostly in drugs because it is something the members know well from their days with the IRA. Now it seems they are expanding their interests here in the north. This has put them in conflict with the Albanians, and soon I think they will hear from the *Milieu*.'

He saw Mowgley's blank look, and explained. 'The *Milieu* is our listing of high-level criminal groups native to France. They are unhappy that foreign gangs are moving in.'

'Blimey again,' said Mowgley. 'Unfair competition, eh? I knew the EEC was set up to encourage competitive trading, but I bet they didn't think that would include gangsters.'

'No. I think not.'

'So are you telling me there's a turf war going on between

the Albanians and the remnants of the IRA, and your home-grown gangs don't like it? Sounds nasty to me.'

Degas nodded. 'Yes. It is'

'So your man was tailing one of the Irish gang members?'

Degas reached for the cigarettes again. 'No,' he said heavily. 'I think he was meeting one.'

~

Another beer and another cigarette, and Degas continued. 'When you called in about seeing Aittif's car I checked, and he was off duty at that time. I asked a colleague and friend in another *department* to check things out, and when he told me about the hire car company I thought we might have a problem.'

Mowgley shrugged. 'It could have been coincidence, and whoever he was meeting didn't turn up. Or he might have been checking something out before coming to you.'

'That is what I hoped,' said Degas, 'but not so. My friend put someone on to watching Aittif.'

'And?'

'And a day later he had a rendezvous with the man in the Range Rover. It was an isolated place on the marshes near Carentan, and well picked. No trees and few hedges. My officer had to drive past then stop at least a kilometre away. The meeting lasted for nearly half an hour.'

'Did your man get a look at the other driver or passengers? Any photos?'

Degas shook his head. 'No. Aittif got into the Range Rover and his contact did not get out.'

Mowgley rubbed his chin. 'So is it enough to make you think Aittif is dirty?'

'Yes. It is one of several episodes which have made me think he is...dirty. I did not have enough reason before to put someone on to him, but thanks to your call it seems he is doing something with some bad people.'

'And he could be useful to the Irish gang?'

'Of course. He could let them know information of our movements and actions, and he could do the things to be helpful. You should know that there is always someone ready to pay a policeman.'

'That's true,' said Mowgley thoughtfully, 'but it might not be just the Irish he is getting in to bed with. And it would explain a couple of things which have been making me itch.'

'What do you mean?'

'Nothing, yet.'

~

All was quiet at the *Bad Penny*.

He had hoped to be welcomed by Mangetout, but found only Nelson and Bébé on guard duty. He was allowed on board in exchange for a Curly-Wurly fairly divided between the two, and had got as far as uncorking one of the bottles he had brought when he heard a bark.

Lady Sarah was approaching, with Mangetout on a lead, and he looked as if he was not used to being restrained and not at all happy that he was.

'I took the liberty of boarding,' called Mowgley, holding the open bottle aloft in case mollification were needed.

'I'm sure you're good at that.'

'What, opening bottles?'

'No, taking liberties.'

After an obviously contrived show of unconcern from Mangetout at his absence, Mowgley offered him a whole Curly Wurly and Lady Sarah a glass of Merlot. Then he put two cigarettes in his mouth, lit them and offered one to her.

'You know I only smoke roll-ups,' she said, nevertheless accepting the Gitanes.

'I know, but I've wanted to try that since I saw Alain Delon doing it in *Rififi*.

'I think you'll find he wasn't in *Rififi,* but I know what you mean.'

They smoked and drank companionably for a few moments, then he said: 'It was good of you to take Mangetout for a walk.'

'I didn't,' she said. 'I've had to go and collect him each night.'

'What, he's been doing a runner?'

'Yes. He's been fine to hang around during the day, then he disappears at dusk. I was frantic the first evening because I knew how upset you'd be, then I got a call from Mimi to say he'd been seen outside Yvette's bar. She thinks he was looking for you.'

Mowgley blew out a cloud of smoke and looked dubious. 'Mmmm. Sounds nice but don't forget that his owner's in the hospital just up the road from my place.'

'Don't spoil a good story. Anyway, are you going to adopt him legally or just have a casual relationship? I advise the latter.'

'Why?'

'It's France. You even have to give your new dog a name starting with the letter allocated to that year.'

'Are you serious?'

'Very. If it's an 'F' year, you have to call him Fido or Frangipan or whatever.'

Mowgley looked bemused. 'I think you're right. No official adoption or registration. We'll keep our relationship on a casual basis.'

She smiled and reached down to toy with Mangetout's undamaged ear. 'I've heard that before. Anyway, pour me another drink if you want some good news.'

Mowgley did as he was told, and Lady Sarah pulled an envelope from her bag and waved it at him.

He frowned. 'I've won the lottery? I've been identified as the bastard child of a multi - zillionaire who's on the point of death?'

She shook her head. 'Not quite, but it is financial in nature. It's from the solicitors who were sniffing around on your ex-wife's behalf *visavis* the sale and division of funds accruing from the sale of *La Cour*.'

He winced. 'I hope the legal talk is not going to cost me dear.'

'Not yet. Anyway, I wrote them what we used to call in the trade a grade 'A' shitty letter, telling them that if we heard another word from them or their client, we would be forced to take pre-emptive action in a French court. They would have to attend with all the associated costs, and we would then claim ours from them. Just to rub it in I did it all in French and hinted that under French and European Human Rights laws, my client - you - could be entitled to a significant percentage of the value of the home you surrendered to her.'

'Blige. Is that so?'

'No, the human rights bit is total bollocks. And anyway it's a bit late for that sort of thing, and especially as you're a man. But they wouldn't spend the time finding that out. It always was just a kite they were flying, and I wanted to have some fun on your behalf.'

He looked at the envelope. That would certainly give me pause for thought if I was them. What do they say?'

'That having considered the situation, they feel it best to advise their client that there would likely be no benefit to pursuing any claim.'

'Good stuff. And did you pretend to be a French avocet?'

'It's *avocat*. An avocet is a bird, and Advocaat is a Dutch drink. No, I pretended to be me, only not disbarred.'

'Wasn't that risky?'

She smiled and reached for her glass. 'Not really, I would have denied all knowledge and said you sent it if they checked the rolls and wanted to make anything out of it.'

'Thanks.'

'No problem. That will be another glass of wine as my refresher for the day.'

She put the letter back in the envelope, stretched and then said: 'You haven't told me how your time in England and your meeting today went. Looking at the label on this bottle, you must have had, to use the police vernacular, a result.'

'Spot on. Excuse me for a moment then I will reveal all.'

She gave a mock shudder: 'As long as you don't reveal all before you pee.'

After being accompanied by Mangetout to relieve himself over the port rail, he returned and told her of his farcical tailing job in London and then his meeting with Derek Jardine at *Le Plat d'Or*.

'So, if your client's partner calls you to take you off the case, you send him a big bill on behalf of Yann and everyone - especially Yann - is happy.'

'That's right.'

'And if he doesn't call you off?'

He shrugged. 'I get Mimi to send the bill in anyway.'

'Hmmm. Has it occurred to you that they might decide to collude and deny there was a problem and you did nothing and so are not entitled to a sou?'

'Not really. Mimi would have got Fowldes to sign a contract. If they do renege, you can send them a stiff letter, or Yann can pay them a visit.'

'That would definitely cost you, but I think Yann is good at recovering unpaid debts. So what of your other current case - the Golf Widow?'

He tried to repeat his two cigarette trick, failed, and did one at a time. 'We don't know she's a widow yet.'

'That's what you think, though, isn't it?'

'It's possible.'

'But wouldn't it be a bit silly to call you in to investigate if she's had the old man buried in the garden or out on the marshes and is having it off with the gardener?'

'Not if she thought I was too stupid to suss her out. And making such a fuss about how much she's missing him and calling us in would be a good indicator of her innocence if the body was found, wouldn't it? Anyway, I'll go and see her tomorrow and try and move things on.'

'Good luck. Perhaps she is genuine and just not the sort you would get on with anyway. Perhaps she's being ratty because she's missing her husband.

He smiled. 'I think perhaps it's her husband's money she's missing.'

~

The *Bad Penny* moved almost gracefully as a gin palace slid by. Lights were strobing in the salon, changing colour with the deep bass thump of the music. A fat, bald man of late middle age was sitting at the wheel in the upper steering position, and he turned to look idly across the gap between them. Beside him, a very brown and very shapely young woman in a bikini had one arm resting possessively on his shoulder.

'Would you like to swap places with him?'

Mowgley turned to look at where Lady Sarah sat on the garden bench, Bébé on her lap and the other two dogs at her feet.

It had begun to rain softly, so he stood up and went into the wheelhouse to fetch an umbrella. When he got back, he looked across the growing distance between the two boats and said: 'That would depend.'

'On what?'

'What the truth is.'

Lady Sarah reached out with one hand to take the umbrella, and with the other for a refill. 'What do you mean, the truth? All truths are subjective are they not?'

'True. I suppose I should have said the facts not evident from the available evidence.'

She took a drink. 'Carry on, my learned counsel.'

'Well, the guy at the wheel could be a skint mate of the owner, or working for him. The girl could be his daughter, or someone else's bit of crumpet. And he could be dying of cancer...or be run over by a bus tomorrow.'

She smiled. 'So could you. Be run over by a bus I mean.'

'True,' said Mowgley, 'but I know everything about me, and very little about him. I was just pointing out the danger of making assumptions from what you see,'

'All very well, she said, 'but don't detectives - public or private - have to make assumptions all the time?'

'Again true. That's why we get it so wrong so often.'

21

This time the door was opened by the gardener rather than the lady of the house.

He was a tall, slim young man, with a mane of black hair and his teeth were very white against a deep tan. Mowgley followed him into the drawing room, where he was asked in stilted English to wait.

He took a seat by the French windows leading to the balcony, looked out over the manicured lawn and considered the significance of his reception. For sure, Madame Annie Cross/deVere was making him wait to underline their relative positions of employer and employee. Whether the gardener was more than an employee and, if so, why she had got him to answer the door was a more interesting consideration.

Nearly ten minutes passed before she swept in, and she had clearly spent the time working herself up into a suitable mood for the encounter.

Before she spoke, he knew that there were only two explanations for her behaviour. One was that she was genuinely distressed at the continuing absence of her husband. The other was that she was going to call him off and refuse to pay the bill.

In fact, he was half right. As before, she seemed completely genuine in her desire to find out where her husband was. But, perhaps because the near-tearful appeal of their last meeting had yielded no results, she had obviously decided to adopt what was known in legal and police circles as the Threats and Menaces approach.

She crossed the room swiftly and stood over him; when he attempted to stand, she waved him dismissively back into the chair. After looking down with a perhaps contrived expression which was a mix of distress and justifiable anger, she said: 'No word for more than a week, and I have to call your office and ask you to come and tell me what's happening.'

As she had planned, he felt awkward and disadvantaged having to tilt his head upwards, so in spite of their proximity he got up. They stood like two boxers at the weigh-in, until she literally and figuratively backed off.

He looked over her shoulder to where the door remained ajar, and wondered if anyone was on the other side of it. Then he said: 'I'm sorry, Mrs deVere. I did make a report of my activities, including a meeting with a friend of your husband, but this morning my secretary told me she had not posted it to you yet. The normal process is a written report of activity and costs incurred every week-'

She waved an impatient hand. 'So who have you spoken to?'

'I went to see Ralph Ferris a few days ago. He is I think an old friend of your husband - and you.'

He watched as he delivered the name, and was rewarded with a downward twitch of her mouth and slight narrowing of the eyes, before she replied. 'He is certainly not an old friend of mine; my husband was a customer of his. And what did Mr Ferris have to say?'

'As I said in my report,' he lied, 'Mr Ferris said that he had not noticed anything different or unusual about your husband's mood when they last met, and the first he knew of a problem was when Mr deVere did not show for their golf match.'

'And did he have any ideas where James might have gone, or why?'

'No.'

'And that's it? That's the sum total of your efforts to find my husband?'

Mowgley tried to look hurt. 'I've also spoken on the phone to the other two members of your husband's golfing circle.'

'And what did they have to say?'

He avoided the temptation to give a Gallic shrug. 'More or less what Mr Ferris said. He - your husband - seemed to be his normal self, and how surprised they were when he didn't show for the match. Both said he was a stickler for routine and would never have let them down without calling.' He paused, and then said as if he had just remembered: 'One of them - Mr Telforth - did say how smart he had looked in recent weeks.'

She looked at him almost incredulously. 'What? What has that got to do with anything?'

Mowgley cleared his throat and deliberately fiddled with the tie he had for some reason put on for the visit. 'Mr Telforth commented on how - excuse me -' he made a great play out of pulling out his notebook and pretending to read from a blank page - ' "well-turned out" your husband had been of late.'

'Are you serious?'

Mowgley put his notebook away. 'I'm just telling you what your husband's friends said.'

Annie Cross was not stupid, and must have known that Mowgley was not the pedantic plod he was playing. Her face flushed and she looked as if she would like to hit him. In a tightly controlled voice, she said: 'So is that it? Nothing else? That's all you've got after a week?'

He maintained his pose and said mildly: 'I have been working on other cases -'

'Do you mean you've been charging me for doing other work?'

'No, of course not. I've only booked a day on your account so far.'

Her lip actually curled before she said: 'And what have I got to show for it? You say you've spoken to James's friends, who said they noticed nothing different about him except how well turned-out he was? That's going to help find my husband, isn't it? I could have picked the phone up and spoken to Ferris and his cronies myself. So what you are actually saying is that you have no ideas at all of what happened to James or where he is?'

'Well, I did intend speaking with some more people who knew, sorry know your husband, and I thought I would ask around locally.'

'Well you had better get on with it, hadn't you?'

He nodded. 'Just one other thing.' Mowgley watched for any reaction as he continued. 'When we first spoke, you said your husband looked after his own dry cleaning. Can you tell me where he took it?'

No more than a tetchy, puzzled frown passed across her face as she said. 'His dry cleaning? What on earth has that got to do with anything?' Then: 'There's a place in Carentan. Near the square. I think he went there about once a month. Why do you want to know?'

Mowgley silently stepped back and away from her so he could get to the half-open door quickly and check if there was anyone behind it. 'I found several tickets in the bedside table when I looked round his room last week.'

Her lip curled even more extravagantly. 'And?'

He shrugged. 'Just that he might have visited the shop and mentioned something when he picked the clothes up. It's just what we call another line of enquiry.'

He moved towards the door, then paused and turned back. 'Of course, the clothes may still be there...'

~

An unassuming town that around 6000 people call home, Carentan lies between marshland and sea on the shoulder of the Cotentin peninsula. It sits on the site of an ancient Gallic port and at the confluence of three rivers. Together, they feed a canal, where battered scows and workmanlike boats rub shoulders with visiting yachts, often out of Paris. The canal leads to lock gates and, when the tide is right, to the open waters beyond. At most times, beyond the gates lies a shining, smooth wasteland of mud, relieved by fields of tall and slender reeds.

The canal is also remarkable for the fact that it passes over rather than under the busy main road down the spine of the peninsula. Carentan is also remarkable for being a key location in the D-Day landings.

It was market day, and the square was filled with stalls, vans and people. Housewives were queuing to pay more for vegetables, meat and cheese than they would have cost in the local shops, but that was the tradition.

After asking directions from a man on a moped with a small dog as a pillion passenger, Mowgley drove round a barrier with a no-entry sign on it, past the church and towards the quay.

All the machines in the Carentan *Laverie* were in use, their users sitting and staring at their clothes rotating as if watching a television soap. With a combination of sign language and the help of a student temporarily separated from his jeans, Mowgley learned that there was a dry cleaning service, but it was out of service. Through the translator services of the student, a harassed young woman in a wrap-round overall explained that the person who offered the service was away. If monsieur had come for his clothes, she would try to find them.

There being nothing on the rack for Mr deVere, Mowgley thanked her and asked where the nearest local's bar was.

~

The *Bar du Coin* lived up to its name, occupying a corner of a narrow, traffic-free street leading to the marina. A few hundred metres closer to the water, it would have been in different hands and dedicated to providing visiting yachties with trendy drinks and expensive food.

Here and in the hands of its big, brawny proprietor it provided local people with cheap drinks, a dish of the day between 12.30 and 2pm, and a place to meet and talk about their world and what was wrong with it.

Accompanied by the student he had lured from the laundromat with the promise of lunch and a twenty Euro note, Mowgley walked into the comforting fug. He was pleased to see and smell that the national non-smoking regulations obviously did not apply to the *Bar du Coin*.

A heavy silence did not descend on the premises as he stood on the threshold, but it was obvious from turning heads and paused conversations that the bar was not used to strangers. He smiled vacuously around then led the way to the bar between the closely-placed tables and chairs at which a handful of people were eating. Arriving, he nodded to the barman and ordered two coffees.

He was further pleased that the man behind the bar understood what he had said, and that there was no gleaming espresso machine occupying the back counter. After shouting a command to someone in the room behind the bar, the man took Mowgley's five Euro note and made change from an old-fashioned cash register. There was, Mowgley noticed, no registering of the cash amount added to the till.

He let the man - who he assumed was the owner - put his

change on the counter, then invited him to have a drink. When his invitation received no more than a disinterested frown and a shake of the head, Mowgley shrugged and ordered a glass of apple brandy for himself and a beer for his translator, who was still unemployed. The man looked slightly more interested, and reached for an unlabelled bottle on the back shelf. As he did so, a small, thin-faced and careworn woman with escaping hair hurried in from the room behind the bar, holding a strangely shaped, wooden-handled saucepan in one hand and two small cups in the other. She placed them in front of Mowgley, tilted the saucepan and poured out a stream of black liquid which looked so thick it would be reluctant to leave the spout. He nodded his thanks, took a mouthful, resisted the urge to shudder, then chased the coffee down his throat with the home-brew apple brandy. As the combination of the sweet, thick coffee and the sting of the Calvados found its way to his stomach, the woman topped up his cup and returned to the back room.

Mowgley reached into his inside pocket, pulled out his packet of Gitanes and looked enquiringly at the man behind the bar. Receiving a nod, he drained the brandy glass and pushed it across the counter. This time the owner accepted his offer, and poured himself a large glass of the Calvados.

~

An hour, two beers and another brandy later, Mowgley was on first name terms with the proprietor of the *Bar du Coin*. He had also made a new friend in the form of an elderly lady sitting at a table close to the bar. She was peeling potatoes rather than knitting, but had the same sort of grimly satisfied expression Mowgley imagined Madame Defarge would have worn while watching the heads of *aristos* rolling into the basket.

In the process of building up a bar bill he hoped his employer would sign off, Mowgley had learned that the name of his host was André, and the elderly lady was his mother-in-law. He had also learned that the *laverie* was open 24/7, and that its owner was urgently looking for someone to operate the dry cleaning service. According to Madame Defarge, the woman who had previously provided that service had recently had the good news that her aunt had died in a nursing home in the south.

The old lady had left her a large house and a small amount of money, and Mademoiselle Bisset had travelled down to the Ardeche to claim both, and probably start a new life. She was not, confided André's mother-in-law, a local woman, nor was she beautiful, or young. But she had been well-liked, and always ready to help her customers. With luck, her good fortune would attract a suitable man before the lady was, as the old lady cackled, past her sell-by date.

Having heard what he had come to discover, Mowgley thanked Madame for her company, Andre for his hospitality, and the student for his services.

As he drove with overtly due care and attention away from the *Bon Coin*, Mowgley reflected on his good fortune that Guy the student had been on hand and employable and that Andre's mother-in-law was clearly the local community's unofficial archivist. Having to adapt to changed circumstances and demands in a new job and a new country could be an interesting challenge.

In spite of or probably because of Guy's help, the session had demonstrated how necessary it was for him to learn to speak French properly if he were to succeed and even prosper in his new life and profession.

~

For obvious reasons deciding to steer clear of the arterial highway, Mowgley took the coastal route back to Cherbourg. He was in no hurry and it was a lovely part of the peninsula. There was also a profundity of roadside bars *en route*.

Dusk was falling as he followed the winding road round a series of coves on the approach to the town. This was a high point of the generally flat eastern coast of the peninsula, and the terrain sloped sharply away from the road and down to the beaches. It was not a sheer drop, but free of the glow of the apple brandy, Mowgley would probably not have chosen to take this road. He would also probably have paid more attention to the road and less to the twinkling lights of distant vessels.

The first he knew of the incident was the blaze of lights in his rear view mirror, then the neck-jarring impact on the rear of the Citroen. As his car slewed sideways towards the edge of the declivity, he had time for several fleeting thoughts. One was that it would have been better to have taken the inland route and risked a confrontation with a breathalyser-bearing policeman. Another was a sense of regret for all the things he had not done that he might have liked doing.

His final thought as the car lurched over the edge was that he was heading alone in a strange land towards a possibly painful and probably messy death.

22

Cables jammed, machinery groaned and its operator cursed fluently and savagely as he ran to switch off power to the winch.

This was what came of working foreign waters, he thought. Considering the history of this part of the country, the nets could have snagged on a sunken warship. It could even be an unexploded bomb. Given his luck and the odds, it was very unlikely to be a treasure chest.

Until recently, Deniel Jézéquel had spent his working life in his home waters off the coast of northern Brittany. Some fisherman liked to cast their nets wider, but he had always made a decent living close to his home port.

Then, for a short while, he had made an even better living by filling the holds of the *Petit Corbeau* with humans rather than fish. He had made more in a month of ferrying illegal immigrants across the *Manche* to England than in a season of long hours and backbreaking work.

It had all been so simple and virtually risk free. The foreigners turned up in the early hours in a closed van, money changed hands and the frightened individuals and families were herded on to the boat. It always happened in the grey dawn or the dark night, when it would have been quite normal for the fishing boats to leave harbour. Depending on the tides and winds, a dozen hours later they would pull in to a quiet cove on the southern coast of England and the passengers would be dumped over the side. Some owners made them swim, but Deniel had a soft heart and would get as close to shore as possible without endangering the *Corbeau.*

He and his crew of one would watch them reach safety, then turn the boat around and head for home. Nobody had been harmed, he and Allain had made some good money, and the illegals had been set on the path to their dream of a new life. England was a magnet for these people, and as far as he could see it was the fault of that country's liking for handing out more than generous benefits to people from poor parts of the world. In the past when fish was scarce and times hard, he had himself thought of moving his wife and children to what was for some reason called Big Brittany, but not for long. The weather might be the same, but from what he heard of the food and the behaviour of the people, he was surprised even the illegals paid to go there.

Life had been good until recently, but then, like the melting away of a huge shoal of fish the good times had come to a sudden end. Luckily for him and his mate they had been late for a rendezvous and found the harbour swarming with uniformed and plain clothes *flics*. The cops had questioned them, but there was no evidence they had been planning to do anything more than set out on a fishing run. So it was only the boat owners caught in the act who had been prosecuted.

The problem was that though the tap had been turned off, the cops and government agencies were still making life a misery for anyone who wanted to do an honest day's work on the water. With a typical overreaction and even though it was all over, there was a constant police presence in and around the harbour and even ludicrous stop-and-searches at sea.

That was why he had decided to try his hand along the coast, just until the fuss died down. He and Allain missed their families, but so far the fishing in this part of the world had been good. There was plenty for all in Norman waters, not that this had made the locals any more welcoming.

Now there was this problem with the nets. He had been this way before, and had seen the sterns of boats dragged beneath the water and even sunk when prompt action had not been taken.

He stood with a hand on the power switch as Allain joined him in looking into the grey sea as if the answer could be found there.

The choices were, of course, limited.

He could risk damage, start the winch again and hope the nets would tear free. Or they could sacrifice the nets and face the cost of the loss.

The two men looked at each other and Allain shrugged in an up-to-you way.

Deniel thought about it for another moment, then swore savagely and re-started the winch.

There was a further grinding and groaning as the cables took up the slack, a moment of fear, then the boat jigged upwards, the groaning ceased and he offered a thanks to the patron saint of fishermen. But there was another potential snag. From many years of experience and the action and sound of the motor, he knew that the nets had not just torn themselves free.

He could also tell they were not empty. Whatever they had caught on was coming up with them.

~

Walking across the swing bridge, Mowgley saw Colonel Degas and Catherine McCarthy standing on the quayside by the line of rusty buildings the fishing fleet used. They were in the midst of a cluster of police officers, officials and vehicles.

Arriving at the taped cordon, he was recognised by one of Yvette's regulars. The uniformed officer nodded, waved the small knot of spectators away and lifted the tape. Mowgley walked through the array of police vans and cars and a couple of rider-less motorbikes with lights flashing. As he arrived he saw the centre of attention was a ragged-edge blue tarpaulin. It was covering something, and water was seeping from beneath it and running towards a puddle by the edge of the quayside.

A plain clothes officer saw his approach and touched Degas on the arm. He and Melons turned and saw him, and Degas nodded as she walked towards him.

'Thanks for the call,' Mowgley said. She looked at the livid bruise on his forehead and said. 'I hope you've got a season ticket for the Pasteur? Or at least you're getting regular user discount?'

'It's free so far,' he said. 'I think. At least I haven't had any bills yet.'

'I can see how you are,' she said, 'but what about the car?'

'Bit like me, actually - just another dent.'

When the car tail-ended him, the Citroën had been shunted into a spin, lurching off the road and towards the steep slope to the beach fifty feet below. There were, in the French way, no barriers, but his car had come to a halt when it smashed into a curious Dalek-looking object. He had been told later that it was one of the many roadside monuments marking places where significant engagements in the D-Day landings had taken place. Ironically, the reminder of violence and death and injury had saved his limbs and perhaps his life. The only damage to the car was the impact point on the rear offside wing, and the door which had made contact with the mini-monument. It was the passenger door, so Mowgley was not too worried. He did not anticipate carrying any passengers, and as the hood was permanently down access would be possible. Even with insurance, the repair bill would have been ludicrous, and the assessor was bound to find all sorts of faults and issue an unroadworthy ticket. So he and the car would live with the damage. When he started making from his new job he would buy something better. Perhaps.

He would not in any case have been able to put in a claim against the owner of the car, as it had sped off into the darkness after the collision. It could be that the driver - like him - had been drinking. Or it could be something more sinister.

A couple leaving the pizzeria opposite the scene of the incident had seen what happened and had called the police and ambulance service. The paramedics had shown little interest apart from advising him to wear a seatbelt in future, and Mowgley had assured them he would when he got one fitted.

The occupants of the two-man patrol car had shown a lot more interest, and were about to invite him to breathe into the piece of equipment known as the 'soufflé' when he had used the magic word. The driver had called in to HQ, and after a brief conversation with Colonel Degas had not pursued that line of enquiry. After checking his car, they had driven off at speed, leaving him to consider how advantageous it was to have friends in high places.

Catherine Mc McCarthy absorbed the information, then asked: 'And what about this mystery driver?'

'What about him?'

'Well,' Melons said, 'there's only two choices, aren't there? Either it was a drunk or someone who hit you accidentally and buggered off for obvious reasons. Or...'

'Or what?'

'Or it was deliberate. Have you thought about that and who it might have been?'

'I'd rather not.'

She persisted: 'But what about the evidence? The driver must have left bits of his car on yours or at the scene.'

Mowgley shrugged. 'There was some white paint in the dent. But do you think the local cops are going to order and pay for a full spectrographic analysis and trace of the car colour pantone and model and make because a Johnny-come-lately would-be private investigator thinks a shunt was a deliberate attempt on his life?'

She pursed her lips. 'They would if René suggested it.'

He smiled. 'I bet he'd do most things if you asked him, but I think I've had enough favours for the moment. Anyway, what are you doing here? You didn't say you were coming over.'

She looked slightly awkward. 'I flew to Maupertus. René thought we should have a briefing session.'

Mowgley scratched his chin. 'Are you sure you don't mean de-briefing session.'

She raised a warning finger. 'Watch it. Don't forget you're a civilian now. I could arrest you for insulting behaviour. Or even better, an offensive tie.' She made a face. 'What on earth is that about?'

He raised a defensive hand and twiddled with the knot; 'I suppose it's a sort of substitute.'

'For what? Good taste?'

'Seriously, it's a problem not having any authority, and having to put up with people being as lairy as they like. I thought the tie might give me a bit more gravitas.'

She snorted. 'Perhaps if you'd have chosen one a bit less...risible.'

'Risi-what?'

'Don't start.'

He looked over her shoulder. 'So what's so interesting beneath the tarpaulin? Not another body?'

'Two.'

'Blimey. This is getting like a really-over-the-top episode of Midsomer Murders. Anyone we know?'

'I think you'll recognise one of them. Come and have a look.'

She led the way to where a man in a white coverall was kneeling by the mound, unlatching a shiny metal case.

René Degas held a hand out to Mowgley, who pulled out his cigarettes and thanked him for his recent help with the situation on the coastal road.

The colonel gave an it-was-nothing shrug, and they watched as the forensics officer powdered his hands then drew on a pair of rubber gloves.

'So,' asked Mowgley, 'who fished them out?'

'A fisherman,' replied Degas. 'He was dragging his equipment along the bottom when it got caught. It nearly sunk his boat, because the parcel was heavily weighted.'

'And are they familiar faces?'

'One is, but not the other.'

Degas looked at the man kneeling at their feet, who nodded, reached out and pulled back the tarpaulin.

By design or coincidence, the two bodies were fixed in a parody of a loving embrace. They were facing each other with arms entwined, and bound together by lengths of heavy, rusting chain. Their dead white faces were in profile, but Mowgley recognised one immediately. He shook his head and said: 'I guess it's too late now to ask him what he was up to.'

As they watched, the forensics officer reached over and gently but firmly prised apart the blue lips of the man on the right. Then he turned and fired off a sentence to Degas, who grunted agreement.

'What did he say?' Mowgley asked.

Degas shook his head sombrely: 'He said that Inspector Aittif could not have told us anything, anyway. Someone has taken his tongue away.'

23

Mowgley did not think much of the Loire Valley.

It seemed to him that, compared with his home territory of Normandy, the landscape was unremarkable, the roads full of traffic, and there were far too many overblown castles. He also thought it was typically pretentious of the area to name some of their villages after famous wines.

He - or rather Mimi - had planned his route southwards to where the dry cleaning from Carentan lady had gone to take up her inheritance. Courtesy of Madame Defarge, he knew the name of the region and probably the town. According to Mimi, the Ardèche was a nice place to visit, but perhaps not to live.

She had, she said, worked out a route which would pass through some fine examples of the varying French landscape without being too tortuous. The route would also avoid all toll roads. Although she had not said as much, Mowgley knew the detour was not to save the company money on road charges, as the customer would have been paying. Neither was it just to show off the richness and variety of the French countryside. Perhaps she had planned the route to avoid giving him cause for panic on the expressways. Or perhaps it was really to avoid imposing him and his driving habits on other users.

Having passed through the region of grand castles and where they had come up with the idea of eating frog's legs, he still had another two regions, six departments and at least five hours of driving ahead. He was tired, thirsty and hungry and needed to pee, and Mangetout had been sending out signals that he too needed a comfort break.

Mowgley assumed there was a subtle difference, but so far it seemed that all the dog's signals and blandishments consisted of sitting and staring at his new master with an unwavering and unblinking intensity which was almost hypnotic. It would be interesting to know if Mangetout was attempting thought transference and, more importantly, if he, Mowgley could tune in and even respond. He tried sending out images of a promise of a dog bowl full of food and then both of them relieving themselves, but there was no apparent response. Then he saw an establishment with a very direct approach to transmitting ideas and suggestions.

It was a squat, flat-topped and garish building, sitting in an ocean of mostly empty car park. On its roof sat a huge neon-lit crossed knife and fork, and alongside it a similarly scaled plastic hamburger and bun with a side order of chips the size of railway sleepers. Even in his relatively short time as an expatriate, Mowgley had observed that France could do junk food equally as badly and crassly as Britain, and often be even more over-the-top in its promotion. This looked a prime example. The fact that it was the time of the *midi* yet not a single lorry or commercial vehicle sat in the car park was a further clue to the range and quality of food on offer.

~

Watching Mangetout take a long and clearly satisfying pee against the nearside front wheel, Mowgley wondered why dogs liked to piss on tyres. He also thought about joining him. Even though that would be quite common in France, he resisted the impulse and led the way into the Happy Burger.

As the car park had indicated, no more than a handful of customers were sprinkled around the vast seating area. He went to the bar, and using a combination of menu French and sign language, ordered an Americano coffee, two Maxiburgers and a bowl of water.

He paid in advance and chose a seat, automatically patting his breast pocket. There were non-smoking stickers everywhere, which made the place seem even more un-French. He would have to have a smoke outside before they left. It was not much fun on the road, as cigarettes smoked themselves at a furious rate in a car with no roof.

He put the water bowl down and unwrapped and gave Mangetout the chocolate-covered nut which came with the coffee. That earned a predictable reaction from the elderly couple in the next aisle. For some reason, the French regarded giving a piece of chocolate to a dog at the same level of irresponsibility as Michael Jackson dangling his child over a balcony.

Having registered the prescribed level of outrage, the old couple returned to their meal. They were both short and very overweight and looked like they had come straight from Central Casting as Old Peasant Farmer and Wife. Out of keeping with their image, they had each chosen a small, wrinkled pizza and were eating as if it was a necessary chore and not a pleasure. Neither looked up, and certainly not at each other. It was as if they were still trying to work out how they had spent the best part of their lives with each other.

Nearby, a weary-faced mother was constantly nagging a child, who took no notice as he used the empty tables and chairs as climbing frames. Further along and across the aisle a young woman in a business suit was earnestly tapping away at a laptop computer. Mowgley wondered if she were totting up some figures, or perhaps sending a message to a lover. He hoped it was the latter.

All in all, it was a depressing tableau of Modern Times. Some things, he thought as the waitress arrived, are the same either side of the Channel.

~

Two hours and a hundred miles on, and he had arrived in a different world.

Hills thickly carpeted with firs had given way to a sometimes rugged landscape dotted with olive and chestnut groves and cottages which looked lifted from a picture postcard. The sky was a huge blue tent, and ahead lay France's Grand Canyon.

Around a hundred million years before Mowgley's arrival, a small spring had risen in the midst of a place of volcanoes and plains. It had wound its way westward, taking the least resistant way through the soft limestone. Now, a million visitors a year came to look down from the thousand-foot high cliffs lining the spectacular route of the Gorges of the Ardèche.

Soon after the river leaves the chasm, it is crossed by a century-old suspension bridge. It was never meant to be in competition with the nearby wonders of nature, but it was, Mowgley thought, a small response and a fine example of Man's own creative ingenuity.

On one side of the bridge was a welter of hotels and *chambres d'hôtes*, and on the other an ancient fortress and medieval village, contrived to look as people liked to think a medieval village should look. It was here that Mowgley came to the end of his long journey.

After walking Mangetout along the bank, he sat outside a mock-medieval bar and enjoyed three very cold beers and two cigarettes in quick succession. Then he made some enquiries inside, returned to his car and drove back across the bridge.

Unsurprisingly at this time of year, the first three hotels he tried were full. There was also no room at the pretentious bed-and-breakfast establishment looking loftily down on the river, and the proprietor seemed to take offence at a man with a dog on a string even asking.

After further fruitless enquiries, he found a bed in a bungalow on the outskirts of the town. It was far from the river and the view from his window looked over a concrete yard, but the price for the night was about the same as a quayside hotel in Cherbourg. It was at this time of year, he reflected, a seller's market.

Paying in advance, Mowgley invited Mangetout on to the bed as he lay back and reached for his phone.

His call was answered after half a dozen rings. The woman's voice was low and mellifluous and heavily accented.

'Do you speak English?' he asked.

'Yes, of course,' she said, as if familiar with the question.

'I'm looking for a room for the night,' lied Mowgley. 'Everywhere in town is full, but the man at one of the hotels on the river said you did bed and breakfast.'

There was a pause, then the woman said: 'No, I am sorry, he is wrong.'

'But he said you had moved down from Normandy to open a *chambres d'hôtes*.'

There was a longer pause, then the woman responded, her

voice subtly changed in tone and level. 'That is true, but we have only just begun the work. We will not be ready until next year. Who is this calling?'

'Ah,' said Mowgley, ignoring the question. 'That's a shame. Is it possible I could speak to Mr deVere then?'

This time the voice was edged with anger. 'What do you want?'

'I just need to talk to him for a few minutes.'

'About what?'

It was Mowgley's turn to pause. Then he said: 'I am being paid to find Mr deVere. I think it would be better if I spoke to you and him before I do anything else.'

24

The big old house stood at the end of a narrow lane leading from the riverside road. It was square-set and solid-looking, the sober stone front elevation enlivened by an explosion of bougainvillea.

The disappointingly tinny buzz of the bell was answered by, he presumed, the woman he had spoken to ten minutes earlier.

She said nothing, but looked at him round the edge of the door as if she were using it as a shield.

'Thanks for seeing me,' he said for something to say.

She made no reply, but opened the door a little further, then turned away and walked into the gloom of the passageway.

Taking that as an invitation, he told Mangetout to guard the car and followed her into a large room. It was full of furniture of an age and style which would have suited people of her parents' age.

She did not invite him to sit, but stood in front of the fireplace, one hand resting on the marble mantle. She was, like Annie Cross/deVere somewhere in what people called middle age. But there the similarity ended. Where Annie deVere had the slim figure of someone who worked at it, this lady was of a comfortable but somehow voluptuous build. She was short, but wore no compensatory heels, and was dressed in a simple cardigan and skirt. Her dark hair was pulled back from her face as if she found that the quickest and thus the best way to deal with it. She wore no makeup that he could detect, and her face, though obviously reflecting the tension she felt, was unlined and untroubled. Now having met both women in Jimmy Cross's life, Mowgley could see why he had chosen this one.

When he refused to start the conversation, she said: 'So, what is it that you want?'

He shrugged. 'As I said, to see your partner.'

'As I also said, what for?'

'To talk to him.'

'Why?' Her face and voice became suddenly angry, 'You've done your work and found him. Now all you have to do is tell her and take the money. There is nothing more to talk about and it is none of your business. He - we - have done nothing wrong.'

Mowgley nodded his agreement. 'Of course not.'

'So why do you want to see him?'

'I want to make him an offer which I hope he will not refuse.'

~

In the flesh, James Cross looked much the same only a little older than the photograph in the glove box of the Citroën. Average height and weight, middle aged with an enviably full head of hair. The only remarkable thing about his small featured face was the badly broken nose supporting the heavy tortoiseshell spectacles. It sat at odds with his overall persona and the combination gave him a look of almost disguised menace. Of course, Mowgley reflected, lots of people with broken noses had never had a fight in their lives.

In the ten minutes since Solange Abadie had summoned her lover, she and the atmosphere had thawed considerably. Cross had been extremely candid about his situation and intentions, and he and his new partner seemed to have been reassured by Mowgley's remark that he was there to do no more than talk.

They were sitting in front of the fireplace, in which sat a vase of freshly-cut flowers. Mowgley had been invited to take the armchair, and the people he had come so far to find shared a comfortable-looking settee. They sat shoulder-to-shoulder, and she had his left hand in both of hers, cradling it on her lap. She was still protective of her man, Mowgley thought, but much less hostile now he had explained his proposal. She had even opened a bottle of something local and red and poured them each a glass.

'What I don't get,' said Jimmy Cross, 'is how you made the connection between me and...' he turned and looked reassuringly at his new partner, 'Solange. Surely not because of a dry cleaning ticket?'

Mowgley smiled his agreement. 'That would have been a very thin lead. It was a combination of things, and your friends, mostly.'

He frowned quizzically. 'My friends?'

'Your golfing friends. Something they all said was how you had spruced yourself up in the past couple of months...and how happy you were looking. Graham Telford said he had never seen you so smart and that your dry cleaning bill must have shot up. Ralph Ferris said on the phone that he thought you had found a new lady, and that he hoped so. All I did was ask around in Carentan, and a lady in a local bar told me about the inheritance. She also said the house was in the Ardèche, and thought you had said it was near the river and the suspension bridge at the end of the gorges.'

Solange Abadie smiled grimly. 'Ah yes, the resident songbird of the *Bar du Coin*. I think it is she who should be the detective. But how did you get my phone number? I asked Giselle not to give it to anyone.'

'My secretary called the laundromat and said she was from the department of income tax and needed to speak to you about your inheritance. She said your friend must tell her how to get in touch with you or you - and she - could be in trouble. Mimi - my secretary- said that would scare anyone.'

Cross passed his glass to his partner for a refill. 'So what happens now? Like I said, whatever happens I'm not going back to Annie. She was becoming more and more demanding and angry about everything. I think she hated being in France, and blamed me for everything.'

Mowgley reached out his glass. 'Can I ask why you moved here?'

'Not much choice. I lost nearly everything in the last property price collapse and mini-recession. To be honest, I left a few debts behind - not to small businesses, but to finance houses - and to some not very nice people who have a say in what goes on in South London. That's why I thought you had come looking for me.

'We needed to get away and it was here or Spain, so not a hard choice. The people who are after me have lots of friends in Spain. But Annie was not happy to leave her life in London. Our relationship was more or less finished before we came over, and it just went on getting worse. Solange speaks good English and I got talking to her when I took my stuff in to the cleaners. Then I asked her out for a drink, and...'

Mowgley nodded. 'So why do you think your former partner asked me to find you? Does she want you back - and does she know about the financial situation?'

Cross made a rueful face. 'I doubt she wants me back, just any money she thinks I've got left. She met me in the good times, and must have known we were in trouble, but not how much. I reckon she wants to know where I am so she can ask for more money, or else.'

'Or else?'

'Whenever we had a ruck about her spending, she'd mention the people in South London and how she reckoned they'd like to know where to find me.'

'And are you going to see her alright?'

Cross shrugged. 'There's nothing much more I can give her. The house is paid for and there's a few grand in the bank, but that's it. She can have that in return for being disappointed in me and what she thought I was going to be.' He paused, turned to his new partner and smiled. 'At least Solange was not after my money. She's always known I'm near to skint. That's what we're doing here. Plan 'A' is to turn this place into a bed and breakfast. Everywhere here gets booked solid in the summer. We'll just lead a quiet life, and I'll keep my head down and forget about improving my golf handicap. At least, that was the idea until you showed up.

'So,' Cross looked steadily at Mowgley through his heavy tortoiseshell glasses, 'the big question is what are you going to do now you've found us? Telling her where we are won't help her, and it may be the finish of me. Is there any chance you might forget that you found us?'

'I can't do that,' said Mowgley. 'But I can tell her I found you somewhere else, and that you said you were moving on, and gave me a handwritten letter for her.'

Cross sat up, the relief obvious on his face. 'A letter? What do you want me to say in it?'

'That's up to you. You could tell her all the things you've told me, or none of them. And perhaps that you're sorry but you want to start a new life - and that she gets to keep the house and what's in the bank. That way at least she'll know you're alive and she has to get on with her life. If she wants to keep it to herself and have you declared dead in seven years, that's up to her. For what it's worth, I think she really was worried about what had happened to you.'

Cross looked fleetingly at his new partner. 'I still don't get what's in it for you.'

Mowgley gave a don't-ask-me shrug, almost spilling his wine. 'I suppose I like happy endings. I was being paid to find you, not to arrest and detain you. I've done what I was asked to do. I still get my finder's fee either way.'

Cross still looked puzzled. 'But what if Annie refuses to pay?'

Mowgley smiled. 'You haven't met my boss. He was a policeman and he's quite scary. He also knows the law and a few bailiffs and cops and lawyers. I think the lady will pay, eventually.'

He looked at the couple and made a questioning face. 'Is it a deal?'

Cross drained his glass. 'Only if we seal it with a decent drink. If I ask my partner-shortly to be my wife - nicely, I think there's a couple of bottles of papa's best bubbly in the cellar. Oh, and I don't suppose you fancy coming back all this way to be the best man?'

Mowgley gave his fourth shrug of the day: 'Only if you can't find a better one – and that shouldn't be hard.'

25

Yvette's bar was busy.

It was mid-afternoon, and there was the usual mix of locals, on and off-duty policemen and those who made an official and unofficial living from the port. It reminded Mowgley of a parallel universe version of his former local at the Portsmouth ferry port. The main difference was that here he was just another oddball customer.

Colonel Degas was waiting at their usual table, and Mowgley signalled for drinks with a wave to the barmaid.

He passed Racine, who was deep in conversation with a distinctly dodgy-looking white man in a turban. Mowgley's guide to the seamier side of Cherbourg smiled and nodded as they passed. Mangetout gave him a friendly growl, then did his usual round of the tables to seek out food and affection.

Degas half-rose to shake his hand. 'I did not recognise you with the beard. Is it to stay?'

Mowgley shrugged. 'Who can say? It might grow on me.'

Degas frowned. 'I suggest it already has.'

'No, I mean I might become attached to it.'

The frown deepened. 'I thought you already were. Attached to it.' He shook his head and sighed heavily. 'What a language.' They both sat, and the Colonel said: 'So, what do you think of the rest of our country?'

'Very big,' said Mowgley, producing a substantial dried

sausage from the carrier bag he had put on the table. 'I liked the Ardeche, but not as much as Normandy. It was a bit wild and...foreign...for me. Do you think Yvette will like this?'

'I am sure she will. What other souvenirs from the Ardèche, did you come with?'

'Some candied chestnuts and other stuff; wine and a lot of receipts and expenses claims for Mimi, and some food and drink for Lady Sarah and the dogs.' He returned to the carrier bag and took out a bottle of clear, innocuous-looking liquid and something in a paper bag. Putting them on the table, he said: 'You can only have them if you know what they are.'

Degas smiled. 'Easy. That is a bottle of *eau-de-vie*, probably made from the fruit of the mirabelle. It can be used to remove paint or start tractors as well as a palate-clearing *aperitif*. It is not to be compared with Calvados of course, but a passable if tasteless substitute when the circumstances require one.'

'And this -' he reached into the bag and extracted what looked like an oversized haggis: '- is a *maouche*. Cabbage and pork, forced into the stomach of a pig.' He weighed the object in his hand then held it to his nose and sniffed appreciatively. 'Wonderful. It is a speciality of the plateau area of the Ardèche and must be cooked very slowly. But it is worth the waiting, like most good things.'

Mowgley shrugged non-committedly 'I'll take your word for it. It reminds me a bit of a diseased organ I saw at a post-mortem. Talking of post-mortems, how did you get on with Inspector Aittif and his close friend?'

Degas waited as their drinks were served, nodded to the barmaid then pointed at himself to signify the round was on him. 'We know a little more about Inspector Aittif now. As you know, I thought he was too fond of cars and women and the other things money can buy...and was being watched.'

'Does that mean you know why he was killed, and by who?'

'No, not yet. But it is certain that he was being paid by someone, and probably because he was a policeman. As you know, when you told us about his activity in the ferry port I had him followed. At the same time I started an investigation into his affairs, but it will be a long process. He obviously lived to the limit of his income, but that is not a crime. It is not hard to take steps to hide money unless you are very stupid and put it all in the bank, and Inspector Aittif was not stupid. Just greedy,

I think. Already we know he had an undeclared holiday apartment in the south, and there will be money somewhere.'

Mowgley tapped his cigarette on the saucer in the middle of the table and watched the ash collapse. 'Silly question, perhaps, but what would he be being paid for?'

A shrug from Degas, and then: 'As I said, it is too early, but a policeman on your side is always worth a good price if you want to know what is going on in the inside. It could be active help with information, warnings or losing evidence, or it could be just looking the other way. What we have to do now is find out if he was working alone, or if there are other bad fish in our organisation.'

Mowgley persisted: 'But you have nothing...concrete? Nothing to prove what he was doing, or why?'

Another shrug from Degas: 'It is too soon to make judgements. As you know, there has been an explosion in smuggling of people and drugs in this part of France, and the business is attracting a number of criminal organisations, including our own home-grown gangsters. There will always be policemen tempted by some extra and easy money.'

'And the man with him in the nets - was he the same man he met on the *marais*?

'No. He is another of our Albanian friends. Another gangster.'

Mowgley fingered his beard. 'So, let me get this straight. The man in the nets was a member of the Albanian mafia, and we think the man Aittif met on the marshes was a former IRA man - or at least driving a vehicle belonging to a company set up with IRA funds.'

Degas nodded.

'So,' continued Mowgley, 'Aittif could have been working for or being paid by either- or both.'

Another nod, then Degas said: 'That is so. He was perhaps the man in the middle.' Another tug of his beard, then Mowgley observed: 'So the ex-Boyos could have found out that he was two-timing them, and knocked him off - and his Albanian contact as well for good measure. Would that also account for the missing tongue?'

In unconscious imitation, Degas stroked his clean-shaven chin. 'That's it. It was probably a sign that he had been talking to the wrong people, or an additional punishment.'

'You mean it was done before he died?'

'Of course. His lungs were full of water, so they must have torn out his tongue, then thrown both the men into the water at night to drown.'

Mowgley grimaced and shivered. 'Not very nice people, then.'

'No, my friend. And there is more to tell you. It will be me who has to pay for our pub crawl. You were right about Mooney.'

'Right about him?'

'Yes, that he is not dead. Or at least the body in the old mill was not his.'

Mowgley increased his beard-fingering activity. 'But the DNA results...?'

'They were fake. Somebody must have switched the blood sample from the body for a sample from Mooney. It may have been Aittif, or perhaps there is someone else who is obliging the bad guys.'

Mowgley sat back and shook his head. 'Blimey. So how did it come out?'

'Come out?'

'How did you find out the switch had happened?'

Degas smiled. 'A simple error. The sample was taken twice, but by different attendants at the mortuary on different days. The first report came back saying the blood belonged to Mooney. That's when I told you about it. Three days ago, another report arrived with the same serial number for the body, saying there was no match, so the DNA of the dead person was not registered. Fortunately, the same person here dealt with both reports. He immediately asked for another sample. The body had not been disposed of because of the ongoing enquiry, and so a third sample was sent. It came back this morning; We do not know who the body belonged to, but it certainly was not Sean Mooney.'

Mowgley lit a cigarette. 'So he's still around, then.'

Degas nodded. 'It seems so.'

More beard fingering and ash-flicking, then Mowgley said: 'Okay. So, can we go through this nice and slowly? And over another drink?'

Degas nodded again and held up a hand to summon the barmaid.

'So,' Mowgley said, 'Mooney is more than probably alive, and got Aittif or A.N. Other to swap the blood samples to make you think he was dead?'

'Yes, although I do not know who this A.N. Other is?'

'Never mind.'

There was a pause as the drinks were delivered, then Mowgley continued: 'So as Mooney bought the mill, it's a safe bet that he was involved in or even behind the smuggling of the drugs and perhaps the people in the cheese lorry.'

Degas shook his head. 'That is not likely. The bodies were Albanian, remember. As was the man who tried to kill you at *La Cour.*'

Mowgley reached for his glass. 'So where does that leave us, apart from being confused?'

'It indicates perhaps that Mooney was somehow involved with the Albanians to some degree, at least to start with.'

'Then he got greedy and tried to take over?'

Degas frowned. 'I think that unlikely. He would not be so silly as to try and take on the Albanian gang himself.'

'So is this where the Old Boys from the Brigade come in?'

'Yes, perhaps. We know that Mooney had contacts within the IRA. It is possible he was working with them all the time, or that they approached him when he was dealing with the Albanians and suggested he work as a sort of double agent.'

Mowgley shook his head and puffed out his cheeks. 'A dangerous game. So we think that Denys Simone and Sylvie Mooney - and your protection officer - died in an act of revenge by Mooney?'

'Perhaps that is the most likely answer.'

'But what about the Albanian guy who tried to kill me?'

Degas stubbed out his cigarette and reached for a fresh one. 'It could have been Mooney suspecting you had not in fact been persuaded to retire, but were working undercover. It has happened before.'

'And the body in the mill and Aitiff and his mate in the nets?'

'The body must have been somebody Mooney and his colleagues did not like. But we cannot be sure about Aittif. You saw him meeting the man from the Irish ferry. It could have been Mooney in the car and at the meeting on the Marais.'

'But whoever it was, why kill Aitiff?'

Degas gave another shrug. 'Perhaps he too was playing a double game - or they thought he was?'

'There could be another solution to all this killing, of course.'

Degas looked sharply at him. 'You think so?'

'Yes. What if Mooney is a psychopath? He's found out that he likes killing people.'

Mowgley emptied his glass, put it on the table and shook his head. 'For sure there are more questions than answers, and a nice array of suspects. While we're at it, perhaps we should include Colonel Mustard in the Library with the lead piping...'

'I beg your pardon?'

'I'll explain later. Anyway, what we know for sure or think we know for sure is that Mad Mooney is still on the scene.'

Degas nodded and reached out to lay a hand on Mowgley's arm. 'Yes, my friend, I think so. And I think we must take very good care of you until he is off that scene...'

26

'Is that staying?'

'Not you as well.' Mowgley's hand reached automatically for his beard. 'Don't you like it?'

'I am indifferent,' said Lady Sarah. 'As I hope you know. I believe we should each be free to express or not express ourselves in the way we live and act and look. It is a basic tenet of democracy. In short, I agree with whoever it was who said that we should all be allowed to go to the devil in our own way...providing it does not hurt other people too much, or frighten the horses.' She paused and picked up the open bottle of *eau de vie* and looked at the handwritten label. 'Oh Lord, did I just say all that? Or was it the diesel fuel talking?'

They were sitting on the garden bench at the stern of the *Bad Penny*. There was no more than a breath of a breeze stroking the quicksilver surface of the water, and the late summer sun was loitering above the marina clubhouse as if reluctant to leave such a perfect day.

They had dined well on the best the Ardèche could offer in cured meats and *crottins* of cheese, which Mowgley had now learned were so called because the small round lumps resembled the droppings of the goats from whose milk they had been made. They had finished their late picnic with a chestnut-flavoured mousse which to Mowgley seemed an inappropriate blending, but which had met with the full approval of Bébé. Mangetout and Nelson were elsewhere, preferring to scavenge from the bins and plastic sacks behind the yacht club restaurant.

Mowgley lit two cigarettes at the same time and passed one to Lady Sarah, who said 'Well done.'

He took a lungful of smoke, then asked: 'For what?'

'You've been trying to do that trick for weeks, and now you've got it just right.'

'At least I've got something to show for my time here, then'

'I think you've got a bit more than that.'

'The beard, you mean - and there's Mangetout.'

She sniffed loftily. 'Don't be so pathetic. You're doing quite well with the language - I noticed the lady in the bread shop didn't wince so dramatically when you spoke to her this afternoon. And you've solved your first two cases as a *detective privé*.'

Mowgley grunted as he threw a crust of baguette at a large herring gull sitting on the roof of the wheelhouse. 'I wonder if it's the same one?'

The gull neatly caught the piece of bread, took a couple of hops and then flew off towards the setting sun. Lady Sarah watched it flap away, then asked: 'The same what?'

'The same one-legged gull I met on the ferry coming over last month.'

'If you like to think so - though I fancy there are quite a few seagulls with only one leg.'

'Yes,' he agreed, then said reflectively: 'I'm not so sure about solving any cases. It was just a matter of finding a couple of people and letting them know what I knew.'

'I think it was a bit more than that.' She looked at her cigarette end, blew on it and then said: 'You certainly have taken an original approach to your new job.'

'What do you mean?'

'I think most trainee detectives would have just put their reports in and taken the money. You acted as if you're some sort of Old Testament avenging deity, bringing justice or retribution or forgiveness to erring mortals.'

'That's a bit strong,' he said mildly.

She shook her head. 'Not really. First of all you put two men in hospital because you think they're muggers. Then you act as a gay marriage counsellor, and decide a woman shouldn't know where her husband is, even though she was paying you to find him.'

'That's not entirely true.'

'In what way is it not accurate and true?'

'Well, she hasn't paid me for finding him yet. And now at least she knows he's alright and just doesn't want to be with her.'

Lady Sarah smiled grimly. 'That's all just fine and dandy, then.'

'Come on,' he said. 'I haven't done any harm, have I? I just like things to work out okay and even have a happy ending, except when someone needs a bit of - as you put it - retribution. Anyway, you really haven't got much room to speak, considering what you did for a living and how it ended up.'

She nodded in acceptance. 'Touché. Give me another cigarette, please.'

He did, and waited for her to go to the wheelhouse and return before he lit it. She was carrying a parcel, which she held out to him as she sat down. 'You can only have it if you can guess what it is.'

He turned the book-shaped package over, then said: 'I've already played that game today. If it's not a Ferrari or a new three-piece suite, could it be a book?'

'Jolly good. Carry on.'

He pulled off the brown paper wrapping, and turned the extravagantly bound book over, looked at the time-worn front cover and said 'Is that who you think I am?'

'No, but close. Have you read it?'

'No, but I know the story. It's about a mad bloke who tilts at windmills, isn't it?'

She smiled and drew on her cigarette before answering. 'Well, I suppose that's a simple interpretation. It's actually about a man who sets out to revive chivalry, right wrongs and bring justice to the world.'

'So what's wrong with that?'

'Nothing, except he goes potty and achieves nothing in the long run apart from causing a good bit of damage. Then he dies of a fever.'

'Oh.'

Lady Sarah reached out as if for the book, then laid her hand on his. 'Don't be depressed. If everyone in the world were like you, it would be a better place, and certainly a more interesting one.'

She took her hand away as if she felt it had been too extravagant a gesture, and said: 'Anyway, apart from all that, have your plans worked out as you would have wanted them to? How do you feel about your first month as an expatriate? And don't encourage that bird or there'll be shit all over my wheelhouse roof.'

Mowgley looked up and saw the big gull had returned and brought a friend or relative. He tore off two chunks of bread, smeared some mushroom terrine on them, then threw them at the birds. 'It's been a lot better than I thought,' he said, 'but I don't know about plans. I never intended ending up here. My wife insisted on buying *La Cour*, and then decided to leg it with the bloke I bought it from. I needed to jump rather than be pushed from the Force, and I had no home in England. Being here just sort of happened. I think that's how life works out for a lot of people.'

'Yes,' she said. I think you may be right. But you are a funny man.'

'Funny?' he said. 'In what way? Funny ha-ha or funny peculiar?'

She leaned over and tickled Bébé between the ears. 'Both. I can see why your sergeant used to get so exasperated and is still so fiercely loyal to you.'

'How do you know that?'

'Oh, we speak on the phone now and then. Mimi gave her my number.'

'You mean you've taken over supervising me while I'm here?'

She smiled. 'Someone's got to, have they not?'

~

The sun had long since left them. Two empty wine bottles stood amongst the debris of their meal, and both the tide and the level of the *eau-de-vie* had dropped further.

Lady Sarah shivered and pulled her shawl closer around her shoulders. 'I think it's time to turn in,' she said, throwing the stub of her cigarette overboard. 'How about you - are you staying?'

Mowgley stretched and yawned. 'If you'll have me.' He stood up and stretched again, then picked his cigarette packet and lighter up from the rickety picnic table. 'I think I'll just take a stroll and try and hold back the tide with a small contribution.'

He edged past the table and, mindful of the statistic that more sailors drown after falling drunk from marina pontoons than at sea, took his time going down the gangplank.

The quay was deserted as he turned towards the water and unbuttoned his fly.

He whistled, then put a cigarette in his mouth as Nelson and Mangetout appeared out of the darkness.

He lit the Gitanes, and looked across the calm, moonlit waters and the entrance to the harbour. It was strange to think that just a month ago he had been a policeman, doing what he saw as his duty at the ferry port. As he had said to Sarah, he had not planned to be where he was, or to be doing what he was doing. But so far, it was not turning out badly. He might even get to like his new life.

He heard the roar of the engine over Mangetout's frantic bark, but never saw the car that hit him.

Interim Report

DATE: As attached sheet/1

Case No: 678764/2

Investigating Officer: DI Tennent 745982

Status as to date:

Following information received from Europol (7896Div/Degas), Sean Mooney was arrested when alighting from a private plane at Manchester airport. He was held overnight and subsequently charged with various crimes including a number of counts of murder (see appendix 'a'). He was also charged with associated crimes including participating with known and unknown associates in the illegal transference of proscribed substances within the European Union (see appendix 'b'). Further associated charges relating to the illegal transfer of persons known and unknown within European Union territory are detailed in appendix 'c'.

The arrest and detention of Sean Mooney can be directly attributed to the work and efforts of Detective Sergeant Catherine McCarthy (18934) during her attachment as liaison officer to the

French Special Investigation Unit headed by Colonel Rene Degas of the Gendarmerie National. Mention should also be made of the contribution made by former CID DI John Mowgley.

The case against Mooney and his associates and accomplices is ongoing, and further reports will detail all victims and associated criminal acts.

Other books by George East

Home & Dry in France
René & Me
French Letters
French Flea Bites
French Cricket
French Kisses
French Lessons
French Impressions: Brittany
French Impressions: The Loire Valley
French Impressions: The River Dordogne
French Impressions: Lower Normandy
French Impressions: The Brittany Blogs
Home & Dry in Normandy (compilation)
French Kisses (compilation)

Also:

A Year Behind Bars
How to write a Best-Seller
The Naked Truth about France and the French
The Naked Truth about Women
The Naked Truth about Dieting
A Balkan Summer

The Mowgley Mysteries:

Death Duty
Deadly Tide
Dead Money

Also by La Puce

Life's a Beach
150 Fabulous Foolproof French Regional Recipes

LA PUCE PUBLICATIONS
e-mail: **lapucepublications@hotmail.com**
website: **www.george-east.net**

Printed in Great Britain
by Amazon